Praise for *Mr. Dick...*

"[Silva] nicely captures the spiri... ....
from his desk or from fights with his wife, his long midnight
walks around London. . . . She convincingly portrays Dickens'
restless energy. . . . [Silva] tunes herself to Dickens' imaginative
frequency. . . . She inhabits Dickens' sensitivity to London's
atmosphere, its chancellors and urchins, its cobblestones and
fog." —*The New York Times Book Review*

"Poignant . . . Impeccably delivered in a sprightly prose that
wants to be read out loud . . . Silva, one senses, is a natural-
born giver, a writer who most likely leaves a candle burning in
the winter nights, inviting restless perambulators in."
—*Chicago Tribune*

"Comical and haunting." —OprahMag.com
("Best Christmas Books of All Time")

"Lively . . . Graced by the ghostly presence of Mr. Dickens
himself . . . Promises to put you in the holiday spirit."
—*USA Today*

"Funny, clever, and touching, with a surprise ending that is a perfect Dickensian fit . . . Just in time for this holiday season."
—*NPR's Reader's Corner*

"This clever, original debut brilliantly imagines the writing of *A
Christmas Carol*. . . . Wildly moving, chock-full of Dickensian
atmosphere and written in a style as rich as a Victorian Christmas dinner." —*The Daily Mail* (UK)

Mr.
Dickens
❧ and ❧
His Carol

SAMANTHA SILVA

FLATIRON
BOOKS
NEW YORK

MR. DICKENS AND HIS CAROL. Copyright © 2017 by Samantha Silva. All rights reserved. Printed in the United States of America. For information, address Flatiron Books, 120 Broadway, New York, NY 10271.

www.flatironbooks.com

Designed by Anna Gorovoy

The Library of Congress has cataloged the hardcover edition as follows:

Names: Silva, Samantha, author.
Title: Mr. Dickens and his carol : a novel of Christmas past / Samantha Silva.
Description: New York : Flatiron Books, [2017]
Identifiers: LCCN 2017028500 | ISBN 9781250154040 (hardcover) | ISBN 9781250154033 (ebook)
Subjects: LCSH: Dickens, Charles, 1812–1870, —Fiction. | Christmas stories. | GSAFD: Biographical fiction. | Historical fiction.
Classification: LCC PS3619.I544345 M7 2017 | DDC 813/.6—dc23
LC record available at https://lccn.loc.gov/2017028500

ISBN 978-1-250-15405-7 (trade paperback)

Our books may be purchased in bulk for promotional, educational, or business use. Please contact your local bookseller or the Macmillan Corporate and Premium Sales Department at 1-800-221-7945, extension 5442, or by email at MacmillanSpecialMarkets@macmillan.com.

First Flatiron Books Paperback Edition: 2020

10 9 8 7 6 5 4 3 2 1

For Atticus, Phoebe & Olive

Such dinings, such dancings, such conjurings, such blind-man's-buffings, such theatre-goings, such kissings-out of old years and kissings-in of new ones, never took place in these parts before.

—CHARLES DICKENS

Part I

1

On that unseasonably warm November day at One Devonshire Terrace, Christmas was not in his head at all.

His cravat was loose, top button of his waistcoat undone, study windows flung open as far as they'd go. Chestnut curls bobbed over his dark slate eyes that brightened to each word he wrote: this one, no, that one, scribble and scratch, a raised brow, a tucked chin, a guffaw. Every expression was at the ready, every limb engaged in the urgent deed. Nothing else existed. Not hunger or thirst, not the thrumming of the household above and below—a wife about to give birth, five children already, four servants, two Newfoundlands, a Pomeranian, and the Master's Cat, now pawing at his quill. Not time, neither past nor future, just the clear-eyed now, and words spilling out of him faster than he could think them.

The exhilaration of his night walk had led him straight to his writing chair by first morning without even his haddock and toast. He'd traversed twice the city in half his usual time, from Clerkenwell down Cheapside, across the Thames by way of Blackfriar's Bridge, and back by Waterloo, propelled by a singular vision—the throng of devoted readers that very afternoon pressing their noses against the window of Mudie's Booksellers, no doubt awaiting the new *Chuzzlewit* installment, with its flimsy green cover, thirty-three pages of letterpress, two illustrations, various advertisements, and the latest chapter of pure delight by the "Inimitable Boz" himself! Why, it was plain to him that humanity's chief concern, now that Martin Chuzzlewit had sailed for America, was the fate of Tom Pinch and the Pecksniffs, and he considered it his sacred duty to tell them.

And so Charles Dickens didn't hear the slap-bang of the door knocker downstairs that would alter the course of all his Christmases to come.

Like any man, he'd known a good share of knocks in his thirty-some years. Hard knocks at lesser doors, insistent *rap-rap-raps* on wind-bitten, rain-battered doors whose nails had lost all hope of holding. And with fame came gentler taps at better doors, pompous, pillared, and crowned thresholds in glazed indigo paint, like his own door two floors below, where the now-polite pounding was having no effect at all.

Because there are times in a man's life when no knock on any door will divert him from the thing at hand, in particular when that thing is a goose-feather pen flying across the page, spitting ink.

2

When the fusee table clock on his desk struck straight-up three, a smallish groom (as was the fashion) with fiery red hair (as wasn't the fashion at all) appeared at the study door with a tray of hot rolls, fancy bread, butter, and tea. Dickens dotted his final *i*, brandished his pages, and stood.

"Topping! I've just this moment finished the new number."

"Wot good news, sir."

Dickens took a roll and tore a bite out of it, his hunger returning. Everything—the whole house—seeped back into his awareness. Oh, glorious Devonshire Terrace, a house of great promise (at a great premium), undeniable situation, and excessive splendor. He was glad for the great garden outside, the clatter of crockery and clanging of tins in the kitchen downstairs, the chatter and play of his children somewhere above. And here was Topping right in front of him, vivid as ever, in his usual tie and clean shirtsleeves instead of a livery, with no sense of impropriety, and a kindly expression that asked what more he might do, because doing was what he liked best. He was the longest-lived of the household servants, and Dickens regarded him most like family of them all, something between the father he'd always wanted and the brother he wished his were.

"Oh, Topping." He leaned in, clutching his pages. "I believe I have once again . . . stumbled upon perfection."

Topping squinched his eyes as a way of smiling without showing his teeth, which went in every direction except straight up and down. Dickens felt a great affection for him, for everyone, even the handsome house itself, which had subdued itself all day in the service of his art. He was sure he had Topping to thank for it.

A sustained holler from the bedroom upstairs announced Catherine Dickens in the full tilt of a labor of her own. The two men looked up and held their breath until it stopped. Dickens smiled with one corner of his mouth, wistful. Another child was nearly born, he knew, if stubbornly resisting its arrival into the world.

"I suppose it altogether too much to think Catherine would hear it now," he said with a playful frown.

Topping's caterpillar brows arched and fell in ironic agreement. "Well, sir. Masters Chapman and Hall are downstairs."

"Chapman and Hall, here?" Dickens returned the half-eaten roll to the tray and trusted his pages to Topping. He sprang for the mirror to quick-comb his hair, fasten his green velvet waistcoat, and fluff his blue satin cravat. "Apparently even my publishers cannot wait to know what happens next!"

"They do sit a bit on the edge of their seats, sir."

"Splendid. I shall read it to them!"

Topping looked at the pages, curious. "May I ask, does Chuzzlewit's man Tapley have, this month, a line or two?"

"Or three, or four." Dickens turned with a wink, retrieved

the pages, and tapped them three times for luck. "I think it far and away my finest book."

Topping blinked in solidarity and stood aside. Dickens rounded the brass ball at the banister and skittered down the stairs by twos. He had that feeling of finishing that had always been for him like floating, air under his feet and lungs like full sails. It seemed wrong to be going down when he should be soaring instead, but down he went, pages tight under his arm, edges ruffling as if with their own excitement. He thought it only his due, Chapman and Hall at *his* door instead of him at theirs. And so, like an actor expecting an audience squeezed into the pit and overflowing the gallery, he bounded into the drawing room to greet them, only to find the publishing partners sitting stiffly in a pair of pink parlor chairs, looking like cold fried soles.

"Chapman! Hall!" Dickens offered his hand as the partners stood. "What a surprise."

"I hope not an unpleasant one," said Hall, with his fingertips-only handshake, limp as old lettuce.

"Certainly not." Dickens gave Chapman a warm double-hander. "Of course, normally you wouldn't be the first to hear it, but never mind that."

He stepped onto his favorite footstool and bowed theatrically, stirring the air with his pages. "Gentlemen, I give you the next installment of everything that matters."

"Charles," interrupted Hall. "We've come on a matter of grave importance."

Dickens peeked over his pages. Hall gripped his top hat with sharp white knuckles. Chapman mopped his beading brow.

"In fact, we drew straws," said Chapman, pulling a broom bristle from his pocket.

"His was the shorter one!" said Hall.

Dickens looked from one to the other, confused. "Yet here you both are."

A long loud shriek from above caused Hall to grimace and Chapman to sink. "But we've come at a bad time," said Hall.

"Nonsense. I think you'll find this new number strong to the very last word."

A string of sharp yelps from upstairs punctuated their discomfort. The visitors gazed at the ceiling in horror.

"Oh, that," said Dickens. "You mustn't worry. The louder it is, the nearer the end."

"The end?" Chapman pressed his kerchief to his lips.

"A child!" Dickens beamed.

Chapman and Hall looked at each other, grim. Dickens was used to the way they were—the obverse of each other in temperament and gesture, but ringers when they shared the same end. It had been Edward Chapman, short and excitable, who years before had stumbled on the notion that certain comic etchings about the exploits of Cockney sportsmen might be in want of a hack writer. But it was William Hall, tall and stern, who'd found the young Charles Dickens—court reporter, freelancer, would-be actor, and playwright—then hungry for recognition and income, in fact, any at all would do. Hall had a knack for computation.

"Charles. I'm afraid it's a matter of money."

Dickens lowered his pages and stepped off the stool. If it was a matter of money, it could be one thing only. "My father's been to you for a loan again, hasn't he?" Dickens started for the slant front desk by the window with a frustrated sigh. "I shall pay it at once, as always."

"It's not your father this time, Charles. It's *Chuzzlewit*."

Dickens turned, his face pinched with worry. Martin Chuzzlewit had become, like so many of his characters, as good as an old family friend. He watched the partners trade glances, grave indeed.

It's not selling one-fifth of *Nickleby*," said Chapman.

"Not one-fifteenth of *Twist*," added Hall.

"There must be some mistake."

"A few of the booksellers have been forced to sell at . . . a discount," said Chapman in a whisper, knowing the word would pierce the author's heart.

"A discount?" Dickens flopped onto the gilt-wood settee, dangling an arm over the edge. He could swing like a pendulum, from hot to cold, light to dark. "It's the name. When the name isn't right . . . I had so many others: Sweezleback, Chuzzletoe, Chubblewig—"

"The Americans do not like it," blurted Hall.

"The name?"

"The story."

"America, the republic of my imagination?"

The partners nodded as if their jaws were wired together, like puppets.

"Where I have never shaken so many hands, been so feted and accosted for autographs, had orange peels and eggshells filched from my plate, locks of hair snipped from my head and fur from my coat?"

"They now take you as a . . . misanthrope," said Hall.

Dickens pulled himself to full height. "I? A misanthrope?"

"You've portrayed them as hypocrites, braggarts, bullies, and humbugs," said Chapman.

"Humbugs?" Dickens puffed his chest, indignant. "Bah!"

He drew back to wait for a retraction, or a reaction, at least. As his renown had grown, he'd learned that a small, tactical tantrum could work wonders. Not this time. The partners were unmoved, faces expressionless. Dickens put a palm to his fore-head, feeling warm and dizzy. "Sales are definitely down, then?"

Hall nodded to Chapman, who patted his pockets and pulled out a thin velvet box. "But we've brought you a pen."

Dickens stared at the offering in Chapman's hand. He could not think of a quill in the world that would ease this terrible sting. "At least my own countrymen do not abandon me. Why, only yesterday I saw a crush of people at Mudie's—"

"Waiting for the new Thackeray, no doubt," said Hall, doubling the blow. He took a copy of *The Times* from the breast of his coat and read from above the fold. "Charles Dickens has risen like a rocket, but will sink . . . like . . . a . . . rock."

Dickens snatched the paper and read it himself, twice to be sure. "Well! From now on I should simply ask my public what it is *they'd* like to read."

The partners seemed to admire the novelty of his thinking, but before they could say so—

"Should Little Nell live? Sikes not kill Nancy? Should Oliver want some *less*?"

"Charles," said Hall, retrieving the paper from Dickens' grasp, "we are simply suggesting perhaps the public needs a bit of a—"

"Christmas book!" said Chapman, unable to contain his zeal.

"A Christmas book? But I'm in the middle of *Chuzzlewit*. And Christmas is but weeks away!"

"Not a long book," said Hall. "A short book. Why, hardly a book at all."

"And we've organized a public reading of the book on Christmas Eve!" said Chapman.

"A public reading of the book I have not written?"

"We have every confidence you will," said Hall.

"And have brought you a pen," Chapman tried again, with a toady grin.

"We were thinking something festive," said Hall. "A bit Pickwickian, perhaps."

"And why not throw in a ghost for good measure?" Chapman knocked his chubby knuckles together. "The public adore spirits and goblins in a good winter's tale."

"A ghost?" Dickens spluttered. "I am not haunted by ghosts, but by the monsters of ignorance, poverty, want! Not useless phantoms that frighten people into . . . inactivity. I do not abide such nonsense."

"Perhaps the ghost is wrong." Chapman tried the gift one last time. "Anyway, it is a pen."

Dickens took the velvet box and turned it in his hand. He shook his head and thrust it back, calm in his new resolve.

"Gentlemen. I will not write your Christmas book."

Hall cleared his throat and withdrew a contract from a second pocket. "I'm afraid there's the matter of a certain . . . clause," he said, opening it with a flick of his wrist. "To the effect that in the unlikely event of the profits of *Chuzzlewit* being insufficient to repay the advances already made, your publishers might, after the tenth number, deduct from your pay—"

"Deduct from my pay?"

"Forty pounds sterling per month."

"But I alone have made you wealthy men! Such a loss will ruin me."

Hall handed him the contract, as another ear-puncturing yawl echoed through the house, shaking its walls.

"*Chuzzlewit*, Charles, will ruin us all."

3

When Catherine's labor stalled by evening, and the doctor advised there would be no baby before morning, Dickens knew he wasn't any use at all. Lying on the sofa did nothing to relieve his torment; a late trip to the larder for a cold lump of steak produced only indigestion and regret. He cleaned his nails and rearranged the furniture, but it didn't help. The house had gone maddeningly quiet. It couldn't contain his worry, and worry would do nothing to ease Catherine's confinement or *Chuzzlewit*'s fate. Both now seemed fraught with danger. His brain flooded with the sort of fears night brings on: What if Catherine were lost to him, his children motherless, his work unable to save them from the maw of poverty, the poorhouse their only refuge? His nerves, one by one, prickled and popped under his skin. His legs, as they often did, twitched for elsewhere. With nothing left to do for it, he traded his writing slippers for a pair of seven-league boots and set out for his great palace of thinking—the city of London itself.

Vigorous night walks of some twenty miles were his own

regular fix for a disordered mind that no amount of fighting with the bedsheets could defeat, the city's vivid restlessness in the dark a fitting mirror for his own. From his earliest writing days, all of London had been his loyal companion and cure-all, by day and night, even in the most unforgiving weather. The city forgave. A map of it was etched on his brain, its tangle of streets and squares, alleys and mews a true atlas of his own interior. The city had made him. It knew his sharp angles, the soft pits of his being. It was a magic lantern that illuminated everything he was and feared and wished would be true. It *was* his imagination—its spark, fuel, and flame. From the highest Inns of Court to the lowest crumbling slums, Dickens had found his writing here, filled his mental museum with all that he'd seen and smelled, heard and felt worth keeping. But he had also found himself.

His best friend, John Forster, liked to say that his famed perambulations about the city had become a sort of royal progress, with people of all classes tipping their hats as Dickens passed. He was ubiquitous. Everyone knew his conspicuous attire; next to Count d'Orsay, he was the best-dressed dandy in London, in high satin stock, shiny frock coat, velvet collar; an excess of white cuff and rings, his waistcoats the most boldly colored, his cravats the most brave. But it was his face, with its kind, searching eyes, variously reported in the press as chestnut brown, clear blue, not blue at all, glowing gray, gray-green, and glittering black, that drew people to him, and a smile that threw light in all directions.

Fashionable ladies stopped him in the street wanting to know, before anyone else, what plot turn was coming next. Cigar-smoking men in top hats and tails liked to think they had guessed. Omnibus drivers knew him by name; gin-shop illiterates, the piemen, even the beggars called out to "Boz" cheerfully, and got a coin in return. The men who smelled of drink, Forster told him, knew him no less than those who smelled of rank.

And now he had sunk like a rock. There was no escaping it. Even the gray marbled moon low in the sky taunted him from the moment he turned out of Devonshire Terrace, no matter how fast he walked, or how far. He had stood his ground with Chapman and Hall, that was one thing. Charles Dickens could not allow himself to be pushed about by mere publishers, who were reliably first at the trough when the trough was full. But around the next corner he was bound to them, too, their futures inextricably tied.

At least he had cover of night, and a layer of smoke that washed everything in the same dull hue. He didn't want to be seen or, worse, seen and passed by. He could hardly bear the thought that his reading public, who'd followed his career from its bright morning to its dazzling noontide, would turn away and forsake him.

Failure was not in his repertoire.

Dickens quickened his steps, counting them off in his head. He could hear himself breathe, feel his heart like a knuckle-thump in his chest. When he crossed the stinking Thames, holding his nose against the feculence that rolled up in clouds, he felt relief to leave behind the midnight world of elegant theatergoers jostling into late hansom cabs. Tonight he wanted a nether London with only poor down-and-outs to keep him company, a ragtag procession of beggars, brawlers, and drunkards whose seeming houselessness echoed some emptiness inside him.

When the last low public house turned out its lamps and the voice of a straggling potato-man trailed away, a street-sad loneliness prevailed. The air was still and heavy, not enough to flutter even a curtain at an open window. He felt himself the only person alive, as if the magic lantern had snuffed itself out, throwing his own darkness into bright relief. He didn't know where his bleakness came from, or why, but it followed him like a shadow through the black streets of Bermondsey and Southwark, a shroud for his own low spirits. This was the land of smoke-spewing tanners and bone-boilers, sawmills and breweries. It smelled of yeast, dung, and carcasses; ash and murk pushed on his lungs, made him strain for each breath. The night was as grim as Pluto. Dickens worried the dawn might never come.

When it did, at last, he found himself in the comfort of Covent Garden, where the city sparked to something he recognized as life. An early constable surprised two street urchins sleeping in baskets and drove them away, shaking his stick. Growers' boys stretched and yawned under wagons spilling over with cauliflowers and cabbages. Costermonger carts jingled across the piazza, tea-sellers set up tables against its pillars, itinerant dealers lined its sides. Everything was on offer: oysters, hot eels, and pea soup; gingerbread, cough drops, and pies; secondhand clothes, violins, and books; ginger beer, tea, and hot cocoa. The sellers nattered and called to each other, holding entire conversations in a single grunted syllable. Dickens stopped to take it all in and thought it as good as a party. The gentler light of day faded his low feeling and restored some mighty faith in the marvelousness of everything.

And so, rekindled by the fires of the first breakfast-men and the smell of fresh coffee and toast, he remembered there was a child about to be born, and made his way, quick-footed, for home.

4

The coincidence of births and books in the Dickens household was by now old hat. Twelve-year-old Charley preceded publication of a three-decker *Twist*; Katey greeted the first monthly installment of *Nickleby*, Mamie followed neatly the last. *The Old Curiosity Shop* was elder brother to Walter, little Frank to *Barnaby Rudge*. But today the five Dickens children, dressed and breakfasted by half seven, sat stairsteps on the uppermost landing, bored with books and babies both.

The mild weather was making them glum. With not a smidge of cold nor any sign of snow, Christmas seemed all but forgotten. Even the family Newfoundlands, Timberdoodle and Sniffery, and Mrs. Bouncer the Pomeranian, appeared lacking in holiday cheer. There was not a holly sprig in sight, not a whiff of plum pudding, and no talk at all of the big Christmas party, which had grown in length and girth each year of their young lives. By now they should be counting the days to their father's abracadabra conjuring spectacular, a homespun holiday theatrical, and a riotous game of blind man's buff. Even the traditional trip to Bumble's Toy Shop seemed on no one's mind but theirs.

"We must all do our headwork to solve it," said Katey, twirling her fat sausage curls. The charming schemer of the lot, she was dressed in plum silk to her calves, pleated, ruffled, and trimmed. Mamie, the quiet one in the pinafore, read to Walter, who rested his chin on a fist, watching Charley try to balance a marble on his shoe. Little Frank sucked on a barley candy, now and then wiping his sticky fingers on his small sailor shirt.

"What is Christmas without Bumble's?" Walter traded one fist for the other.

"I suppose Mother and Father have just forgotten, that's all. Though I should think Mr. Bumble will be sad not to see us," said Mamie, ever thinking of the feelings of others. Little Frank began to cry.

"Why are you crying?" asked Walter. "Crying won't help."

Katey sat up tall and rapped Walter lightly on the crown of the head. "That's it! I've hit upon the very thing that will save us!"

Downstairs, just returned from his night walk, Dickens stepped inside quietly, listening for some sign of new life. Hearing nothing, he closed the front door, relieved to be on the lighter side of it. If he hadn't eradicated Chapman and Hall from his mind altogether, at least they were tucked quietly into a far corner instead of the drawing room of his own house waiting to lower the boom. Yes, they had nipped at his thoughts all the way home, but only as ambient mumbling, easily ignored. Still, he pressed his forehead against the door and gave himself a good talking-to in any case, a little lecture on the importance of putting on his most inscrutable face and not blemishing the day.

"Oh, Father," said Katey, swishing down the last flight of stairs. "It is another boy!"

Dickens turned, snapping to. "A boy?"

"But we prefer girls!" Katey fell into his arms, playing it up for sniffles and sobs. The boys rushed down behind her, crying on cue. He knew it was a conspiracy of false tears, but Dickens winked sideways to his sons and put an arm around Katey. "As do I, my Lucifer-Box. But never mind us."

He wanted to leap for the stairs to greet his new son, but here were his children already born, clamoring for his attention and compelling as ever. Katey was his Lucifer-Box, the pet name he'd invented in honor of her fiery petulance. Young Charley was Flaster Floby or the Snodgering Blee. Walter was Young Skull for his fine high cheekbones. Frank was Chicken Stalker, after a comic character in *The Chimes*. But dear Mamie was Mild Glo'ster for her quiet, reliable nature, like the cheese. She hung back now, as she often did, searching his face for some clue to his true state of mind. She was a worrier, like he was, and could sense unease in the smallest gesture. So he gave her sudden merriment, all play. Walter wanted a magic trick. Little Frank, still sucking his barley candy, tugged on a pant leg. Dickens hoisted him onto a shoulder, sticky fingers, sticky face, and all. Katey seized her chance.

"Father, we were just thinking of poor Mr. Bumble, who must miss us so."

Before he could answer, Catherine's maid, Doreen, appeared at the top of the stairs, preceded by her own heavy sigh. She was red in the face, as if her mistress's mighty labor had been hers as well. Dickens looked up, eager for news.

"Does she bid me come to her?"

"This is number six, sir." Doreen dabbed her ruddy neck with an apron hem. "She bids you stay well away."

But he couldn't wait another second. He swung Frank down with a growling kiss on the cheek and started straight for the stairs. Walter yanked on Katey's dress. She tried one more time, calling after him.

"Oh, Father. Can you think of nothing to cheer us?"

But he was two flights up already, and didn't hear her plea.

5

Catherine Dickens, in a white satin bed gown purchased specially for this occasion, leaned against a hillock of pillows, holding the newest member of their family. Dickens paused inside the door, struck by a buttery glow in the room. His wife looked weary but happy.

"A boy?" he whispered, tiptoeing toward them.

Catherine nodded. Dickens kissed her forehead and sat on the edge of the bed beside her. He leaned on an elbow to pull aside a corner of blanket, enough to glimpse his newborn son, whose little chest rose sharp and quick, each breath a startling discovery of air. The baby had one tiny hand curled against his own pink-perfect cheek; the other clutched instinctively at his father's ink-stained finger, seeking an anchor in the world.

"Oh, my," said Dickens, overwhelmed.

"I do hope you've a name in mind."

"Oh, Cate. Just in this moment I've no confidence in my naming skills whatsoever."

"What is it, Charley?"

Catherine was sensible to his ups and downs. She could read between the lines of his face, kept a running tally of the faintest furrows on his brow. It took some effort to mask the worry he'd walked in with. "Nothing," he lied gently. "I am bursting with happiness."

Catherine looked at their son. "How clever he is to have come in time for the Christmas party."

"Christmas," said Dickens. "Yes." He had not the heart to tell her the *Chuzzlewit* news. Not now. Catherine depended on him; they relied on each other. There was a going forward about them, as if life should be an ever-expanding affair—more children, a bigger house, better things. Dickens himself was known to be quick with the sterling, and generous to a fault. Every charity and beggar in London thought him an easy mark. Catherine was fond of fine fabrics, fresh flowers in every room, and had more than once mentioned having spied a magnificent marzipan in the shape of a goose that might be the perfect centerpiece for the party this year.

"Do you remember our first Christmas at Furnival's Inn?" she asked. "When you told me to close my eyes and declare my heart's desire?"

Dickens did remember, in exquisite detail. How lovely his new bride was, cheeks flushed in the firelight, dark curls delighting the sides of her face, eyes sparkling with hope. His first romantic attachment to one Maria Beadnell had ended badly, but Catherine was just the remedy. The eldest daughter of an esteemed music critic, she was an unsentimental Scottish beauty whose wit and wants were a match for his own. They had begun their life together when she'd joined him at his three small rooms at Furnival's. It was elbow-to-elbow in the early going, but they found a gladsome affection between them, a comfortable ease. Their shared memory of it was a touchstone.

"So close them," said Dickens. "And tell me again."

"All right, then." Catherine closed her eyes. "I wish for a home."

"A home. Well wished, my dearest pig."

"For happiness."

"For what is a home without happiness?"

"And children with which to share them."

"How many children?"

"Neither too few nor too many, of course."

"Then just the right number."

"Just." Catherine opened her eyes to find her husband's gaze. "And that every Christmas will be more splendid than the last."

Dickens recalled those days at Furnival's with fondness, too, how they'd lived well with less, pretending it was more. Tomorrow would make good whatever debt there was today. It had always proved true. Each Christmas *had* been more splendid than the last. And why shouldn't it be so? He was Charles Dickens, after all. Catherine believed in him. Chapman and Hall thought better of the trough, perhaps, but even they would eat again.

"Is it too much to ask for," she asked, "even now?"

"For Mrs. Charles Dickens? Whose husband is believed to have great prospects?" He could still recite each word he'd pledged when he waltzed her about their modest rooms at Furnival's all those years ago, giddy with thoughts of their life to come. "Why, we shall have such dinings, such dancings, such kissings-out of old years and kissings-in of new as have never been seen in these parts before!"

Catherine held their newborn to her cheek. "Oh, darling. I thought we had just the right number of children, but today I feel sure of it."

How often he and Catherine had repeated this very scene,

often in quick succession, each child greeted with trumpeting joy. Children were an act of optimism—sheer belief that the future will outshine the present. How he longed for that feeling now, the heart breaking open and flooding one's veins with love, breaching even those banks to wash the world with it, so that every worry fell away. Everything but this.

Dickens took the swaddled child in his arms and considered his sweet-sleeping face.

"Number six," he sighed. "I suppose we shall need a bigger house."

With a heavy-lidded wink, Catherine patted his knee and settled back to rest. "Perhaps a small refurbishment will do."

Doreen alerted them to her presence with a gravelly cough. She flung back the curtains and threw open a window. The air hung thick; dust pooled in a shaft of light. A cobweb joined the flocked fuchsia wallpaper to a yellow damask chaise. The creamy glow of the room turned to glare. Doreen took the child in her doughy arms. "When it's summer for winter," she said, shaking her head, "sure enough the world's about to go topsy-turvy."

Dickens stood to go, kissing his wife on the top of the head.

"I do hope the weather improves for the party," said Catherine, rallying long enough to suggest that if her husband had any influence in the matter of snow, he might use it now.

"I'll see what I can do, darling mouse."

Catherine reached for his hand; he let his fingers twine and linger in hers. "We are bursting with happiness, aren't we?" she asked.

"We are," he said, as if willing it so. He let go and turned for the door.

"Oh, and don't forget Bumble's for the children, dear. They've been waiting for days."

His hand gripped the knob like a vise. The mere mention of Bumble's Toy Shop, their annual rite of merry excess, wrenched him back to the tight spot he was in. The bill would come due soon enough, and if Chapman and Hall were true to their word, sterling would be scant. But surely they were wrong. The new *Chuzzlewit* chapter would fix everything and all would be well with the world once again.

Books had always been the thing to save them.

6

John Forster sat behind a carved mahogany desk pulling hard on his bushy muttonchops. Dickens liked to say that the hair on his friend's face—in the hierarchy of whiskers, somewhere between flapwings and a chin muffler—could never quite agree to meet in the middle and make a beard. It didn't matter. Forster was thickset, pugnacious, and pompous, but the truest friend there ever was. The son of a butcher, he had long ago decided he preferred books to beef. If there were those who believed no one should be a writer who could be anything better, John Forster believed no one who *could* write should do anything but. He'd risen to prominence as editor and critic, but was best known as Charles Dickens' greatest enthusiast. He was first in line for the latest installment on Magazine Day each month, and the last to sleep. "You know him?" people in line at Mudie's would ask. "Boz himself?"

"Know him?" Forster was known to bellow back, "I represent him!"

On this particular afternoon, he watched with consternation

as Dickens paced back and forth in front of him like a newly caged animal.

"Chapman and Hall have rubbed bay salt in my eyes. And on the birth of my son!"

"A book *this* Christmas?"

"Precisely."

"But Christmas is only weeks away. Why, it's not humanly possible."

Dickens stopped briefly to consider whether it was, in fact, humanly possible. "Well, perhaps I could do. But refuse!"

"As you must."

A flying rubber band stung Forster on the side of the head. It was meant to be an earnest office with only grown men in it, but here were the Dickens children in the anteroom, tending to their boredom with the amusements of rubber bands and paperweights. Forster watched Little Frank pull a linty candy from his pocket, discard a piece of gullyfluff, and stick it in his mouth.

Dickens took Forster's grimace as a gesture of solidarity. He stopped, awaiting some further expression of indignation to match his own.

"Why, you cannot leave Chuzzlewit stranded in America," said Forster.

"My point exactly." Dickens slumped into a slat-back chair. "And yet what is the point? My public have abandoned poor Martin, and with him, me."

"We must not panic."

Dickens inched to the edge of his seat, tapping the contract on Forster's desk. "But what about this clause? You never mentioned any clause."

"I never thought they would invoke it. It's nothing but legal mumbo jumbo."

"Well, they have threatened to 'mumbo jumbo' me to the tune of forty pounds sterling. On a monthly basis!"

"Preposterous! We must not succumb to this sort of blackmail."

Dickens swayed from pique to self-pity, like the rising and falling flames of the fat office candles. "You are my fixer, John. What do you advise?"

Forster had been his fixer, his bulwark, bully, and protector, from the early days of *Pickwick* onward. When hawkers stood on street corners yelling, "Git yer Pickwick cigars, corduroys, figurines!" it was Forster who'd run down the factory middlemen and demanded his friend's fair share. The two had been ardent allies ever since, thick against the thieves of the publishing world.

Forster pawed the contract from his desk, eyes darting from clause to clause. Another rubber band struck his nose. He batted it away, impatient. "Besides writing the book?"

"Yes!"

Forster sighed and tugged on his muttonchops, appraising his friend's pleading eyes. "Well. I suppose you could . . . cut down."

Dickens cocked his head as if hearing a language yet unknown to human ears. "Cut down?"

"That is . . . cut back," said Forster, as gingerly as he could manage.

Dickens gazed at the ceiling, where his thoughts sometimes congealed. "Cut back," he said, trying out the sound of it.

7

Christmas had been hiding in the streets all along. The Dickens children marched behind their father in obedient single file, but their eyes were bright and round as new pennies. Shopkeepers stood on ladders, decking their windows with evergreen boughs. Old men roasted chestnuts in crowded courts; the poulterer had a hand-painted sign for his goose-and-brandy club, the butcher his roast beef, the grocer his plum pudding. Never mind the warmish weather or the clatter of carts and coaches. The air smelled like it had hailed nutmeg and snowed cinnamon.

Dickens couldn't see or smell it. He barreled forward like a racehorse with blinders on, headfirst, locked jaw and neck, crunching on his bit while rehearsing an impromptu speech about the virtues of "cutting back." He was unaware that his children could barely keep up. It took them two strides for each of his, except for little Frank, who needed three in double-time and a skipping step. But as they took the last corner for Bumble's Toy Shop, there was no mistaking the elevated beating of their little hearts.

"This must not be our usual spree, children. We are merely looking, that we may comprehend our *one* Christmas wish."

"But Katey said—" Young Charley took a sharp elbow to the ribs.

"Yes, of course, Father," said Katey as she turned to the sibling behind with a wink. "Merely looking. Pass it on."

"Because Christmas is not in the end about *things*, children. It is about *feeling*."

"It *is* about feeling, Father," Katey parroted. "Pass it on."

Dickens was only midway through his lecture when he watched them, one by one, break ranks and rush ahead to wonder at Bumble's famed window display, a profusion of garlands, ornaments, and fat red bows. A thousand tiny white dots had been painted around the edge of the glass, pretending to be frost. The boys admired a tinplate toy train on a track lined with painted trees. Katey imagined herself the master of a French puppet theater. Mamie fell in love with a doll.

Dickens' shoulders sagged. This battle would be hard-won.

At the first jingle of the bell over the door announcing their arrival, the children pushed past him, scattering to every corner. Dickens froze at the threshold, gut bracing at the sight. Stacked floor to ceiling, cranny to nook, were dollhouses, drums, and music boxes, guns and swords, bows and arrows, toy soldiers, rocking horses, blocks and kites. There were toys of wax, wood, rubber, and brass; toys that rolled, toys that pushed, skipping ropes, hoops, ninepin skittles, and battledores. He had stood here a hundred times before, enchanted, but today the elaborate exhibit of childhood trappings threatened to swallow him whole.

He had a sudden urge to flee, but Bumble had spotted him, with that twinkle in his eye suggesting money and merriment would soon change hands. The Dickens children were a reliable bunch. "Ah, Mr. Dickens!" Bumble pranced toward him on spindly legs, spectacles bouncing on his beaklike nose. "Wonderful to see you!"

"We are merely looking, Mr. Bumble."

"Of course, Mr. Dickens," said Bumble, with the usual fluttering and flapping about. "Look all you like. But how glad I am you've come, as I was hoping to put you first down for our Christmas fund for the Field Lane Ragged School. It is your prized position, Mr. Dickens, and no one else shall have it as long as I live and breathe."

Forster's counsel to "cut down" drummed in Dickens' head, against all his instincts. The ragged schools had been his great cause since a visit to Field Lane when he was writing *Twist* showed him wretched children no charity school or church would admit. The poor boys had no place to go and no one who'd have them, save the Fagins of the world, who would use them up and toss them away like chewed-up, spit-out food scraps. What they needed was a school, and it was Dickens who'd led the charge. But he couldn't carry it alone, not now. He tugged at his cravat, his face contorting, trying to find a way to say so.

"I admire Field Lane, as we all do."

"You more than anyone," said Bumble.

"Admire, and yet, sometimes it seems—"

"That we cannot do enough. I know."

"Yes, but sometimes enough is—"

"The best place to start. I quite agree."

Dickens was never at a loss for words, words with precision and punch. But here he was, stumbling through his own thoughts, trying to find a way out. If he could not state the simple fact of being hard up for guineas, how would he ever write a book again, any book at all? Bumble seemed to take the stalling as computation. He licked the point of his pencil, ready to write any sum whatsoever, Dickens supposed, especially a big one. He couldn't blame Bumble for expecting it. He had always given more each year than the last, where now he just hemmed and hawed.

When the bell tinkled over the door, Dickens saw his chance. "I shall detain you no longer, Mr. Bumble. Do not miss a customer on my account."

"Not to worry, Mr. Dickens. I shall be rid of him at once."

Bumble flitted toward a rotund fellow with a red bulbous nose, capacious waistcoat, and a white wig perched on top of his head but not quite right. Despite his reprieve, Dickens couldn't help listening in. "I shall remember," said Bumble, lifting his spectacles to inspect the fine print on the man's business card: "Fezziwig and Cratchit."

"Good names!" Dickens marched toward them, momentarily forgetting his own predicament. He plucked the card from Bumble's hand. "'Fezziwig and Cratchit.' I shall put them in my mental museum."

Glad to see his best customer's enthusiasm waxing, Bumble cut in: "Mr. Dickens. Let me introduce you. This is Mr. . . . which one are you again?"

But on hearing "Dickens," the man attempted a sidestep toward the door. Dickens gently blocked his way, surveying the man head to foot, everyone a potential character.

"Hmm. I take you as more a Cratchit than a Fezziwig."

"Oh, no, sir!" Cratchit blushed like a beet. "Smith is my name. Cratchit is no one's name, I assure you. Why, it is hardly a name at all."

"It's a name to me!" Dickens gazed upward, considering its possibilities. "Hmm, sounds like scratch, and crutch, or better yet, cratch, like a rack, a cradle, a manger! Yes, I like it very much. And if Mr. Cratchit be not present in body and soul, why, I shall do him the honor of a place in my newest book."

"But, sir! If that be so, Cratchit shall throw himself into the Thames!"

"Ah, yes. So he shall," said Dickens. "Couldn't write it better myself!" Blithely unaware of the terror he had struck in the poor man's heart, he lifted Bumble's pencil from between his fingers and dug in his pockets for a blank mem-slip, one of the scraps of paper he carried for writing down fresh ideas. By the time he looked up, the man was hotfooting away as fast he could.

"Oh, dear," said Bumble. "I guess not everyone wants a place in one of your books."

Dickens looked at the card one more time, and put it in his pocket with a shrug. "Oh, well. There's always Fezziwig."

"But never mind him, sir." Bumble retrieved his pencil and licked the end to freshen its point. "Where were we? Ah, yes. We could start with the usual array of gifts for the boys at Field Lane."

Caught at last, Dickens felt a tug at the hem of his coat. He looked down to find Walter with a black cape tied about his neck, a magic set in his arms, eyes brimming with wonder. "Look, Father. A conjuring set!"

Dickens knelt across from his son, forehead to forehead, all resolve teetering.

Outside Bumble's window, a pair of dark eyes watched Dickens' every move without blinking. They were shiny brown with coal-black lashes, and belonged to a small ragged boy whose face was smudged with pencil lead. There were faint freckles beneath the grime, and a barely detectable dimple on his left cheek. He had twigs for bones and clothes too big by half, a man's clothes, rolled up where necessary to fit his tiny frame. An old tattered jacket, patched at the elbows, had five buttons, but no two that matched. He wore a pair of corduroy trousers rubbed bald at the knees and turned up twice at the hem. They were pinched high on his waist with a makeshift rope belt. His small hands, in fingerless wool gloves, holey and thin, clutched a dog-eared sketch pad to his chest.

The boy studied how Dickens tousled his son's hair, perked his ears to listen, nodded now and then, and seemed even once to laugh. He pulled off his brown cloth cap and leaned closer to the window. His breath made a small circle of white vapor on the glass. But no one saw him. Not even Bumble, attentive to all possible comers, paid the boy any mind.

People had a way of looking past him.

Inside, Dickens was losing ground fast. "Oh, all right, my little Young Skull. Perhaps just the magic set."

"But what about the rest of us, Father?" asked young Charley.

Soon all the children gathered around him with armfuls of toys. Dickens dropped his head back to roll his eyes at the ceiling, but a brightly colored Chinese lantern grazed his face. He batted it away. "What Walter may or may not get has nothing to do with the rest of you." When they looked at him with long faces, he could feel himself wavering. "We must think not of those who have *more* than we do, but of those who have less!"

Little Frank whimpered. Mamie hoisted him onto her hip. Katey put a hand on her sister's shoulder in solidarity.

Dickens looked at their cherub faces, his voice faltering. "We cannot all have whatever it is we want . . . whenever we want it."

But soon enough the jingling bell over the door signified

their departure, all carrying whatever it was they wanted, wrapped and ready for Christmas Day. Mr. Bumble waved after them.

"I shall save your spot in the holiday fund, Mr. Dickens! Never worry!"

Dickens smiled weakly and turned to bring up the rear, balancing the tallest stack of the very presents he had sworn against. The children gabbled and clucked ahead of him, all shouting over one another with excitement.

He muttered under his breath, "Cut back, indeed. Well done, Mr. Dickens."

8

Half the distance to home, Dickens' children scattered behind him like quail. He turned to see Mamie pressing her nose to Mudie's window, clutching her new china doll with a sweet green bow about its neck. She never passed without stopping, wanting to see the latest installment of whatever he was writing, usually front and center in an elaborate display with framed illustrations, a sketch of "the author," and knickknacks on tiered shelves behind swags of gold satin.

Young Charley pulled to Mamie's left. "Look, Father," he called.

Dickens edged closer. He peered over his gifts to a stack of unsold numbers towering in the window, and a sign: FREE WITH PURCHASE OF TEA— *Martin Chuzzlewit.*

"Good Lord. They cannot give them away."

Young Charley leaned lightly against his father's shoulder. The other children made a half circle around him. Mamie threaded her gloved hand through his arm. "Perhaps the warm weather has people in less than a reading mood," she said.

He tried to think of something reassuring to say to them, but he had no words for this. The older children knew well that by now every copy in the city, if not the country, ought to be long sold out, sometimes within the first week after Magazine Day—that monthly literary riot here at Mudie's and bookstalls everywhere when readers of every variety lined up around the block long before opening, in wild anticipation of the newest Dickens number. They'd crowd the window taking turns to catch a glimpse of the illustrated cover, pointing to their favorite characters, chattering about last month's twist at the end, venturing guesses as to which way it would turn. Forster called it a veritable Boz-o-mania. From *Pickwick* on, his popularity was unrivaled. Now here he was, quietly taking in a new universe of possibility in which Charles Dickens was no longer at the top of the heap.

A tap-tap-tap on his shoulder sent a jolt down his spine. He spun around, ready to pounce, to find a gentleman in a high-collared coat and sharp-pointed shirt. Dickens judged, by the small leather journal the man held in his hand, that an admirer had appeared just in time.

"Would you do me the honor of an autograph, sir?"

"Why, certainly I will," he said, loud enough for his goslings to hear.

Katey and Mamie gladly relieved him of the presents he was carrying. The man slid an album into Dickens' open hand. It was only a little larger than his palm, thin and wider than it was tall, and gold-embossed. He leafed through to a fresh page, pulled a pencil from his pocket, and flapped his elbows, preparing to write.

"To whom shall I make it?"

"Marley, sir. Jacob. A man who's never missed a word you've written."

"My favorite sort of reader." Dickens signed with a flourish. He sensed his children watching, felt Mamie squeeze his arm. He handed the album back with a satisfied smile. "Jacob Marley, I am ever in your service."

The gentleman flipped to the page to review his newest get. "Dickens? I thought you was Thackeray!" He tore it out, crumpled it into a ball, and tossed it into the street, stomping away.

The children watched their father's autograph be further insulted by the wheel of an omnibus clip-clopping past.

Dickens narrowed his eyes. "Well. How sad Mr. Marley will be when I introduce him in my new number, only to kill him off in the next."

"He should be dead to begin with," said young Charley.

"Dead as a doornail," said Katey.

"So he shall. So he shall."

The matter settled, Dickens turned for home. His children trooped behind in cautious silence.

In the spot where they'd stood, five scruffily clad street urchins appeared, watching the author disappear down the street, his top hat bobbing in the crowd. Their "captain" was a beetle-browed, hairy-lipped youth of not quite seventeen. He wore a series of three scraggy coats: one had no buttons, another no sleeves, and the last a lapel but little else. The captain picked up the crumpled paper from the street and flattened it against his dirty tweed trousers. He couldn't read, but he could put pieces together.

"Dickens, eh?" he said, with a menacing glint in his mud-brown eyes.

9

Dickens stared at the sheet of foolscap that had vexed him for the better part of a week. Each day he'd redoubled his commitment to rescuing Martin Chuzzlewit from the clutches of foreign snobbery, yet had barely the bones of a paragraph, the remains of a sentence. He found every reason *not* to write and very few in its favor. All he could think of was the money trench he was in, with only a handful of weeks to dig himself out. Today, having vowed to stick to his chair, he was stuck. He adjusted his inkstand an inch to the right, the glue pot to the left, picked a different quill, then another with just the right fineness and ink flow, changed the nib, thought long and hard on the merits of blue or black ink, decided firmly on iron gall, and dipped.

Still nothing.

The clock on his desk ticked louder and louder. In the early days, Chapman and Hall had wooed him with punch ladles and silver spoons; there was an oil portrait on one occasion, a celebratory dinner on another. But nothing had pleased him more than the fine fusee clock, with its burled wood, clear chime, and brass bezel. It greeted him every morning, with its gilt Roman dial and matching moon hands. He'd wind it three turns to the right with its heart-shaped key—it seemed to be a clock always in want of winding—and only then could begin to write. But now each agonizing tick-tock marked another precious second gone with nothing to show for it. He tried covering his ears, but it tapped on in his brain. Dickens wanted to scream. Instead, he stood, opened the window, and pitched the clock out. The defenestration ended successfully with a bang at the bottom of the garden steps. He listened for the silence, closed the window, and wiped his hands of the deed.

Back in his chair, Dickens scrunched his eyes shut and put a finger to each temple, trying to image forth a mental picture. But nothing came to him at all.

He was saved by a light knock on the door. "Good Lord, just come in!"

Topping popped inside, carrying an unwieldy stack of letters. "Interruptin', sir?"

"I should think that unlikely. Haven't managed to write one good word all day."

"Just the post. A few bills, past due. Usual contingent of beggin' letters . . ."

"'Tis the season," Dickens said with a sigh.

Topping deposited the first letters on his master's desk, one at a time. "Various confirmations of yer speeches and engagements: Royal Theatrical Fund . . . Poor Man's Guardian Society . . . Royal Hospital for Incurables . . . Second Annual Dinner of the Charitable Society for the Aged, Infirm, Deaf, and Dumb . . ."

"Has Charles Dickens ever met a cause that was not good?"

"Only if it was bad, sir—"

"Which apparently requires twice the effort." He rested his

chin in a hand, watching the pile of mail lean precariously to the left.

"Oh, and an invitation from the Ebenezer Temperance Society." Topping held up the letter with an arch of his ginger brows.

Dickens stood and grabbed it from Topping's hand. "Can these teetotalers not see I am set upon *improving* the pleasures of those who have nothing, not denying them what little they have?"

"Relieved to hear it, sir."

"These Ebenezers . . ." Dickens curled the fingers of his right hand into a tight fist, as if he wanted to punch the letter itself. "I'd like to screw and bruise them, scrouge and scruze them!"

"Only wot they deserves, sir."

"Why these people continue to vex me, I do not know." Dickens tore the letter into tiny bits, opened the window, and tossed them in the direction of the clock.

"Speaking of vexing, sir, your father—"

"Not here, is he?"

"Just arrived. Downstairs."

"Well, send him away. Make some excuse."

But it was too late. John Dickens appeared in the doorway clutching the brim of his faded brown bowler. His son sank at the sight of him. His father was north of sixty, but by temperament still a good deal south of death. He was maddeningly sanguine for a man who lived on other people's money. It puzzled him how his father affected an affable, confident air, no matter how down on his luck, like someone who had known money, or at least met it once or twice, and still considered it a friend. Never mind that the seams of his snuff-colored coat were hanging on for dear life.

"Hello, son."

"Father. What a surprise." He signaled to Topping that he could go.

The old man walked into the room with a limp, the result of a nagging left hip. He steadied himself with a hand on the back of a tall leather chair.

"I've come to inquire after the new child, of course. All fine fettle, vigor, and salubriousness, I presume?"

"Seems to be thriving, thank you."

"Have you a name?"

"No name yet."

"Well, at least he's got 'Dickens.' That should be name enough for anyone."

His eldest son was in no mood. Dickens leaned back in his chair, crossed his legs, and tapped a letter opener against his thigh, waiting for the inevitable. His father sat across from him and leaned in, as if all news were good news. "Charley, as long as I'm here—"

"Yes, let's have it, then. I've only a moment."

"Why, a moment is all I need for a matter regarding certain contemporaneous events which require perhaps a small anticipatory pecuniary effort—"

"Only a small one?"

"It so happens I've stumbled upon an opportunity for a most expeditious domiciliary arrangement."

"You live over a drinking house, Father. I should think that expeditious enough."

"Oh, but a man seeks ever the augmentation of his particulars, and but for a small stipendiary emolument—"

"Rent's come due, has it?"

"I do find myself somewhat short in the pocket."

Dickens dragged a checkbook from a desk drawer and skimmed a thick collection of stubs that nearly blinded all reason.

Coals, £12; wages, £46; £30 each for the dairyman, doctor, and chemist; various checks for pleasures, presents, and smoking; wine, washing, new clothes all around, and various household refurbishments. And that was last month alone. Only one check remained. He dipped his pen and filled it out.

"Somethin'll turn up, son, and I'll have it back to you in no time."

"Please, Father, you cannot continue to ask my publishers and everyone else connected with me for money."

"Everyone knows that I am good for it."

"Everyone knows that *I* am good for it." Dickens slapped the desk with a loose hand and pulled a pair of scissors from the drawer. He wanted his father to stop him, tell him to put the scissors away, close the drawer, it was all a bad joke. Wished he did want to see the new child, or his *own* child, sitting right in front of him, or at least sense his distress. Offer him, if not money, some whiff of that undying optimism when he needed it most. A sympathetic ear, a word of wisdom, a shoulder to lean on, when he felt so unsteady himself. Some sign that the natural order of parent and child was intact. It was ridiculous to need a father at his age, when he was a father himself, now six times over. But he did. And said nothing.

He scissored off the check with three sharp snips and held it out, barely able to meet his father's gaze. "There you are."

John Dickens put his hat on his head and stood. He folded the check with his knobby fingers and deposited it in a frayed coat pocket. "Mightily Christmas-like of you, Charley."

"It is still November, Father," he said, pulling at his collar. "And an August-like one at that."

But John Dickens patted his pocket lightly, a faraway glimmer in his milky blue eyes. "Still, son, Christmas begins—"

"In the heart. Yes, I know." He stood, too, trying to find something redeemable or reassuring on his father's puffy, grizzled face. But he found nothing. It was a rare silence between two men who relied on words to secure the necessities of life.

"This must be an end on it, Father."

10

When November rounded its last corner, Christmas preparations at Devonshire Terrace were at full pelt. Festive fabrics cascaded over a settee. A decorator hung a kissing bough; a housepainter studied a wall. Mamie practiced carols at the piano while Katey turned the pages and sang. The boys scrambled up and down the stairs playing pirates. Catherine, still meant to be convalescing, instead reclined on the drawing room settee in her velvet robe and slippers, embroidering a holiday sampler while dictating to a cook.

". . . four turkeys, a goose, mince pies, filberts, and candied fruits. A Christmas pudding, of course . . ."

Dickens lingered in the threshold, gripping the household ledger to his chest, marveling at how the entire house seemed to spin and whir around Catherine's calm center. He was acquainted with her gusts of postpartum activity. Not one to cut the social scene during pregnancy, she would linger at a ten-course dinner well into her seventh month, and even once, when she should have been spending her last weeks in bed, was spotted with a friend getting out of a carriage and galloping on foot up the Strand. Once a baby was born, she'd refuse to stay in bed any longer than four days, far short of the custom. She would remove to a sofa as soon as possible to resume direction of the household affairs, and if a party was afoot, all the better for her mood. Because her mood was the thing. The halo of euphoria that surrounded each birth was often short-lived. The first week she might be happy, the second, fine, the third, not well at all, and by the fourth it was possible Catherine could be found, at odd times of the day, crying in a heap. It was not the "delicacy" of pregnancy Dickens feared for his wife, it was this. He must approach all subjects, especially money, with tenderness and tact.

The painter poked his head around. "This the hall to be painted green, mum?"

"Not so green as to spoil the effects of the prints." Catherine turned and spotted her husband. "Oh, thank goodness. I need your additions to the guest list. Party invitations post tomorrow."

Dickens walked in and perched beside her slippered feet, the ledger on his lap.

"Careful, dear. The chintz."

He rearranged himself and cleared his throat. "Catherine—"

"Do you think one goose enough, darling? The guest list is twice as long as last year. Perhaps two would fit the bill."

"Is it really necessary?"

"The goose?"

"I was only thinking—"

The new baby screeched in its blue-bowed bassinet. It was a high thin cry, like a needle piercing Dickens' brain. Catherine signaled to Doreen, who swept the child up in her ample arms and took him away. Mamie hit a stretch of inharmonious keys.

"Never mind, Mamie," said Catherine. "Play quickly through

and no one at the party will notice." She turned back to her husband. "I'm sorry, Charles. Here I am now."

Dickens crossed one leg, then the other. Searched the ceiling, the floor. He had scarcely mentioned the doomed meeting with Chapman and Hall to her, a few days before over a shared lunch of Scotch broth and fresh herrings. Most of it he had said into his napkin, between fortifying gulps of red currant wine.

"Cate. I was only thinking that if I am not to write this cursed Christmas book—"

"Of course you shouldn't."

"I'm so relieved you agree," he said, not convinced she did at all.

Somewhere below them a persistent hammering began. Each blow was a smack on the back of his head, a jolting buzz between his ears. Catherine must have seen it on his face.

"Oh, ignore that, dear. Probably the new coat hooks for the children. Or maybe the wreath on the door. Which I'm having done in deep varnished red."

"The door?"

"Indigo is past season. Though I am thinking imperial yellow for spring."

"Right. Well, that brings me to the thing, which is, Cate, I thought, regarding Christmas, we might be a bit sensible this year—"

"Sensible?"

"Yes, you see . . . I've been reviewing the household expenses." He tapped the ledger with twitchy fingers.

Finishing a row of cross-stitches, Catherine looked up, her focus now clearly on him. "Wait. Your father's been to you for money again, is that it?"

The mere mention of his father felt like a pebble in his shoe. Dickens could see him even now, kneading the brim of his sloppy hat, the way he sat in the leather chair upstairs pretending to re-joice at the birth of a grandson, but only for his own benefit. He wished he could love his father more, wished he could feel something besides guilt and contempt. But Catherine had touched a nerve.

"How long he is growing into a man! Why, never once in my father's shabbily cheerful life has he managed to make one end meet the other. Which is precisely my point."

"What point, dear?" Catherine put down her sampler to re-view the list from the cook.

"The point that we are simply living beyond our means—"

"You needn't be so dramatic, Charles."

"Catherine, our living has no relation to our means whatso-ever."

"Oysters, I should think, as well," she said, handing the list back.

His shoulders rose and fell, but Catherine was well known for not missing a beat.

"When have we ever been sensible regarding Christmas? Think what it means to the children, our friends. And you! Who loves Christmas more than anyone. And now to throw water—"

"It is humane to throw water when there is a fire burning out of control!"

His vehemence stopped her, spun her state of mind like a top. Catherine pulled a silk kerchief from inside her pagoda sleeve and pressed it to her lips. She looked out the window, eyes puddling. "If only it would snow, the Christmas spirit would return to you at once."

Dickens stood, catching the spine of his ledger on a corner of fabric that wrapped around his forearm. He wrestled it off. "It is not snow we need, but sterling, or there shall be no Christmas at all!"

She blotted the corners of her eyes. "You're making me very sad, indeed."

"Catherine, it is the having of babies that brings your sadness on—"

She wiped a sniffle away. "But the buying of chintzes which often cures me. And Christmastime."

Dickens exhaled. He was wrong to have come to her, wrong to have asked that she take on his troubles, when she was busy enough defending against her own low state. A frenzy of activity was *her* cure for a disordered mind, as night walking was for him. Now standing behind the settee, he put a hand on her shoulder. He couldn't bear to deny her anything at all that might aid her restoration.

"Then of course you'll have them, Cate."

Craning her neck to look into his eyes, she seemed to find something to match the tender regret in his voice. She put her hand on top of his. Dickens found some small peace in the warmth of her touch. There was so little of it these days, with the hullabaloo in the house, the birth, the book. He missed it sorely. There was no want of affection between them, just no time. Each day's demands and necessities, never ending, never done.

He rubbed his forehead. "This money madness of Chapman and Hall's has rendered me vexed and alone."

"You're not alone, darling." She patted his hand. "Why, all the world loves you and your books."

He didn't want to be patted or patronized. He wanted true human feeling, and everything else was rote gesture, a reminder of the very thing that was absent.

"Not so *Chuzzlewit*."

"Don't worry, dear. If your public don't appreciate it now, they will . . . someday."

"Do you mean after I'm dead?"

She turned back to take up her embroidery hoop. "I don't think I did mean that, but then, you wouldn't be the first."

Dickens stared at the back of her head. "If they could like it a little more while I'm still alive, that would do fine."

But Catherine was lost to the golds and greens of her holiday floss, and he had lost the will to make a fuss. When he turned to go, the boys launched into the room with play-swords, swinging and cursing. So many other times he would have led the charge, with "ahoys" and "mateys," black patches and snickersnees. But there was no pirate in him today. When Walter challenged a fringed lamp to a duel, Dickens' nerves tumbled over the edge.

"Boys!" he said, but they were too busy fencing their way over the footstool, pretending it was a ship's plank, to hear. Katey sang louder to spite them. The baby, upstairs, continued to bawl. The hammering below pulsed in Dickens' chest. He could feel redness rise in his face, a terrible tightness in his scalp. He rubbed the back of his head, trying to make it go away, when little Frank started pounding the piano keys.

"Frank! Mind your sticky fingers!" His thundering voice surprised even him, and drowned out all the clamor of the house. Everything stopped: the music, the singing, the pounding, the swords. Even the baby's distant howl ceased. They all looked at him, wide-eyed. Little Frank ran to bury his face in Catherine's lap. Anger flashed in her eyes. Dickens opened his mouth to explain himself, but not one word came to him, neither admonition nor apology.

With nothing to say, and more irritation than regret, he lumbered into the foyer, hesitating just long enough to consider the new expanse of pine-green with cherry-red trim that would no doubt cost him a pretty penny.

"Hope ya like Christmas, sir," said the painter.

Dickens gnarled and trudged upstairs.

Fury falls away in dribs and drabs. Dickens took an early supper alone in his study, but to no effect. After a few more hours of not succeeding at writing anything, he became aware of an unusual quiet in the house, except for the sound of sweet whispers somewhere above. He tiptoed up the stairs toward the little voices, and paused outside the boys' attic nursery. Young Charley, Walter, and Frank were bathed, hair combed. They knelt at their beds in plain muslin nightgowns and caps, hands folded in prayer, eyes shut tight.

"Make me kind to my nurses and servants and to all beggars and poor people," they recited in unison. "And let me never be cruel to any dumb creature . . ."

Dickens leaned his head against the doorjamb. It was the prayer he'd written for his children long ago, when his firstborn was no taller than his trouser knee. It warmed the cockles of his heart to hear it.

"But please remember the croquet set," said young Charley.

"And another cat, all my own," added Walter.

"And a bag of peppermint sticks as big as a house!" said little Frank.

Dickens crossed his arms and set his jaw. Catherine appeared beside him, her hand in the crook of his elbow. "You see, dear?" she whispered. "What Christmas means to them?"

"I think I'm beginning to, yes."

Catherine turned to face him. "Charles, you don't owe Christmas to anyone. Not even to me. But you owe it to yourself to believe in yourself. You've always done what you set your mind to, what was necessary."

"You mean write the book?" he asked, surprised by her change of heart.

"Only if you think it best."

Catherine grazed his cheek with a kiss and disappeared as quickly as she'd come, leaving him to his own dilemma. Whether she was friend or foe, in that moment, he didn't know, nor what he owed and to whom. He admired the steady confidence of everyone around him that they would all survive. At least envied it as much as he minded. He turned back to his fresh-faced boys settling under the covers, tucked up to their chins, satisfied they had recited not only their duty to God, but God's duty to them as well. He let go a long, frustrated sigh.

"I think without a Christmas book, we are done for."

11

Dickens was at his desk by half-past nine, with just the right quill, fresh nib, and virgin sheets of rough bluish paper, folded crisply and torn in half. His desk was the way he liked it: a vase of fresh flowers, his little gilt rabbit on a leaf next to a bronze statuette of two toads fighting a duel with swords. Everything was in apple-pie order, the house all hush-hush. He breathed in and out, as if to fill his own well, dipped his pen, and spoke as he wrote in a small, neat hand.

"*A . . . Christmas . . . Wreath.*"

He narrowed his eyes to look at the title, first this way, then that, crossed it out, and dipped again.

"*A . . . Christmas . . . Prayer,*" he tried, but without success.

"*A Christmas Pudding?*" He rejected this before even crossing the *t*.

He waved away the morning post. Lunch was brought on a tray, but refused.

When Topping tapped on the doorjamb in late afternoon, Dickens sprang from his seat. "Topping! Where is my clock?"

Topping indicated the window, briefly miming the defenestration.

"Right. Oh, well," Dickens said, missing his clock terribly.

Topping produced the full day's stack of mail. Dickens reached for his letter opener, a man eager for battle, or any distraction at all.

"Bit thick with bills today, sir." Topping handed them off one at a time. "The poulterer, the butcher, the baker . . ."

"No candlestick maker?" Dickens huffed as he stuffed them in a drawer already brimming with debts owed.

"And then yer charities . . . Destitute Sailors Asylum . . . Discharged Prisoners . . . Fishmongers . . . Lost Dogs . . . Female Missionaries to the Fallen Women of London . . . Invalids, Idiots, Imbeciles . . ."

"Imbeciles, indeed." He tossed the lot straight into the bin.

"A second cousin once removed, money difficulties . . . Likewise a friend of a friend of yer uncle's . . . Oh, and this from yer brother Fred—"

Dickens took the letter and held it to his forehead, acting the clairvoyant. "I sense a rather lengthy dissertation on Fred's newest scheme. Hmm. Another automatic smoking machine, perhaps?"

"Or the cane that turned into an umbrella—"

"Or the ventilated top hat."

"And the stamp-licker. I remember that one."

"Whatever it is, it's a money-spinner for sure," he said, tossing it with the others. "That is, if I'm willing to spot for it."

Topping wrinkled his nose, saying nothing. Dickens admired that his groom knew nook-and-cranny details of Dickens family life, but stayed sensibly out of the fray.

"And an invitation to dine at Mr. Forster's this evenin'."

"With the usuals, I presume," said Dickens, setting it under the dueling toads. "I am in no mood for a literary bash, thank you."

Topping held up the last of the lot. It was an elegant envelope, pale pink and perfumed, with a Penny Red stamp. "Oh, and this, sir. From a Mrs. Winter."

Dickens couldn't breathe. He'd swallowed his own heart, which now lodged in his throat. With the tips of two fingers, he pinched the envelope from Topping's grasp, as if it were a thing easily sullied by human hands. He waved it lightly under his nose, taking in the aroma of frankincense, vetivert, and rose. An abrupt melancholy swelled inside him, a bittersweet remembrance. Topping waited for some instruction, but Dickens couldn't think what to say.

His reverie was broken by a horde of children—his own horde, in fact—careening down the hall, yelling and laughing, in pursuit of two galloping Newfoundlands. He stormed into the hallway to intercept them, but it was a game of round-and-round, up-and-down. The mob had already disappeared down the servants' stairs. Dickens planted himself, shouting after them.

"Children! How am I expected to think, much less write?"

Still gripping the letter opener in one hand, the perfumed letter in the other, he was overcome by an odoriferous assault that trumped the frankincense, stifled the vetivert, and pummeled the rose. Topping looked down at a steaming pile of dog excrement pooling around his master's shoe. Dickens saw it, too. "Well, this tops it all!"

A ferocious tongue-lashing gathered in his mouth, interrupted by a persistent striking of the door knocker downstairs. "What now?" he moaned, as Topping rushed off to answer it.

Fred Dickens stood in the open door nervously squishing his hat in his hand. He was Charles' younger brother, specializing in the sort of speculative ventures that were the order and hum of the day. His were built on whim and folly, but upheld by an un-relenting optimism, inherited from their father. Fred was amia-ble and kind, but hapless.

"Has he read my letter, Topping?"

Topping seemed to look right through him, as if he weren't there at all. Fred, it was well known, suspected this of everyone. "About my new scheme?"

"Is there a tree in yer scheme, sir?"

Fred turned to follow Topping's gaze. An old Saxon wagon drawn by four horses stood at the front of the house. Two deliv-erymen finished unloading an evergreen tree taller than both of them put together. They were hauling it straight up the walk, its long quaking branches brushing the rails of the black iron gate.

"Tree for Mr. Dickens! All the way from Germany!"

Upstairs, Catherine had arrived on the scene, hoping to mollify the warring parties. But the smell choked her, too. She watched her husband balance on one leg to scrape the offense from the bottom of his shoe with the letter opener. A kerchief over her nose did double duty to mask her amusement.

"I'm so glad you find this funny, Cate."

"Not funny so much as fitting."

Dickens scowled and scraped. Topping appeared at the land-ing. "Sir. Yer brother Fred is downstairs—"

"Good Lord! Am I only some duck to be plucked for my relatives' own purposes?"

"—and a very large tree, sir."

"Oh, the tree!" said Catherine. "Tell them to put it in the front parlor, would you, Topping?"

Topping turned back down the stairs to do so.

"A tree?" demanded Dickens. "*Inside* the house?"

"A Christmas tree. From Germany."

"Have we no trees in England?"

"The Queen and Prince Albert insist on it. It's a new tradition."

"Traditions are not new, Catherine. They are old. And we cannot afford the ones we have."

Walter and Frank appeared behind their father in makeshift magicians' capes, in rehearsal for their Christmas conjuring act to come. Walter wore his father's top hat. Little Frank used a long candy stick for a wand. He pulled on his father's pant leg.

"Fingers, Frank!" Dickens snapped.

"But Father," said Walter, "Frank's my assistant and we've learned to conjure a penny from a hat."

"Well, you'll have to conjure far more than a penny if we're to continue to live in this manner!"

Catherine glowered at her husband but said nothing. He took it to be one of her punishing silences, nothing close to sympathy for his view, which made him cling stubbornly to his ground. He could match her muteness word for word. Every fiber of his being marshaled to the cause. Where she blushed furious red about the neck of her aubergine dress, he bulged blue at the temples.

Katey and Mamie, unaware of the impasse, pattered down the upper staircase and skidded to a stop in stockinged feet, flushed and giggling. They wore fine party dresses, the newest fashion no doubt, striped silk, sashes, and frippery, their hair in fresh ribbons and corkscrew curls. Even Mamie had discs of bold rouge on her fair white cheeks.

Katey handed him a piece of paper. "Here's the list of all the rest of our Christmas wishes, Papa. And in ten minutes' time Mamie and I shall give waltzing lessons in the drawing room. A penny a dance!"

Dickens looked from one child to the next, all staring at him with great expectation, seemingly bottomless, that he had no idea how to satisfy. His usual playfulness had evanesced. What few drops remained of his patience simmered to a boil. "My own flesh and blood, and all you think of every minute of every day is yourselves, and what you will get! Not what you already have! Never how much even a single meal would mean to the starving children of India!"

The children stared at him, stupefied. They were accustomed to his occasional outbursts, but they looked at him as if this were an attack on Christmas itself. Walter took off his father's hat and looked at the floor. Little Frank sucked on his candy and sniffled; Mamie bit her lower lip. Even Timberdoodle dog-sighed, and Sniffery hung his head. Catherine glared at her husband in a way that ice might admire.

"I shall now go out," Dickens said, with no moves left.

Topping, short of breath, had returned again to the landing. "Sir, your brother Fred? Downstairs?"

"I shall now go out the back!" Dickens extended a stiff arm to Walter. "Hat, please."

Walter surrendered the hat without looking up, his small shoulders rising and falling beneath his cape. Dickens stomped down the servants' stairs, leaving his family in his wake. Katey folded her arms defiantly across her silk-sashed waist.

"I've never understood how, if I should eat all the food on my plate and lick it clean, that would possibly help the starving children of India."

Mamie's shoulders dropped when the back door opened and shut with a thud. Walter started to sob. Catherine pulled him close, trying to contain her own rising ire.

No sooner was Dickens out the door—creeping like a thief out of his own house—when he flinched at a figure rising from behind a hedge. Fearing it would be Fred, he found instead a street urchin in three tattered coats with a thin curtain of bristle on his upper lip, his palms cupped in front of him.

"Alms for the poor, Mr. Dickens?"

He didn't recognize the young ruffian, who seemed quite familiar with him. "You've been lying in wait for me?"

"Never mind, sir, 'aven't waited too long."

"Do I know you?"

"Don't believe you've 'ad the pleasure, sir. But I knows you." He pulled a wrinkled piece of paper from his pocket, straightened it on his dirty trousers, and handed it to Dickens, who recognized his own discarded autograph for Jacob Marley.

"Where did you get this?" Dickens demanded.

"Never mind." The captain of the ruffians clipped the paper from Dickens' hand. "It's mine now."

Flustered, Dickens took whatever pence he had in his pocket and pressed them into the youth's moth-eaten glove. "There. I don't know what you want, but it's all I have."

The captain did a rough tabulation of the coins, tightened his fingers around them, and looked up with a crooked smile, his own greasy cogwheels spinning at industrial speed. "It'll do fer now, sir."

Unnerved, Dickens fled into the darkening night with long, determined steps.

12

The chambers at 58 Lincoln's Inn Fields were well known as a magic cavern, the hub of London literary life, a refuge for writers, major and minor, where they were assured of firelight, wine-light, friend-light, and the burly-shouldered, beneficent, but forceful care of John Forster, Esquire. His rooms were the best rooms—part private club, part library—with the most beautiful editions of books covering every inch of wall, even in the bathroom. There were engravings, paintings, easy chairs, and thick carpets. The house smelled of leather, old books, and boiled beef.

Dickens skulked outside a long-paned window, peering into the dining room, where the high and talented literati of the day assembled around gleaming white plates and bright silver. Forster sat at the helm, blocking his view. Dickens leaned to the right of a boxwood to catch sight of Thackeray and the Carlyles, to the left of the drapes to spy Trollope and his wife. Wilkie Collins, the youngest darling of the group, sat at the far end, dabbing politely at the corners of his mouth as Thackeray stabbed the air with a fork.

William Makepeace Thackeray was a year older than Dickens, not quite yet a household name, but on a steady course and with equal aspirations. He stood six-foot-three, and even sitting down used up the space around him like a hulking giant. He was famed for his sharp tongue and cutting wit, to no one's greater benefit than his own. Dickens knew already theirs would always be a race for top spot. They had been polite in print, but this was another thing. He leaned closer to the glass to catch Thackeray's arrows and slings, for it was fulminating or nothing with this crowd. But he heard only gabble and muffled puffs of hot air. Desperate, he pressed his ear hard to the window.

"I should think us all sick to death of these endless social-problem novels with an earnest purpose!" said Thackeray, bayonetting his beef.

"Mary!" Forster shouted to his jittery housemaid. "Mr. Thackeray has no carrots!"

In fact, Thackeray had lots of carrots.

"He *is* Mr. Popular Sentiment," said Anthony Trollope, piling on.

"Mary! Butter for Trollope's flounder!" Forster plunked his knife so loudly on his plate it rattled the window. Dickens clutched his ear, still relieved any strike against "Boz" was an incursion on Forster's own soul. He was grateful to have so intimate a defender.

Ignoring Forster's outburst, the unflappable party continued eating.

"And clean plates all around!" he insisted.

Mary did as she was told, picked up their plates—guests mid-bite—and scuttled into the pantry.

Dickens was sure the unmistakable sound of bone china meeting hard floor would be noted by all. Mary had found him lurking near the larder, and panicked, dropping everything. He held a finger to his lips with an apology in his eyes, and bent down to pick up the bits and shards. He relied on Mary having a long-standing tender spot for him, interrupted briefly when Little Nell from *The Old Curiosity Shop* died and she could not forgive him killing her off. Some years ago, with the aid of Mamie and the elder Thackeray daughter, Mary had taught herself to read—in little moments between dusting and scrubbing, after grate-sweeping, or just before the needlework—so that she could read Dickens. It was Mamie who'd told him so.

"Never mind, sir," Mary whispered, stooping to collect the broken pieces into her apron lap.

Dickens stood and peeked through the door. He had a clear view of Wilkie Collins, who wore a bounteous black satin cravat, his usual, like a spillway over his fine white shirt and black coat. "I love Charles, as we all do," he said, "but the public want scandal and impropriety, not gushing displays of the heart!"

"Still, one must admit," said Thomas Carlyle, "the lower classes eat . . . him . . . up."

"The better for all of you," Jane Carlyle threw in. "Even those who've never read a novel read Dickens."

"He who runs reads Dickens!" said Thackeray, inciting an uproar of catty laughter.

Dickens gritted his teeth, reassured only somewhat by the sight of Forster ripping his dinner roll into twos and fourths. He was having none of it.

Mary stood behind Dickens at the door, balancing clean plates in one hand and a tureen of stewed carrots in the other.

"Tell Forster I'm here?"

"Yes, sir."

"But not the others."

Mary nodded, looking terrified by the assignment. He put

an encouraging hand on her shoulder. "It's only acting. I know you have it in you."

She blinked and pushed through to the dining room, where she set down the tureen long enough to deliver the fresh plates. Dickens watched her take up the tureen and walk slowly, deliberately, to Thackeray's left, where she began piling carrots on his plate, while looking straight at Forster, jerking her head toward the kitchen.

"Mary, why are you twitching so?" Forster asked.

"It's the kitchen, sir."

"Is it on fire?"

Mary shook her head.

"Then do not bother me with it!"

He turned back to his guests, preparing to launch his own fusillade in Dickens' defense. But Mary hovered, resolute. "Perhaps a small fire, sir."

"I see you are entertaining the literary lights of London!"

Despite being discovered in Forster's own kitchen standing in a sea of crunchy china, Dickens was miffed.

"You refused my invitation!" Forster said in his defense.

"And a good thing, too! Just listen to them cutting me down and slicing me up!"

"They do have Dickens-on-the-brain, I'm afraid. For *you* are the 'Inimitable Boz,' and I daresay they cannot bear it."

Dickens pushed the door open a crack to have another painful glimpse. He frowned at the sight of his nearest rival, with wavy hair, abundant brows, and a penchant for taking up so much space. "I'm in a terrible way, Forster. And now Thackeray, sitting in my chair."

Forster stepped beside him, sneaking a look himself. "Thackeray could never replace you in my esteem, nor my affections."

Dickens joggled his head with enough of a smile to express sheepish gratitude. He peered out again. "How's it going, then?"

"The dinner?"

"The novel! *Vanity Fair.*"

They both looked out at Thackeray, tugging at his brows.

"He's a writer," said Forster with a shrug.

Dickens turned to him, desperate. "Walk with me?"

Having made a hasty excuse to leave his own dinner party after the oyster patties but before the apple tart, Forster now puffed at Dickens' heel, purple in the face just keeping up. Dickens took double-length strides, going nowhere in particular, but full steam ahead.

"I have thoughts of the Regent's Canal, the razor upstairs, the chemist down the street . . . of murdering Chapman and Hall!"

Forster stopped, hands on his knees, gasping for breath. Dickens turned to him. "What's wrong with me, John? I'm restless and repressed. I sit, but cannot write. Lie down, but cannot sleep. My children aggravate me. I loathe my father. And Catherine, who should be convalescing, thinks of nothing but Christmas and the piffling party."

"The Christmas party?" asked Forster, seeming glad at last to hear mention of his favorite social event of the year.

"She decorates without prejudice, while I suffer visions of the poorhouse!"

"Is it as awful as all that?"

Dickens knew there was no such thing as pity in his friend,

unless he could breach his thinking ramparts straight to the quick of his feeling heart.

"Oh, mine is a bleak house, I assure you."

Forster mopped his forehead with a kerchief. "What's to be done with you, Boz?"

Dickens stepped closer and pulled the pink perfumed letter from his pocket. It was still sealed with glossy gilt wax. "It's from . . . Maria Beadnell," he said in a hopeful whisper. "I couldn't bear to open it. She might be ill. Or dead."

Forster snatched the letter and sniffed it, repulsed. "If dead, she'd be hard-pressed to write."

Dickens gnawed at the hairs on his knuckle while he watched Forster break the seal and read the letter, dispensing with it as quickly as he could.

"She longs to see you."

"Oh! How the floodgates of my past are open. Those pale blue gloves, that raspberry-colored dress, the charming tendency of her eyebrows to somewhat join together . . ."

Forster raised one brow high.

"Maria was my first attachment . . . my *muse*."

"Who made mincemeat of your heart!"

"I know. I have never since been able to hear her name without a start. And yet, the stimulant of unrequited love did lift me up into this writing life."

Forster grunted and started walking again. Dickens knew him to be a devout single man who could never forgive the injury enacted by a young Maria Beadnell on his closest friend. They had bonded over the cruel memory of it one night with the help of a full bottle of French brandy. Forster spoke so vividly of her heartlessness, it was as if it had happened to him.

Dickens was quick to his side, threading his right arm through Forster's left. He slowed his own step and tried one more appeal.

"I don't know where to turn, John. I am vacant of thought and words. The blank page has made *me* its sworn enemy. Where am I to find my muse now?"

"Perhaps with time, Catherine will be your muse again."

"Oh, dear friend. The love between husband and wife bears the weight of awful responsibilities. What begins as modest inspiration ends . . . in deepest debt."

"Then let debt be your muse!"

Dickens stopped and turned the letter in his hand. "Even now, when I'm in low spirits, a sense comes crushing upon me of some illumination lost. If I could see Maria once—"

"I do not approve."

"It could lead me to write again."

John Forster's face gnarled like a knot on a tree. Dickens had him in a bind, plain and simple. "Very well. I shall arrange it."

Dickens threw both arms around him, nearly lifting his pork-bellied friend off the ground. Forster blushed and stiffened, but Dickens knew he was putty on the inside. It was a scene often repeated between them: resistance, surrender, affection. This was their own round-and-round. The years had made it so.

13

On the day Forster had arranged it, at precisely the agreed hour, Dickens stood in the Winters' parlor at Artillery Place trying to choose a perfect pose to strike. Here he was, at the marbled hearth of his own first flame, long-dead embers stirring inside him. He didn't know what it meant, what he wanted from her, whether it was wrong to have come at all, but the very thing he'd complained of lacking, with no idea how to get, had appeared in the form of a pink letter—inspiration, at last. He pulled the envelope from his pocket and admired the large curlicue letters. It was Maria's own hand, not changed at all, which made him wonder at how clever life can be.

In the most innocent days of his youth, Maria was his sun. What a devoted poor fellow he'd been when even a sideways glance from her made him impossibly happy. She flirted, he doted, writing heartsick letters if he couldn't see her, sometimes twice in one day. But when he declared his hope for everlasting romance and marriage, she laughed at him, called him "a mere boy," pronounced his prospects not good enough, and cast him aside without mercy in favor of Henry Winter, "a merchant of good standing." Her stinging rejection, just before he turned twenty, was, for a time, the all-absorbing event of his life. Forster was right: she had torn his heart to bits. But he had her to thank, too, knowing he'd fought his way out of poverty and obscurity with one perpetual idea of winning her back. Those days were far behind him. She had become Mrs. Henry Winter, and he, a man. But her letter awakened some unexpected longing in him, not for Maria, but for who he was then.

How strange, to return to the place of his own long-ago undoing, in hopes of somehow being redone.

Dickens leaned an elbow on the mantel, a well-chosen stance, he thought, dignified with just the right amount of feigned indifference. He caught sight of himself in a large gilt mirror and straightened his fine magpie waistcoat. It was bold and theatrical, shawl-collared, with broad blue and green stripes. He'd borrowed it from an old actor friend, William Macready, for just this occasion.

"Oh, Maria," he rehearsed in a quiet voice, "how I've dreamed of this day. Why, there are things locked in my breast that I never thought to bring out anymore—"

"Sir, Mrs. Winter," announced her valet.

Maria Beadnell bustled into the room, plump as a fresh-baked meat pie, dressed as near to a peacock as any woman can achieve, and dripping with jewels. Dickens turned to take it all in. Here she was, backlit by morning rays streaming in through tall windows, like the corona of a solar eclipse around her. His memory filled in the dark center.

"Oh, Maria! How I've longed for this day—"

"Charley!" She walked toward him, hands crossed over her heart. "Is that really you?"

It *was* Maria, in all her glory. He'd once thought her voice that of an angel's, high-pitched and jingly, though today it had a nasal resonance he didn't remember at all. She was close to him now, coming into soft focus. It was such a simple question, "Is that really you?" But his tongue lolled in his mouth. The sight and sound of her had flung him back all those years to the idiotic, goggle-eyed young man he'd been when they met. He determined to utter something profound, befitting the man he'd become. He would pay tribute to what she'd meant to him; Maria had ruined him, yes, but he'd risen like a phoenix, all because of her. When he finally concocted the words to say so, a sneeze appeared on her horizon, wiggled and rolled across her eyebrows, which had definitively grown into one. And there it was, the great event itself, like a blast of buckshot across the room.

"Good grief!" Maria laughed and produced a monogrammed silk kerchief. "'Sneeze on Monday, sneeze for danger; sneeze on Tuesday, kiss a stranger.' I can never remember whether it's a sign of good fortune or an omen of bad luck!"

She honked into the kerchief and tucked it back into her lace undersleeve before taking both of his hands in hers. Maria Winter, née Beadnell, had a very bad cold.

"But never mind me," she said, talking in rapid fire. "Just look at you! *The* Charles Dickens! Why, you've not changed one whit. Well, of course, you are famous now, but in every other way—though so very, very famous! I want to hear every detail! Do you know Thackeray? Oh, never mind. I want to hear about *you*. All about you."

Maria installed herself on a carved Empire sofa with great rolled arms and hairy paw feet. Prattling away, she patted the cushion beside her, insisting Dickens should sit.

Dust clouds rose from the gray damask.

14

"She's a featherbrained, flighty, fribbling busybody who cares only for my celebrity, and nothing for who I am!" Dickens moaned to Forster the next day, blowing into a handkerchief of his own. "And as if I had not suffered enough, I must now pay with a raw chest, a dizzy head, and a stuffy nose twice the size of my own."

Forster shook his head.

"She wants to meet again as soon as possible," said Dickens.

"What did you say?"

"What could I? Honestly, I think her in some way in love with me."

"Or perhaps not," said Forster, with a look of knowing more than he was letting on.

"Oh, it was a pitiful display, I assure you."

"That I believe. However, I've done some ferreting around, and the fact is that Henry Winter is a bankrupt."

"What?" Dickens fell flat against the slatted back of the chair. "The divine, industrious Henry Winter for whom she threw me over, quite unceremoniously, with a barrage of small humiliations, one of which was telling me he was a man I could never hope to equal?"

"Yes. That one."

"Why, Maria did nothing but sing his sugary praises, practically from the rooftops—"

"Well, he's in the gutter now."

"So she was begging a favor, like everyone else?"

"I believe she may be greasing the wheels for a loan."

Dickens leaned forward and dropped his head into his hands. "Oh, God. What have I done?"

"I recommend avoiding her."

"But I have nothing to give. Less than nothing."

"Then at all costs, steer clear."

Dickens scratched his fingers through his hair, working his scalp, his embarrassment.

"What you need, my friend, is a jorum of hot rum and egg in bed, with blankets, under the care of your devoted wife."

"Oh, Forster. Had I only listened to you. I've been unfair to Catherine, and in this, her favorite season."

Forster put his elbows on his desk and pulled at his muttonchops. "Well, the season has only barely begun."

Dickens doubled his normal clip, determined to make a fresh start with his family. They were all acquainted with his ups and downs, but Catherine most of all. Of course he would live with the tree *in*side the house, and admire whatever wall covering she chose, even if it created a dizzying concurrence of circles and stripes or fought with the pattern in the carpet. He vowed to speak not a word of the foyer's bold green.

His heart rose as he turned the corner onto Devonshire

Terrace, then abruptly stopped beating. A large green-and-black park-drag coach stood in front of his own iron gate, loaded at the top with steamer trunks. Young Charley was pushing Timberdoodle into the carriage from behind; Walter pulled at his collar from the front. Katey and Mamie, in smart traveling clothes, emerged from the house.

"Girls. Where are you going?"

"To Scotland. Grandmama's," said Katey, putting on her bravest face.

Walter looked at his father mournfully, and sniffled. It was clear he'd been crying. "Is Christmas really canceled, Papa?"

"Why aren't you coming with us?" asked little Frank, sticking his own tear-and-candy–stained face out of the carriage.

Katey walked, stiff-spined, past her father, but Mamie stopped in front of him with a look of sincere concern, more than her usual. "I shall miss you, Papa."

"In you go, children!" said Catherine sternly.

Dickens turned to see his wife sweeping down the front steps in her best traveling suit, with the great tartan skirt. Doreen trod behind her in a hulking wool cape, with their yet-unnamed newborn bundled and tucked inside. Catherine crossed the gate and stopped short of the carriage to face her husband, taking up the long ribbons of her stiff-brimmed bonnet.

"In time to bid us farewell, I see," she said, tying a bow with quick, sharp movements.

"Why Scotland? Is your mother unwell?"

"Mother is fine, Charles. The trouble is with you."

Dickens looked at Doreen, who held fast to her mistress' side, as if she, too, knew exactly where the trouble lay, but relished the thought of hearing it. Determined not to endure her smug stare a second longer, he opened the carriage door and held out an insistent hand. Doreen turned up her nose, grabbed on, and heaved herself inside, jostling the coach and its contents. He clapped the door closed after her, and turned to his wife.

"What do you mean, the trouble is with me?"

Catherine snapped open her reticule, a green silk-velvet purse framed in cut steel, and produced Maria's pink letter. It surprised him to see it in her kid-gloved hand, having banished it from his own mind already.

"Apparently, in your haste yesterday, you left this behind," she said. "Yet Mrs. Winter believed it an important souvenir of your meeting."

"I want no souvenir."

"I believe it *her* souvenir, Charles. She paid us a visit this morning, quite unannounced, to say how much she regretted not having you autograph it while you were in her drawing room, and wondered whether you might do so before returning it to her. At your convenience, of course."

"Catherine. There is nothing between us."

"I should think not."

"Maria Beadnell is a bird-witted gossipmonger—"

"Then why did you go?"

Dickens pulled off his hat and let it drop to his side. He studied the cobblestones under his boots, which offered nothing in his defense. Even if Forster was right about Maria's true motive, it was no excuse at all.

"Because I'm a fool."

"On that we quite agree."

She turned toward the carriage, where the children pressed their faces against the glass. Dickens reached for her forearm, not wanting her to go. She looked at his hand curled around her sleeve, with cool emerald eyes. He pulled away, sheepish, and shook his head.

"Catherine, please."

She tipped her proud chin and waited.

"I realize you cannot be entirely sympathetic to the demands I feel upon me just now. To my state of mind."

"Nor you to mine."

"But you're changed toward me."

"We are changed toward each other."

"Perhaps I've not been at my best—"

"You've been at your worst. Terrorizing the children. Nagging me about the household refurbishments—"

"But you deck the halls as if this were Windsor Palace!"

He gasped as soon as he said it, as if to suck the words back inside. He hadn't meant to be harsh, but the corners of her mouth wilted, and her eyes glossed with tears. These were the weeks of *her* ups and downs, and when the smallest kindness could buoy her he had instead made it worse.

"Oh, Catherine. If you'd only let me explain."

"I think it quite explains itself." She handed him the pink letter and pursed her lips. "Perhaps I do derive joy from things you regard as frivolous, Charles. But beneath it all, I have not forgotten what matters. And until *you* remember, I think it best we be apart."

"You're leaving me?" he asked, incredulous, searching her face for the wife he knew to be patient and fair.

It was Catherine's turn to search the ground at her shoes. She was a proud woman, and could be fierce when called for, even in low spirits. Dickens knew her to rarely change course, once decided. She looked up from beneath the brim of her bonnet to meet his gaze.

"I am, for now, leaving you to yourself."

Dickens looked at the pink letter in his hand. It now seemed so ridiculous and pointless a folly on his part. He wanted to disagree, protest, make his own case, but he knew she was right. He was hardly fit for his own company, much less hers. No amount of groveling or humility would change it. Instead, he opened the carriage door and offered an apologetic hand. Catherine swept up the skirts of her traveling suit and slipped her gloved hand into his, if only to steady her step. He held on tight.

"Will you return by Christmas?" he asked.

"I cannot say. But rest assured, *we* shall have Christmas wherever we are. With or without you."

Catherine stepped into the carriage, releasing her husband's hand. He hesitated, folded the steps, and closed the door behind her. The coachman, who had waited respectfully by, boarded the top and took the reins. Walter and Frank waved through the window. Young Charley put his hand to the glass. Dickens matched it finger for finger, until the coachman urged the horses away, hooves clattering down Devonshire Terrace. He stood alone in the middle of the street and watched the carriage disappear around the corner, listened until there was no sound at all. He was mad at the world, mad at himself.

"Oh, damn it all."

Part II

15

By midmorning on his first day alone, Dickens began to enjoy his ill-gotten peace. He dismissed the cook first thing, discharged two workmen, and drove a decorator to gather his chintzes and flee. He assumed his writing post at half-past eight in good twig and high spirits, with nothing, as far as he could tell, to stand between him and a quick Christmas book. No hammering at the walls, patter of feet on the stairs, or clatter of pans in the basement kitchen. Even Topping tiptoed about.

Dickens did miss his fusee clock, which had been recovered from an azalea bush in the garden and declared a dead loss. But, now captain of his own ship, he saw time stretched out before him, and calm, quiet seas. His bowsprit pointed straight to the unseen shore of a new story. Embarking was never easy, but he could concentrate everything he had on the task now that he was free to be diligent without any distraction at all. He had a full stack of fresh foolscap and a good supply of a new blue ink that was said to dry upon leaving the pen. No more smudges or blotting. Just thoughts and words, paper and quill.

He put a finger to each temple, elbows splayed like a flying jib, filled his lungs with air, and squeezed his eyes shut. But instead of pictures in his head, a bout of seasickness roiled his gut. He stared out over the garden, but all he could see were steel-colored clouds conspiring for a late-morning storm. That first vertiginous thrill of being alone to do whatever he pleased, write whenever he wanted, crashed and died. When the rain did arrive, pelting the windows with drops the size of boiled sweets, he had to slap his own cheeks to keep from nodding off. He cleaned his nails with the letter opener, pulled a few mem-slips from his pocket, and pasted them onto the wall.

When morning rounded the bend for noon and the tempest outside blustered on, Dickens had a clipped conversation with the Master's Cat (who offered no useful ideas at all), took three stretching breaks, a light lunch, and a cold bath to clear his head. By late afternoon he had one half-written paragraph that was illegible for all the scratching-out and barely good enough for the bin. He ran his fingers through his curls until they stood like jagged peaks in all directions. When he laid his cheek to rest on the green tooled leather surface of his desk, he caught sight of the miniature portraits of his children hanging side by side on a far wall, framed in gold and seed pearls, and had to look away. The quiet was more than he could bear.

He supped alone on cold beef, bathed again, and retired to bed early in hopes a good solid sleep would freshen his writing mind. But mostly he tumbled and tossed and lost the usual battle with the bedcovers. Catherine would be halfway to Scotland by now, parted from the husband who had clumsily betrayed her trust. Perhaps a separation was for the best. He had suffered a frenzy of false feeling, a grasping for his past instead of his present. Maria meant nothing to him. But it was a weakness in him to have reached for her at all, to believe she held a clue to something he'd lost along the way. The biggest terror of all was not being able to write, having no inspiration, no source, no reservoir of words and feelings, no one to prop him up or spur him on. No one to be his mirror, to reflect back what he thought he might be.

When the *rat-a-tat-tat* of the rain on the roof subsided, the chime of a clock tower in some distant square called to him. Desperate for a change of scene, he mistook it for company, got up, and went out. His first ten miles, he calculated, were quick ones. He had nothing to do and nowhere to go, but not one desire to turn home. There was nothing for him there, only empty corridors and groaning wood floors. He wanted noise and puddles, action and light. London was a never-ending spectacle, a great floating pageant. Surely he could count on it to fill his head with novel things, or at least show him where to look.

By mile twenty, he despaired of ever meeting a new thought again. He had inklings on every tired subject save the Christmas book, which triggered nothing in him but contempt for Chapman and Hall. There was nothing to do but let his boots carry him farther into the labryinth of the city. The fingernail moon vanished behind a curtain of mist and soot that fit his mood. Fog hovered in the hat brims of cabdrivers, rolled into stairwells to blanket snoring beggars, crept down the Thames bridge by bridge. It was a bludgeoning, hairy mist, he thought, like a prowling thief that would follow on your heels, knock you over the head, steal your thoughts, chew them up, and spit them out right in front of you, tiny particles scattering away on the brackish air. It was just the right weather for chasing phantoms about town.

Everything was strange, and everyone a stranger.

Dickens couldn't remember, suddenly, whether he'd crossed the Thames two times or three. Water lapped hard against a post; old wooden buildings rose above him like menacing monsters.

Rats scurried at his feet. He had come to the river's edge, but which edge, and what way to turn? Sweat pearled on his brow. He took off his hat to wipe his face with a kerchief. When he pulled his watch from his pocket, he startled to find it had stopped at quarter-past ten.

Dickens was lost. Time had abandoned him, all sense of when and where. The fog seemed alive, grabbing at a trouser leg, whirling about his shoulders. He wanted to outrun it, but each direction looked like every other, and his feet were made of lead. The muck on the embankment clutched at his boots; the murky air lay heavy on his lungs. He strained for each breath; his heart pulsed in his neck. There was no one about, no signpost, nothing to show him the way.

He quivered like the thin needle of a compass trying to find true north.

Dickens closed his eyes, three quick puffs of breath and a long inhale. Air in, air out. Just as he'd done as a boy when he sensed the world too strongly, or needed it too much. There was a knowing beyond thinking, beneath words. If he could only quiet his mind, reach for the little voice inside him—an inner-minder who somehow grasped what he did not. So, tucking his chin to his chest, he softened his breathing and listened for it. Air in, air out. And when he thought he heard a whisper from his smaller, wiser self, he tried again and finally willed his feet to walk.

16

When one's whereabouts are hard come by, a city is an impression of itself, a kaleidoscope of not-quite-right things, a variegated jumble of place and memory, all that is and once was. Dickens passed through it like a man with mechanical feet: heel, arch, toe, repeat. It was enough to deliver him safely across Southwark Bridge, where St. Paul's great dome, with its shimmering gold cross, dodged in and out of view, bouncing like a bauble on a high cloud shelf. He thought he knew Cheapside when he came upon it, but only from the waist down, its upper reaches swallowed by a thick froth of air. But when the rough walls of Newgate Prison appeared, Dickens moved along it, hand over hand, and felt his bearings take hold.

Fear became familiarity. The intersection at Old Bailey Street was right where it ought to be, and the row of tottering houses beyond, all the same. He rounded the corner for Snow Hill and there it was, the portal to the coachyard of the Saracens Head Inn, where he and Forster had first dined together, years ago. It was reassuring to find it still guarded by two stone heads looking down on him from either side of the gateway. Had they always been frowning? Dickens couldn't recall. But the inn was its old self in every other way, content to sit at the top of the yard with the painted COFFEE ROOM faintly legible over an old long window. He was on a well-worn path now, his body knew what to do: pause here for the omnibuses clomping westward; stand clear of the cabriolets going east. Pass the pork man, the hatter, the draper, the Old Bell Tap. Head west for Holborn, but stop shy where the road narrows, take the snicket down the hill, cross two alleys, and come at last to the threshold of one's own past.

It was a minor no-name square, hardly a square at all, at the juncture of three insignificant roads. But it had been his universe once, the near-circumference of all that mattered. The dense vapor blurred its far reaches, made black silhouettes of its rooftops, but he knew it all by heart. Over there would be the stage door of the small jewel box of a theater where he'd first acted, down that street the chophouse where he liked to dine, and in the square's very center—he could just make it out—a stalwart brick clock tower he had once relied on for the time, that had long ago ceased to keep it.

The square had no pretensions, no ambitions to be grand, and, when better courts came to be, had fallen into disregard, but for a thick slap of paint now and then on a door here and there. But the fog hugged the little square dearly, and wrapped him, too, with welcome arms. He had long ago outgrown it, the circle of his world growing ever larger from those early days, but looking on it, he could breathe again. His heart let go some anchor.

Of course his feet would lead him here. Feet had memory, too.

He set his sights on the stage door of the Folly, straight

across, where his friend Macready was known to be giving his Hamlet, having recently been banished from Drury Lane upon tepid reviews. The two had traded letters for months, sometimes twice in a day, made plans and canceled them, called upon each other at home but been missed. The exchange of the borrowed waistcoat had been executed discreetly by their grooms, no questions asked. Dickens had never thanked him in person, despite the debacle of the Beadnell reunion, and here was his chance to make good. Muffled voices wafted on the air. Theatergoers streamed into the square and shuttled away, squeezing into cabs, sardining into an omnibus, fighting over umbrellas. The timing was perfect. A glimpse of his old friend was reason enough to have come all this way.

Heel, arch, toe, repeat. Dickens took his first steps with an airy lightness in his chest, an emperor returning from exile, hailed by the most lowly speck of soot. Even the soup-air seemed to part for his progress, cutting a narrow path as wide as his shoulders. And then he heard it. Over his head, the old clock tower rang like a tremolo inside him. It stilled him, made the smallest atom of his being clip to attention. He craned his neck to glance up at the tower, which seemed to look down on him, too, with its bright moon face. It was revived, as was he. Someone cared about the little square after all. How many years it had been since he'd relished the tower's fine clanging sound: so right and true. Such old friends they were, he thought, and glad for each other's presence.

The second chime bounced around the square like a game of rolling-ball, the third celebrated his arrival, the fourth was a tonic for his soul. By the ninth chime, he knew it must be midnight. He had lost track of hours and miles, but the last play-watchers were drifting away. He'd best hurry to catch Macready, who would be in his dressing room and, whether jubilant or despairing—for he was his own best and worst critic—surely grateful for the visit. But the clock's face held him transfixed.

The twelfth chime sounded, shuddering through the square and down to the soles of his feet. He surrendered to it, forgetting why he'd come, only able to pull himself away when the ringing faded to a hum and returned him to the imminent world. Macready, the Folly, old friends, bygone dramas. He should hurry, or he'd miss him. But the pulling away was like taffy. His torso turned in advance of his head, his feet ahead of his gaze. He didn't see her, or she, him. She must have shot across the square while he wasn't looking, maybe been obscured by the clock tower itself. He had cut her off and was now near to toppling a young woman in a deep purple cloak, the color of midnight itself. He caught himself in the nick of time. She stepped back with a gasp.

"I'm so sorry!" he said. "I didn't see you coming."

The woman looked up from beneath her velvet hood. Her face seemed lit from within, a pale pearl glow. She had gentle eyes, some sort of blue—unless the night was playing tricks—and glimmering, without one whit of terror at the prospect of being run down. He was struck by her simple beauty.

"How clumsy of me," he added, tipping his hat.

"No, no. It was I," the woman said, less afraid than amused.

He pointed to the tower above them, muttering an excuse. "You see, the clock, well, my own clock recently met an untimely end. And whenever I hear one chime, I'm reminded of . . ."

"Your lost clock?" she asked.

"No," he said, with sudden clarity. "Lost time."

He hadn't meant to be so blunt, but the answer had arrived on his lips straight from his heart with no thinking in between. She had a clear, calm radiance that invited the truth with no wish to judge it. The young woman studied his dark shining eyes, and appeared touched by his candor.

"Yet isn't there also, in that very chime, the chance to begin again?"

"Begin again," he said, admiring the thought of it. "Yes."

Her smile illuminated the darkness itself. "Well, then," she said, lowering her gaze. "Good night."

She started past him, headed straight for the farthest corner of the haphazard square. He watched her go, purple cloak sweeping gracefully behind. It had its own wind, he thought, made its own weather. The brume seemed to twirl away as she walked, as if it favored her, too. The fog was lifting all at once.

A voice from behind shattered the moment's magic.

"Why, it was at this very theater, not so many Christmases ago, that he first called me his 'sweetling pigsney.'"

Dickens turned to find, as he feared, Maria Beadnell parading across the square, followed by a gaggle of fur-coated friends with matching bouncing plumage about their necks. He could hardly believe his eyes.

"And I'm told he walks these streets still," she driveled on, "no doubt haunted by the ghost of our love . . ."

Dickens cringed at the sound of her tittering laugh, still repelled by his own misjudgment at meeting her. Maria was headed straight for him, but they'd not yet locked eyes. In a panic, he spun around and tripled his step toward the stranger in the purple cloak, who was crossing through the dim mouth of a narrow street barely large enough for a cart to go through it. She startled to find him falling in beside her, walking briskly.

"Do not be alarmed. I am only pretending to walk you home."

"Then I shall pretend not to be alarmed," she said, looking straight ahead.

"I mean you no harm. I am merely fleeing my past," he said,

glancing back over his shoulder in hopes Maria had not followed him.

A few doors from where she'd turned, not thirty feet from the square, the woman stopped at a brick-terraced lodging, low and thin as two fingers. It was a poor, slant-roofed house, nestled in a maze of little courts and alleys where costermongers lived and itinerant traders took rooms. This was the sort of London where rich and poor might mingle in near proximity, if worlds apart.

"Flee all you like," she said, turning to face him. "Your past is quicker than you are and will catch you soon enough."

Dickens cocked his head to wonder at her bit of wisdom, spoken with crystalline confidence, when he was distracted by more voices jangling behind them. From where he stood he could make out Maria's back end being safely delivered into the belly of a hansom cab with the help of two coachmen who pushed her in. Her cackling lingered in the square until the door shut her definitively inside.

"I am saved," he said with heavy relief.

"Then I've served you well."

"Indeed. You cannot know what misery you've spared me." He removed his hat and bowed his head. "I am grateful."

"And *I* am home," she said, putting her hand on the door's rusted iron knob.

"You live here?"

"And work there," she said, pointing back at the theater, a sliver of its stage door visible beyond the clock tower.

"Hmm. I like the efficiency of it."

She opened the door into a pitch-black hall leading to a narrow staircase that dipped hard to the left. "Well, thank you . . . for pretending."

Before he could utter another word, form a sound or even a

thought, the door closed quietly between them. He hesitated, hoping he hadn't frightened her, and stepped back to look at the window above. He scratched his chin, chuckled to himself, returned his topper to his head, and waited for a candle to be lit inside, that he might be assured of her safety, as she'd assured his. When a gentle glow blossomed above, he walked on into the night in another direction altogether, with renewed vigor and miles still left inside him.

17

Dickens wandered into the checkered streets mumbling to himself, eyebrows dancing, replaying the conversation—her parts, his parts—embellishing here and there, what he might have said had he his wits more about him, or she a hundred steps farther to go. He'd forgotten about Macready altogether, the dread of Maria Beadnell, the frustrations of starting a book he didn't want to write. For the first time all night he felt his feet firmly beneath him, as if gravity now worked in his favor.

When next he looked up, his inner-minder had carried him just shy of Leather Lane, straight to Furnival's Inn, as known to him as the knuckle of his right thumb. Once the town mansion of the Lords Furnival, it had long ago tumbled to a more humble purpose as coffeehouse and hotel, where a gentleman might still get a good dinner at a fair price, even if his fellow diners were now less than fashionable. But Dickens loved its withering stucco and worm-eaten wood beams. It had been his first true lodgings, at a smart rent, when he was just beginning his writing life. In three simple rooms at No. 13 Furnival's Inn, he'd found the place of his own becoming. He hadn't thought of it in so long, not until Catherine mentioned it, their first Christmas, those early days. And here he was again, all these years later, looking at it like it was an old friend who'd gone missing for years, only to be stumbled upon happily in the street.

"Begin again," the young woman had said to him. It rang in his ears, as sure as the old clock tower had chimed over his head. This, too, was his past, but the fondest part of it. Whether instinct or luck had led him here, it would be a terrible waste of coincidence to turn away.

The sleepy desk clerk, awakened by a zealous pounding on the door well after midnight, was a thin young man with porcupine hair and a zigzag nose. He had kind button eyes too close together, thick spectacles, a food-stained waistcoat, and a misbuttoned shirt. Dickens stood before him, about to sign his name to the register, when he saw an engraved plaque hanging on the wall: CHARLES DICKENS SLEPT HERE.

"I trust this will be strictly confidential," Dickens said in a whisper.

"What's that, sir?" asked the clerk.

"My stay."

"Oh, the comin's and goin's of our 'clientele' are no business o' mine."

Why, the clerk didn't know him. The young man appeared blind as a bat, and possibly no smarter than a doorknob, but it was a rare event for Dickens not to be recognized at all. Even his less-than-devoted readers seemed to know him on sight. Some part of him took offense, but another took heart. His whereabouts and what-doings, he decided, should be nobody's business but his.

He pointed to the plaque to test his theory. "Dickens slept here, did he?"

The young clerk looked straight at him, with no hint of recognition at all. "So they says. Turned 'is old rooms into a museum. Left everythin' just as 'e did. So they says." He leaned in with a wink-wink. "It's a sideline. Two pence an 'ead just to see it."

"Popular attraction, is it?"

"Oh, not anymore, sir," said the clerk.

Dickens scowled. But the clerk lit up with an idea of his own. "In fact, if you was interested in number thirteen, and didn't mind the occasional—and I mean 'occasional'—visitor, there might even be a discount to ya . . ." He leaned over the register, squinting hard only to see that his new customer had written nothing. "Sorry, sir, but ya 'ave to sign yer name, or we don't know who ya are."

Dickens hesitated, the quill in his hand poised over the register. If not Dickens, who would he be? Until now he'd been famed for his onomastic finesse—a knack for inventing names that epitomized his characters, breathed life into them. His pockets might teem with jotted-down cues from the street, words he liked, even sounds. Public lists, obituaries—his own correspondence—were a vast trove of raw material. But most came from thin air, the outer wings of his imagination, fully-formed on his lips, where all the joy was in the saying: Quilp, Buzfuz, Crimple, Grimwig, Lillyvick, Swiveller, Squeers, and Gamp. Names that sparkled and cracked, hummed and hissed. It was more than verbal dexterity, a stage trick, a pun. A made-up name could hold a truth, even if he didn't know what truth it yet was.

And then it came to him. The invitation from the temperance society that had angered him so. Yes, of course. That was it!

Five minutes at Furnival's and he'd already had an idea. He dipped the pen and wrote in the register, pleased with himself, even making a show of it. He slid it toward the clerk, who read deliberately, a finger under each name.

"Ebenezer . . . Scrooge?"

"Scrooge it is," he said with a satisfied twist of his fist. "Says it all, I think."

"All right, then," said the clerk, seeming curious a man could so admire his own name after having it all these years. "Never met a Scrooge."

"Well, you've met one now."

Dickens took off his hat with near-reverence as he stepped inside No. 13, at the top of the rickety stairs. The clerk used his candle to fire up the cloudy oil lamp on the mantel. It was enough to scatter light across the snug box of a room, with two smaller rooms on its flanks. Dickens recognized the Turkish carpet in the middle of the floor and the two balloon-back chairs in gold velvet—the "mister" now lacking one arm, and the "missus" a few button eyes. But he was most glad to see his old birch writing desk, with its turned legs, two drawers with brass pulls, and a wooden lip around three sides, no taller than a five-pound note. It was the first piece of furniture he'd ever bought, from an old countinghouse near Cornhill whose partners had died within a week of each other, though still, apparently, intending to turn a profit. Dickens had given their poor, set-upon clerk everything in his pocket, and hired a cab to deliver it.

He slid his hand across the dull grain of the old table, its nicks and burn marks, round spots of yellowed wax. He knew them all. This was where his "Boz" was born, so many of the *Sketches* that worked their way into readers' homes and hearts; then *Pick-*

wick, which catapulted him to the literary firmament. Twenty monthly numbers, fourteen guineas apiece—what a fortune for him then. Enough to marry, have a child, move house. He was a blithe up-and-comer who thought nothing of leaving it behind, this desk, now seeming small and precious, when it once was vast, his entire future spread before him.

"Y'admire him, sir? Dickens?" asked the clerk over his shoulder, squatting to light a fire in the hearth.

"I did once."

Dickens sat in the table's ladder-back chair, feeling each chink of its spine. He smiled when it creaked and tilted like old times, having one leg shorter than the other three. He fished out a blank mem-slip from his pocket, folded it in fourths, and put it under the feeble leg, pleased his old trick still worked. Behind him, the clerk pulled a coat sleeve over his fist and rubbed away the grime on a windowpane.

"It's a view, sir. Of rooftops, anyway. If ya like that sort of thing."

Dickens stood beside him and looked out. He could see the outlines of his own reflection in the dingy glass, flames awakening in the small fireplace behind him. Outside, the sky had cleared and the moon welcomed a huddle of crazy chimney stacks, gables, and peaked roofs, all leaning against each other; sleepy windows, some gaping, some broken-paned and stuffed with rags; and in the distance, through a narrow gap, the tip-top of his clock tower peeping over them. If he stood close enough and pressed his forehead against the glass, he could look down to slivers of streets and alleys that led to his little square. His world felt whole again.

"How long'll ya be stayin', sir?" asked the clerk.

"As long as it takes. I'm to write a Christmas book."

"A writer. Now I see. Ya like this room fer luck!"

"I'm hoping. In fact, I wonder if you might do me the favor of the loan of a quill and some ink and paper."

"I s'pose I could," said the clerk, with his signature wink, "if we keeps it strictly confidential."

Dickens smiled, grateful. The clerk started for the door, turning back with a thought.

"But if it's a Christmas book, ya best 'urry, Mr. Scrooge."

The sun rose and fell and rose again, before word got to Forster where his friend was installed. He marched to Furnival's first thing to demand an explanation, but found an unshaven, slack-shirted Dickens hunkered happily over his old table, pen floating side to side. Forster surveyed the room, rocking on a warped floorboard. The wallpaper peeled at its seams where it wasn't scraped away altogether or discolored with damp. The rug had faded into a dirty wash of not-quite-color, its edges more frayed than fringed.

"Are you quite sure about this place?"

"Never more sure."

Forster stared at the "mister" chair, judging whether it was safe to sit on. Its sun-bleached gold velvet was worn to the nubbins and stained.

"I daresay, it's much changed," he said, choosing to stand instead.

"As am I," said Dickens, putting down his pen. He stacked his new pages and rose from his chair, not tired in the least. "But when I stood before it, how my heart yenned for those memless, penniless, worryless days. For the writer I was then. Why, since late my first night here I've been smoky at work, as if this were the very thing I needed all along."

Forster edged closer to the writing table. He cocked his chin hard to the left, trying to make out the upside-down words on the page. "The Christmas book?"

"I've got my steam on for it, Forster."

"Have you a title?"

"Oh, better than a title."

"A plot?"

Dickens buttoned his waistcoat, went to a small three-legged basin, and splashed water on his face, giving nothing else away.

"A character? A scene?" asked Forster, hope flagging. "Have mercy, Boz, and toss me a crumb to nibble on?"

"You shall know soon enough."

"I remind you it's to be to the printers two weeks from today. Two weeks!"

"I don't even know what today is!" said Dickens, glad of the fact.

"Tuesday," said Forster. "With too few Tuesdays left before Christmas."

"It's meant to be a short book. You know I've written more in less time before. And I'm writing again. That should make you happy."

Forster looked around the rooms, waving shafts of gritty light away. "But Furnival's Inn? This frenzy of yours?"

"A frenzy that just may finish it in time."

"Very well. But be watchful, Boz. Word is out that Chapman and Hall have asked for a Christmas book, and there are spies everywhere, wanting to beat you to the punch."

"Don't worry!" he said, toweling his face with a kerchief. "No one knows my whereabouts, I assure you."

18

The pushing, throbbing market at Covent Garden was just the place to lose himself and find inspiration there for the taking. The warm weather notwithstanding, the holiday season had begun in earnest. A brigade of holiday billstickers, armed with paste pot and brush, blinded walls with colorful broadsides promoting this tonic, that corset, a snuffbox, an ale. Costermonger baskets brimmed with holly, its shiny leaves and red berries the best advertising there was. The pilfered greens, extracted at night from the best London homes and walls, were today cheerfully sold back to the very housekeepers whose houses the coster boys had filched them from. But no one cared. Everyone was buying. Even the poor wanted their pennyworth of holly, laurel, and "mizzletoe."

Ladies shopped, hawkers shouted, pickpockets picked pockets.

Dickens fell in with a swarm of shoppers and donkey-barrows streaming in from Long Acre to the Strand on one side, Bow to Bedford on the other. The flagstones were stained green from the tromped-on leaves underfoot, and slippery as ice.

He liked the rattle of iron tires, the hawking and gossip, teasing and fun, but the bell of the muffin-and-crumpet man called to him above all else. He hadn't eaten in two days.

He pivoted toward the smell of fresh bread, when he caught sight of a small figure shadowed in an arched doorway, peering out at him. It was a ragged boy, in a man's clothes, sketching fast with a stump of black lead. His eyes, too big for his face, stole glances at him; the child drew quick, sharp strokes in between. Dickens was used to this, the quick-sketch artists in the street, trading on celebrity and gossip, for their fair share of not very much at all. He didn't mind, as long as the likeness was a good one. He started for the lad, who, seeing him approach, darted into the crowd. He meant the boy no harm, was only curious to see what he'd drawn. If it was good, he might've even been flattered and given the child a coin for it. He stopped and looked in all directions, but the boy had disappeared.

When he turned back, a toothless old woman with a dried-plum face blocked his path. She stuck a roughly tied bundle of dried flowers under his nose. "Lavender for the missus, sir?"

"Oh, no," said Dickens, stumbling over his words. "The missus is . . . away."

"Perhaps a 'miss,' then," said the woman, pumping her woolly brows and cackling like a goose.

Dickens shook his head and stepped around her. It jolted him to be reminded of Catherine's sudden departure, to say the words aloud. She had left him, no, left him to himself, that was her point. She must have known he couldn't bear to be at home without her. Perhaps that was to be his penance. So how propitious that Furnival's had materialized out of the ether to shelter him. The place he'd spent his bachelor days, before Catherine, before marriage and children. It was true certain burdens of daily life now felt lessened by it, and returned him to that younger self, with only his own needs to meet. Hunger the first among them.

He followed the sound of the muffin man's bell receding from the piazza, fixing his eyes on the white apron tied at the seller's back and the tray on his head covered with green baize. Now that it was well past noon, he'd be lucky if a single crumpet remained, but if so, he determined to be the one to have it. He tunneled into the crowd in pursuit, when he stopped short at the sight of flowing purple velvet weaving in and out of the throng not twenty feet in front of him—the cloak of the young woman he'd met that night in the square. He nudged people out of the way to clear his view and get closer; she was grace in every step, finally settling into a small crowd of shoppers with an empty basket over her arm, inspecting a wagonload of winter cabbages. Her hood was down; she wore no bonnet. He marveled at the soft lines of her profile, the milky skin and just-right nose, the bloom of primrose on her cheek. Her light mahogany hair was braided in a wreath at the back of her head, save a loose tendril that danced against her neck. When she happened to look left and catch his eye, she blushed at the sight of him and turned quickly away. Why shouldn't she? He was gawking at her like an infatuated schoolboy. But he seized on the serendipity. The old woman was still clucking close behind him.

"In fact, I will have the flowers," he said. "They may yet brighten someone's day."

He exchanged a coin for them and took the lavender tight in his fist, but when he spun around to the cabbage wagon, the young woman was gone. In her stead, a buxom woman dressed in a riot of fuchsia and green was bearing down on him, blocking out everything else. It was Maria Beadnell herself.

"Is that you, Charley?" she called, elbowing her way to stand before him, in a gushing display of jewels and joie di vivre: a hat in the French style, voluminous pink ostrich feathers spouting from a brown velvet cap, earrings a dangling spray of leaves, flowers, and birds in gold, peridot, and amethyst. If her husband was indeed a bankrupt, it was as if the less money she had, the more gaudy her display.

"Fancy the two of us meeting here, of all places! How I love the low life, don't you?"

Dickens was speechless. Despite his dismissal of her recent attentions, and Forster's warnings about her needing money, the sight of Maria still made his heart stop. He relived the terror of first feelings and the horror of their recent reunion all at once—a dream interrupted by a nightmare. He gave her a lopsided smile and wielded the bouquet between them like a buffer. But they were no defense against her.

"Lavender for me?" she said, a hand to her ample breast. "The very symbol of love, devotion, and purity?"

"Actually, Maria, I—"

"How terribly sweet," she said, plucking the flowers from his grasp. "Why, since our meeting I've been hoping against hope we might find each other again, and here we are, walking down memory lane together."

"Indeed, I'm just now on my way—"

"Oh, don't be silly! This is fate, plain and simple. We have years of catching up to do, Charley, years and years. Don't you agree? Why, we've hardly just begun. In fact, you must come 'round for tea. I insist. I've a cabriolet waiting around the corner."

Dickens was trapped like a rat. "Tea, now? In the afternoon?"

"Haven't you heard? It's all the rage. With dinner so late these days, we all need a light repast to sustain us. You know that terrible sinking feeling 'round midafternoon? Of course, we have the Duchess of Bedford to thank for it, but I'm told 'afternoon tea' will soon be enjoyed throughout the empire. Tea with scones and clotted cream! Shall we be decadent together?"

Dickens had a sinking feeling of his own. Maria wiggled her arm through his, an iron grip on his elbow. Even if she was angling for a loan, he was hungry and had no will to resist her. At the very least, he was assured of a fancy, well-baked bun and perhaps a nice glass of sherry. But he cast a glance over his shoulder as they went, hoping to catch sight once more of the young woman in the purple cloak.

She was nowhere to be seen.

19

Dickens was surprised to find, awaiting them at Artillery Place, a low table laid with a fat pink rose on the side of each cup, hearts of lettuce, thin bread, butter, and pillowy scones baked that morning. It was as if she'd been stalking him with every expectation of success. Once his hunger was sated, he'd suffered politely through the rest, learning more about "little tea," "low tea," "high tea," and "handed tea" than any one person should know. If it was the rage and the thing, it was also a twaddle and a bore. But Maria prattled on.

Over the hoped-for glass of sherry, he endured the requisite false praise and flummery of *him*, followed by a second glass to wash down a gloating, unnecessary discursion on the merits of Mr. Winter—her beloved Henry—which Dickens felt sure was the windup to a plea for money. But the plea never came. A part of him wanted her to ask, beg even, so he could refuse her. Perhaps that's why he'd come, or stayed so long, to exact some small crumb of revenge for the way she'd tossed him over and then pitied his misery. That memory of Maria had haunted him for years. This was torment of another variety.

If there was no satisfaction to be had over tea, the importunate Maria Beadnell was turned quickly to the service of the Christmas book. Back at Furnival's, she inspired him late into the night. A spiteful smile played on his features as he dipped his pen and wrote.

"No sooner did his eyes fall upon the subject of his old passion—her lizard tongue darting out in search of each bite, a dollop of clotted cream clinging to the folds of her chin—than cherished memories of Christmas past were lost to him forever."

Dickens laid down his quill, checked his watch, found it near midnight, and stood for his coat. Outside, a recent downpour had mellowed to a sprinkle, which refreshed his upturned face. He set off straight for the Folly, where he hoped, with any luck, to catch a moment with the purple-cloaked young woman, whose sighting that morning had stayed with him since then, perhaps even helped him suffer through his imprisonment at Artillery Place. He had no plan as to what he would say to her, but the mere thought of being in her presence, however briefly, softened the harder edges of his day.

He lurked near the stage door, waiting as parties of playwatchers burst out of the gallery doors—the half-price pit and box sitters footing it into the muddy street for the gin palaces and public houses, while the more haughtily dressed joggled into hackney coaches and cabriolets. To avoid detection, not only for fear of Maria, who seemed to be all but hunting him, but because he was known among the theatergoing crowd, he turned to face the brick wall and pulled his hat low. Under the wavering yellow gaslight, the playbills plastered on every square inch shouted for attention. Macready's *HAMLET* was buried by advertisements from every theater in town: MONSIEUR PLEGE AND HIS LAUGHING GAS! HERR BOORN WITH HIS LIVING MARIONETTES! MADAME BARIERE WITH HER LIONS, BEARS AND DOGS DINING WITH HER AT TABLE AND TAKING FOOD FROM HER MOUTH! Working his way along, he was promised circus acts, sea battles, a grand bal masqué, and, of course, the to-be-revealed, not-to-be-missed GORGEOUS COMIC CHRISTMAS SHOW, every theater's one assured money-spinner of the year.

At the end of the collage, he found a fresh-pasted poster shouting louder than all the others. It had bright orange type, some words as tall as a head, announcing, FOR THE FOURTH TIME, AN ENTIRELY ORIGINAL, IRONICAL BURLETTA OF MEN & MANNERS FOUNDED ON THE CELEBRATED PAPERS BY 'BOZ!' WRITTEN AND ADAPTED EXPRESSLY FOR THIS ESTABLISHMENT BY W. MONCRIEFF AND CALLED, NICHOLAS NICKLEBY, OR DOINGS AT DO-THE-BOYS HALL!

Dickens fumed. He could hardly count the number of theaters and playwrights who'd stolen his work and made insufferable fluff of it, at times before he'd even finished the book in question. Forster had sued the plagiarists and fought every theater manager in town, nearly to fisticuffs, to no avail. Dickens finally took the matter up on his own, wanting to make an example of Moncrieff in particular, the most relentless dramatic thief, who'd mutilated his work time and again. He satirized him cruelly as "Mr. Crummles" in *Nickleby*, all unbound self-conceit and vanity. Moncrieff responded by stealing *Nickleby*. Apparently, on an annual basis.

"Boz!" He heard a thundering baritone, and turned to find William Macready lumbering toward him, arms outstretched, leaving his flock of fellow thespians and hangers-on to wait by the stage door. Dickens was never more glad for those flat features, irregular nose, and natural scowl, not the look of an actor at all, but eyes full of fire and warmth.

"Macready!" he said, starting with a hearty handshake and ending in a hug.

They were old friends, godfather to each other's children—mutual admirers. It was well established in their circle that Macready, a man of high culture and wide reading, thought Dickens a genius, had sobbed openly over three of his books, and considered him one of only two amateurs with any pretension to theatrical talent. Dickens relished recalling the night Macready confided to him that his own two Macbeths put together paled next to Dickens' public reading of *Twist*. He didn't care that some found Macready a moody, ill-tempered, grumbling egotist; he had never fought with Dickens, and even called him "the one friend who really loves me."

"Oh, Boz. I do hope you haven't seen my Hamlet tonight. Not quite up to snuff, you know?"

"I haven't. Why, is something the matter?"

Macready leaned in, lowering his voice. "I am to quit the London theater."

"Good heavens! Why?"

"All the wrong people are making the money, and none of the right ones are," he said, sweeping his arm across the ocean of playbills.

"I know the feeling."

"I knew you would."

A few more actors emerged from the theater, with stagehands, a musician, a pair of ushers. Dickens was glad to see Macready, but another part of him yearned for a glimpse of purple cloth. He was determined not to miss the girl twice in one day, if only to apologize for his forwardness the night they'd met under the clock tower when he'd nearly chased her home.

Macready carried on, oblivious, eyes flaring with an idea. He grabbed Dickens' forearm and held it hard. "In fact, Boz, do you remember, long ago as young actors together, how we dreamed of a traveling troupe?"

"I do remember, of course."

"Well, a few of us are plotting to put on all of Shakespeare's plays before audiences who've never seen them. Virgin audiences. We sail for India in the new year!"

Macready had his attention now, filled his head with color and spice: fire-breathing red, deep orange-marigold, golden turmeric, Krishna-blue, and the bright green of happiness. Queen Victoria herself had recently introduced curry powder, made of ginger, cardamom, pepper, and mace, which had opened a new world of culinary possibility. It tasted of freedom to him.

"India . . ."

"It is a vast, untapped market!"

"Have you room for one more?"

"Of course! Why, I've always said you were born to theatricals!" Macready waved vaguely to his waiting fans and fellow actors. "Come dine with us. You remember the old chop-house—"

Dickens was tempted to throw in, when his eye caught a coterie of young women exiting the stage door. He put a hand on Macready's shoulder. "No, no, old friend. I shan't intrude."

Macready followed his gaze. "Ah, I get your meaning," he said, with a conspiratorial clap of his friend's back. "Well, think of India."

"I will, indeed. I promise."

He watched his friend's entourage fall in step behind him, the great actor leading them away with a monologue to the night. Dickens smiled and swiveled back to the passel of women clustered under a single gaslight wishing each other a fair night's rest, with flushed cheeks and wisps of falling-down hair. It was strange to him, waiting for someone he didn't know, but his heart pinged when she appeared at the back, velvet hood down, eyes clear and bright, glinting like stars on a country night.

There was something familiar about her, some faint memory of the just-so of her face. He couldn't call it up until a slight turn of her chin made him remember. It was right *here*, at the Folly, not two years past. A light comic burletta. He sat four rows from center stage; she wore a pirate costume in blue bronze and sang a lovely ditty, straight from her heart. Even then, he couldn't take his eyes away.

The women pulled away from each other in twos and threes. Dickens set out after the single velvet cloak gliding across the square in the direction of home.

"Hello, again," he said matter-of-factly, falling in step beside her.

"Hello. Again." She stopped abruptly and faced him. "Though before we take another step together, sir, may I ask, are we still pretending?"

"No!"

"Well, I remember last time that you were 'pretending' to walk me home."

"But this time I quite intend it. Though I *am* pretending to have brought you a small gift of lavender." He held up a tight fist, offering a faux-bouquet.

"Why a gift?" she asked, amused. "What have I done to deserve it?"

"Ah, you see, I felt you bestowed a great favor upon me night before last, and I bought a little bundle of lavender to thank you—"

"Well, then, where is it?"

"Mmm. Donated. But to a lesser cause, I assure you."

Dickens caught a small upward curve of her lips, a near-smile, but he couldn't be sure. The fickle rain had stopped but everything glistened around them, shiny puddles and oily cobblestones. The luster of her swept-up hair.

"I've seen you before," he said, pointing back to the theater. "There, on that very stage. You were a singing pirate, I can see it now, with blue ribbons in your hair."

"Oh, that was long ago."

"Not so long. Why, I can still hear your lilting voice. You are an actress. I guessed as much."

"A seamstress," she said, resuming her trajectory for home. "It was only that one night, when the better actress was ill."

"I saw her as well," he said, striding beside her. "She was not better. She was bad. I remember nothing about her but her badness! You are an actress, no matter what you say. And I ought to know, having played a part or two myself in a theatrical here and there. Why, even now I am thinking of joining a troupe—"

"But you're a novelist, Mr. Dickens."

He slowed his step, taken aback. "You know me?"

She turned to meet his eyes. "Everyone knows you. Are you not Charles Dickens, the greatest living writer in all the English language?"

"Only living?"

She swallowed a laugh, half biting her lip.

"And only the *English* language?"

At last she succumbed, with a laugh that started at the crinkling corners of her eyes, sounding its mirthful notes to the far end of the square. He was bewitched by the unrestrained joy of it. But a few steps more and they were already stopped at her door.

"In truth," he said, surprised by his own serious turn, "the writing comes not as easily as it did once. And in darker moments, I fear might never come again."

She studied his face. Not just his eyes, but his cheeks, chin, forehead—all the parts put together. He wondered what she saw. On good days he thought himself a man on the outskirts of middle age, still possessed of a fine, youthful vigor. On bad, his own wrinkles in the mirror repelled him, crooked lines and creases that bore the history of his years.

"That is too great a tragedy to consider," she said. "The writing will come again, and must."

"In fact, the night we met, I wrote into the small hours, as I hadn't in ages." He paused, coming to an awareness himself. A smile took hold of his face. "Why, it was as if . . . I'd found my muse!"

She smiled easily this time, flattered. "If only it were a living."

"And yet, the greater one's living, it seems, the less one truly lives."

She looked into his eyes. He felt it all the way to his soul, any gulf between them disappearing. Something about the sympathetic fairness of her face made him speak the truth, even where he wasn't yet sure of it himself. The truth of Furnival's, his reason for being there, for being left alone to find his way. How much he wanted to let go the embellishments of life as Charles Dickens, and find what it was just to write again.

There was a quiet moment between them, thinking their own thoughts.

"Well, good night, Mr. Dickens," she said at last.

"But I know a wonderful chophouse . . ."

She hesitated, a hand on her door. "Perhaps another time."

"May I at least, I mean, since you know my name, may I know yours? Miss—"

"Lovejoy. Eleanor Lovejoy."

"Miss Eleanor Lovejoy." Dickens clasped his hands and thanked the sky. "What a marvelous name!"

"For a muse?"

It was his turn to consider her. She had the natural honesty of a wild rose, all briary thorns and pink satin petals.

"No," he said, with a theatrical bow and a tip of his hat. "For you."

Eleanor Lovejoy dipped her chin and curtsied. And then, without another word or glance, she stepped inside, pulling the door closed behind her.

20

The next morning, Dickens sat at Saracens Head Inn gobbling his breakfast as if he hadn't eaten a good meal in days—one plate of beef, another of shrimp, a hot kidney pudding, coffee, and claret—gesturing with his fork between bites and quaffs, as he described minute details of his new-old life at Furnival's Inn. Forster, who had no appetite at all, watched with wonder. He'd seen it before, and took it as a good sign. When his friend was onto a new story in a promising way, his hunger for all things was boundless.

Forster gingerly asked the question most on his mind. "How's it coming, then, the Christmas book?"

"I'm feeling my way," Dickens said, wiping his mouth with a generous napkin tucked in at his collar.

"You've a solid start?"

"More a middle."

"So a muddle," Forster concluded, nicking a piece of fatty meat from the plate.

"Certainly no ghosts, sprites, or goblins, but worthy enough without one."

"Pages, Boz, we need pages."

"Soon enough, I assure you."

"I assure *you* that Chapman and Hall breathe down my neck on a daily basis," said Forster, popping the beef in his mouth.

Dickens forked a final bite and chewed on it awhile. Forster need not be his concern. Not now. This was all on him. "Keep them at bay a little longer," he said. "I'll finish the book, settle the score, and be done with the lot of them." He gulped the last of the claret and set his glass firmly on the table, eyes glinting. "Perhaps even done with the life of the pen!"

Forster rolled his eyes and spit out a piece of gristle.

"Macready sails to India in the new year. He's taking a troupe."

"Boz. The point of Furnival's was to write without distraction."

"Well, perhaps one," he said, pulling his napkin from his collar. "A most inspiring young woman."

"Oh, good Lord. Who is she?" demanded Forster, being the weary but watchful guardian of his friend's time, talent, and heart.

"I hardly know anything about her. Yet fear I cannot write another word until I do."

"Do what?"

Dickens folded his napkin and placed it neatly on the table. He looked at Forster, wistful. "Know everything about her."

In a postprandial burst of energy, Dickens said good-bye to Forster, and set off north toward Furnival's, but soon found himself at Clerkenwell instead, at a small flower market. On a whim he bought a fistful of laurel, thinking he'd offered Miss Lovejoy a false token the night before and wanted to make good on it. He knew he should be writing instead, but what was the use when she occupied every turn in his mind? So he launched into the trapezium of shabby thoroughfares, courts within courts, sorry alleys, and little lanes that would lead him from there to her lodging house.

This was the land of coffee stalls and old-clothesmen, catch-penny broadsides, ballad singers, and lamplighters, sellers of stationery, songs, and last dying speeches. Dickens dodged the beggars and crossing sweepers, narrowly missing a bucket of slop emptied from a window over his head. "Git yer matches! Razors! Scissors and thread!" yelled the Irish costers working their shallow baskets. But as he was neither buying nor giving, they gave him a wide berth.

The clusters of tenements and rows of lodging houses looked cramped and unhappy, with dwarf doors and squeezed windows, broken shutters, if shutters at all, and more paper and rags than glass in them. There was a barber in one front parlor, a herring vendor in another, a cobbler visible through an opening out back. A few rickety balconies leaned hard on thin wood columns as if on crutches, which threatened to drop at any moment. People stood on them anyway, in shirtsleeves, yelling across to each other about the strangeness of the warm weather. Another two feet and they could have reached out and touched.

But something changed when he turned onto Miss Lovejoy's street, at the end opposite the clock-tower square. In the dove-gray light of day, a neater row of lodging houses sat end to end, more sweetly kept, with one or two crude signs painted on brick: LODGINGS FOR TRAVELLERS, 3D. A NIGHT. BOILING WATER ALWAYS READY. The frenetic whir of life settled to a murmur, as soft as the blowing of a kiss. It was wrong to have come, to act out his compulsion to try to find her. But a calm came over him, a feeling of rightness in wanting to thank her.

He stepped up to her tiny slice of a house, which was barely there at all, but with a quiet dignity. Straightening his waistcoat, he looked one direction, then the other, half expecting Maria Beadnell to pounce. A few old women regarded him with pity or puzzlement, like he might be a man who'd lost his way. Disregarding them, he clapped the rusted iron ring three times against the old plank door and waited. When no one came, he knocked again and put his ear to it, but heard nothing. He rapped his knuckles more vigorously; the door surprised him when it fell open a few inches on its own. When he put his face to the darkened crack, it yielded easily, letting him peer inside.

"Miss Lovejoy?" he called up the stairs.

No answer. A single door at the top of the stairway stood ajar, letting out a ribbon of mellow daylight. Perhaps she was resting, or busy at some task and hadn't heard him. He knew he should turn away, but his curiosity was aroused. If she wasn't home, he might leave the laurel for her and a note to say he'd paid a visit and how sorry he was to have missed her. But that would require her to read, and he didn't even know that about her. Surely something in the room would tell him. The mere thought that he ought to investigate made him feel like a spy, but his intentions were pure, he told himself, and something in that beam of light beckoned to him.

He glanced behind to make sure no one was watching, stepped in, and tiptoed up the uneven staircase, one creaking step at a time, holding the laurel as if lighting his way. When he reached the top, he considered the half-open door. It stood ajar in a particular way, almost friendly, with nothing forbidding about it at all.

"Hello? Miss Lovejoy?"

No answer. Not a sound from inside. With the push of one finger, the door squawked open on rusted hinges, an invitation in itself.

He stepped inside the spare single room. Two square windows faced him, like eyes keeping watch, with lace panels for eyelids. The floor was scrubbed clean, pictures of saints graced a near wall. There was a bedstead with a patchwork quilt, a plain square pine table with two plainer chairs, and a dresser for cups and plates. Near the small hearth sat a single tufted armchair, pale green with low turned legs, the finest piece, of so few things, even if worn to the horsehair stuffing. He removed his hat out of respect, having written often of rooms just like this, whose humbleness called to some tender place inside him.

He stepped to the back of the armchair, thinking it *her* chair, ran his hand across the velvet nap, thought he felt the whisper of her presence. The hearth was no higher than his knee, with a small grate, iron basket, and a few lumps of coal burning down to nothing. He supposed she'd just been here, sitting in her chair, no doubt, the best seat in the room. He closed his eyes to image it forth: Miss Lovejoy brushing her hair, or combing it, or embroidering an antimacassar, no—he saw her reading a book.

A woman who worked in the theater might be so many things, literate or not. Dickens knew from his early acting days that putting on a play for the stage was a helter-skelter conspiracy of actors, managers, stagehands, scene-painters, wardrobe women, musicians, and carpenters banding together whether they could read or not. Now that the monopoly of Drury Lane and Covent Garden theaters had ended, the most successful stages moved easily between the great tragedies and the lowest burlesque, usually in the same night. The laborers behind the wings looked more and more like the throngs in the seats. They liked love and murder best, thought most tragedies too long, would have preferred

Macbeth with just witches and fighting, and *Hamlet* with only a ghost and the death at the end. Reading was not required of those who loved or served the theater, just an affinity for human foibles, fancies, and farce.

Miss Lovejoy was one of those, he was sure. But could she read a note of thanks if he left one?

Dickens looked at the tired bunch of laurel in his fist. He was a trespasser, to be sure, though he meant well, he told himself, simply wanting to leave her a token, some small thanks for having awakened him to Furnival's Inn and his old writing life. He reached in his pocket for a mem-slip, finding only a small stub of pencil. Perhaps there would be something he could write on somewhere, an old scrap or a playbill from the theater. But the tidy room had only the barest necessities, nothing superfluous at all. It was then he saw a humpbacked half trunk peeking out from under the bed. Not a foot tall and a little more wide, its tawny leather was scuffed and faded, like an old hide stretched over a skeleton of wood slats and tin. It called to him, like an answer to everything.

He took five steps toward it, and in that span talked himself into and out of the thing he wanted to do. But he couldn't resist. Kneeling, he set his hat on the floor, the laurel bunch on top. He reached under the bed for the leather handle at each side of the trunk and pulled it toward him. It looked bigger in his hands, more important, like a treasure chest, a box of relics, a collection of her most precious things. He blew a soft breath across its fine layer of dust, revealing its patina beneath, the telltale luster that comes from the touch of human hands year after year. The trunk wasn't heavy, but it was too full to close all the way. It had a broken cast-iron latch that begged him to throw it open, to bare what was in it. Drops of sweat dotted his upper lip, his heart doubled its beat. The deed was only half done, he told himself, there was still a way out. He could put the trunk back, retrace his steps, simply leave the laurel—no, *take* the laurel—and go.

Resolved to do the right thing and restore the trunk to its rightful place, Dickens pressed his fingers lightly against it, not wanting to disturb it any more than he had. But a gentle push dislodged a flimsy old magazine that slipped onto the floor. Dickens picked it up and turned it over. The seafoam-green cover was faded and dog-eared, but he knew it at once. It was Cruikshank's illustrated cover of Rose Maylie and Oliver from the last monthly number of *Twist*. It catapulted him back to those days. *Good old Cruikshank*, he thought to himself—though the man couldn't draw a pretty woman to save himself and his boys looked like miniature men, nothing like children at all. A notorious inebriate, Cruikshank soon after became a fanatical, teetotaling Ebenezer, against moderation of any sort. Dickens had replaced him at once. Still, kneeling there, he had only affection for the man and the story he held in his hand.

Now there was no stopping. He pulled the trunk all the way out and flung open its lid to find it brimming with monthly numbers, all his! Each collection was tied neatly with red satin ribbon—the *Sketches by Boz*, the *Curiosity Shops*, *Master Humphrey's Clock*, *Barnaby Rudge*. Only the *Twists* had come loose from their stack.

He picked up the bound *Pickwicks* from near the top. The care with which they'd been aligned, edge to edge—each flimsy cover married to the next—flattered him greatly. Even the soft, slack ribbons had the look of having been loosed a hundred times and refastened into meticulous bows. These were beloved things to her, his stories. He was cherished by Miss Lovejoy, that was clear, and his heart lifted to know that whatever feeling she kindled in him was at least mutual.

Voices! A scuffle downstairs. Outside, loud, and coming

closer. Had he left the door open? He couldn't remember. Dickens snapped his head to look over his shoulder, every hair bristling. He held perfectly still, sure he'd be caught in the act, but the ruckus soon passed. Taking it as a sign that his luck was about to expire, he rushed to set the numbers back in the trunk and leaned over to close it, when the gilded edge of a bound book glinted at the bottom. He dug down for it, holding the volume in his hand, the familiar red calf and gilt over marbled boards, the six-paneled spine with a beaded band and scrolling foliate borders. This was the prize of the lot. For a woman of Eleanor's means, such as he believed them to be, a book like this was a treasure indeed. Dickens held his *Nicholas Nickleby* and imagined it in her fine, nimble hands. He turned the cover, as she would have, to the elegant endpapers inside. And there it was. In a rough but purposeful hand, its true owner's name: *Timothy Lovejoy*.

Dickens didn't know what to do. Put it all back, that first, yes, push the trunk under the bed, scramble to his feet, retrieve his hat at the last second, the spray of flagging laurel, and rush out her door. He closed it clumsily behind him, thought better of it, left it slightly open as he'd found it, and vaulted down the stairwell that now closed in on both sides. He spilled out her door into the street, disconcerted, and thankful the old women were turned away and didn't see him. He was breathing fast, confused and upset. He'd entered the secret places of Eleanor's life uninvited, but it was he who felt aggrieved. There was a man—a husband, surely—she hadn't mentioned. And why should she? Dickens was nothing to her, less even than he was to Maria, who at least believed his acquaintance meaningful. He didn't know why it mattered so. Why his heart, which moments ago had been buoyed, was now sinking to the bottom of the sea.

When he collected himself and turned to go, not ten steps

from her door, he came flat against a flank of street urchins, strip-lings in their late teens, standing shoulder to shoulder, blocking his way. Maybe they'd spotted him on his walk and followed him! They had a roughness about them, the look of lads whose pockets were thick with other people's money. The cleverest sort.

Their captain stepped forward. His three tattered coats, one atop the other, gave him away. He was the same one who'd accosted him at the back of his house but two weeks before.

"Good Lord! You again?"

The young ruffian held out his cupped hands and put on his best "Oliver" voice. "Please, sir. May we have some more?" His scrabby underlings chimed in, one at a time, then all at once, with their own cupped hands and a mocking chorus of, "More, more, more?"

Dickens was red in the face, collar tight, his lips dagger-thin. The captain cocked his head with a smirk, as if pleased they'd had the desired effect.

"I am not amused!" Dickens said, slapping his hat onto his head and sliding past them down the street at a swift clip.

When he turned onto the clock-tower square, he jolted at the sight of Miss Lovejoy walking toward home, a market basket over her arm, radiant and at ease, an innocent to his prying and snooping about. He lowered his head, praying she hadn't spotted him, and took the nearest corner to disappear down Holborn Hill.

21

The mysterious Miss Lovejoy hounded his thoughts, and no amount of fast-walking could cure it. Dickens' mood had plunged from hope to humiliation. He knew that every person was a fiery furnace of passions and attachments, unknown to every other. He had stepped too close and been burned. It was his own doing, but the red-hot pain of it seared all the way down.

When he was sure he'd put enough distance between himself and his petty crime, he began to suffer the sort of hunger stimulated by sneaking about with little expertise in the matter and nothing to show for it. In search of some comfort and a sturdy glass of port, he settled for a dining room stuffed into a little court out of Newgate Street. It was an old room he frequented often, heavy-paneled, dark, and dingy, just the place to hide from the world, with a fire crackling away no matter the season. It had old-fashioned food and tidy waiters with limp white neckcloths who were always glad to leave him in peace for the prospect of a twopence at the end of the meal, and even, occasionally, three. Dickens wanted to be alone to nurse his embarrassment.

Once the monotonous catalogue of roast beef, boiled pork, mutton chop, pigeon pie, and rump-steak pudding was discharged, he muttered his usual order, then snapped open the pages of *The Times*, intending to dine alone with his wounded pride, a chop, and an ale. When the waiter returned after he'd eaten to ask whether a pastry or cheese was wanted to top off his meal, Dickens dismissed him politely, only to find two ladies eyeing him over the daily news. They were well-to-do, judging from the chaos of ostrich feathers and taffeta bows on their bonnets, and no doubt twins, with identical pointy chins, marionette lines down the sides of their mouths, and mauve satin dresses with stiff puffed sleeves and high collars. They had the mean look of audacious gossipers.

"Excuse me, sir," said the first sister. "Are you who we think you are?"

"Charles Dickens?" ventured the second, less convinced than her twin.

Dickens put on the air of a bumptious city clerk with hardly enough time to spare for his dinner and even less for them. He feigned a smile. "I'm flattered, ladies. I often get that. But I am not he." He rattled his newspaper and disappeared behind it.

"I told you so," said the second sister to the first. "The real Mr. Dickens is much better-looking!"

He lowered the paper again to glower at the women, when something pulled his gaze to the dirty window. A single weathered pane framed the face of a young woman who shaded her brow with a hand as she pressed her face against the watery glass to search the room. It was Eleanor Lovejoy herself! He didn't know whether to hide or run, debated the merits of both in his head over the course of three seconds, and finally leapt from his chair. He tossed aside *The Times*, grabbed his hat, and marched straight outside to meet his fate, whatever it was. If, as he suspected, she had found him out and trailed him here, he was sure he could explain somehow.

He was only steps ahead of the waiter, bringing his bill.

"Mr. Dickens!" the waiter called after him.

The twin busybodies, hearing his true name, looked at each other with matching scowls. But Dickens was already out the door, pushing toward Eleanor's side.

"Miss Lovejoy?"

She turned toward the sound of his voice. They were square to each other, as close as they'd ever been. He'd never seen her like this, in the full light of day. The hood of her cloak was down. Loose curls the color of deep autumn graced the sides of her face. Today her eyes were bachelor-button-blue, right to the edge of violet, clear and alive. White florets spiraled away from the dark centers, like clouds reflected from the sky. She was more beautiful, more vivid, each time they met. The little crowded court, all the world, ebbed around her.

"Mr. Dickens! I'm so glad to have found you."

This took some considerable rethinking on his part. "You were looking for *me*?"

"Yes, I followed you here. You see, I found a posy of laurel dropped at my doorstep and caught sight of you in the street, and assumed—"

"Oh, the laurel." He didn't know how to excuse the series of circumstances that had led him to be in her room. "You see, I did bring you laurel, but not finding you home, well, it so happened, your door was—"

"Never mind," she said, dismissing any need for explanation. "I lost track of you in the street, but I've found you now."

Dickens turned his hat in his hand, taking in this turn of

events. Instead of horror at his own behavior, he now felt grateful he'd dropped the laurel *outside* her place, no doubt when he was accosted by the gang of street boys near her door. But there was also a keen satisfaction knowing she had sought him out. Perhaps he was wrong about the husband. A married woman might take offense at a gesture of flowers of any kind, and certainly wouldn't pursue a man who'd brought them. Timothy Lovejoy might be a brother, an uncle, a father, a grandfather. He might be anyone. Who had loved her enough to leave her his collection of novels. Why, he should simply ask her, if he could do so without revealing his own regretful sleuthing in her room. The question was working its way from his mind to his lips when the waiter appeared, waving a piece of paper.

"Sir! Your bill!"

"Oh, of course," he said, fumbling in his pocket for change. He deposited a coin in the waiter's hand.

The waiter looked at the coin and found it wanting. He stood there, hand out, sure there would be more.

"That's all, thank you," said Dickens, eager to return his attention to Miss Lovejoy.

"Quite sure, sir?"

"Quite!" he barked.

The waiter rolled his eyes, straightened his neckerchief, and went back inside.

"The world enters in, doesn't it, when one least wants it," he said to her, exasperated.

"And when we want it the most?" she asked. "What does the world do then?"

Dickens tilted his head to consider her. She had a way of getting to the heart of things, right past gibbering small talk. There was a ready intimacy between them he didn't understand. They had exchanged so few words in their brief acquaintance, but each one carried weight and purpose. If she would forgo pleasantries, so, too, would he.

"Will you walk with me? Somewhere quieter than this."

Eleanor nodded her assent, a small, reassuring lift of her eyes. Even her forehead, the tendrils dancing across it, seemed to say yes. But when he held out his elbow, she stopped to consider it, suddenly shy. He was willing to wait, as long as necessary, when another voice called out to him. It was Topping, ruffled and out of breath, flagging a piece of paper and pushing through the crowd. He took off his bowler hat and wiped his forehead. His flop of red hair was matted like a helmet.

"Beg pardon, sir. I've been looking for you all morning."

"Good Lord, Topping. How did you find me?"

"It's one of yer places, sir. You often come here."

"Well, what is it you want? Can you not see I am otherwise engaged?"

"But they won't deliver without your promise to pay, sir. Four turkeys—"

"I've not ordered any turkeys."

"For the missus, sir. And a goose!"

At the mention of his wife, Dickens mellowed like an old port wine; the tiny muscles around his eyes relaxed, his shoulders dropped an inch. "Is she home?" he whispered, with a subtle upturn of hope in his voice.

"Oh, no, sir. Far from it. The turkeys are to board a coach for Scotland. And the goose!" Topping produced a bill of sale and a sharpened pencil.

Dickens' terrible mood rebounded, his shoulders clenched at his back. He grabbed the bill and ground his teeth. "I trust they're not traveling first-class," he said, spraying spittle as he scratched his name and handed it back. Eleanor, beside him, seemed to blink back a smile.

"Anything else, sir?" asked Topping, as if he missed his master's presence but would never say so, not straight out.

"There was nothing in the first place!" Dickens was altogether losing patience. He had a great fondness for his groom, but these interruptions were maddening. He didn't know what he wanted, except to be left in peace.

Topping scratched his head and stood his ground, shifting from one foot to the other.

"What is it, Topping?"

"The tree, sir. The one in the parlor. Wot should I do with it?"

"I don't care. Do whatever you like. Just don't let the dogs piss on it!"

"Very good, sir," he said, somehow pleased to be of any service at all.

Dickens watched Topping fall into the stream of people wending their way back toward Newgate, his flaming hair disappearing under his hat. He heaved a frustrated sigh and shook his head. It wasn't Topping he was mad at, or Catherine. But what, then? His mood bubbled and jumped, in small spurts, first calm, then furious, then remorseful, now bristling with his own self-importance, then feeling himself no better than a worm. He turned back to Eleanor, who had never left his purview, surprised to find her looking up at him under a thick curtain of black lashes, with a benevolent generosity in her eyes.

"Your family. Are they away?" she asked, breaking his stare.

"Indefinitely, I'm afraid."

"Is it lonely for you?"

The question pierced him like an arrow. "At times, yes. But it's my own doing."

"I'm sorry."

"That I'm so awful a man to chase his own family away?"

"Yes, perhaps. Or so misunderstood."

This hit him like a wall. It was peculiar what she understood, with keen precision, without knowing him at all. That he wanted to be seen, cherished, and cared for, without demands, without the necessity of fixing everything—understood for who he was when he meant well and did what he could. He bowed his head and rubbed the top of it. His abiding aloneness long preceded Catherine's leaving, even the marriage itself. He wondered sometimes how deep it resided. Whenever he got close enough to see it clearly, he dizzied and recoiled. But he couldn't escape it. No matter how full his house, his dining table, his days, there it was again, the sense of being singular and separate from the world. But now he was tired of it all, his own responsibilities, everyone else's expectations. When he raised his chin to face her, he found himself looking through a sheen of his own near-tears.

"So you see, I have no one to keep me company but you."

Eleanor worried her fingerless, crocheted gloves, as if struggling for an answer. He understood. If there was no husband, she was a single woman, and he a married man. Any sensible person might think it a calamity in the making. And yet he found in her a kindred soul, and couldn't help himself. She turned her gaze away, revealing the bare white canvas of her slender neck, the pristine line of her jaw. He wished he were a painter with palette and brushes in hand, because words were inadequate to tell the form of her brow, how light flowed over the surface of her cheek, the delicate indent right below it, the subtle bloom of her lips. He'd been too forward again, but the temperate air and her loveliness had emboldened him.

He put a hand to the fur lapel of his long frock coat, where his heart was. "I shall be a perfect gentleman," he pledged. "No threat whatsoever to your reputation. On my good word."

When no answer came, he followed her gaze. The high-collared busybodies from the dining room were marching outside, matching capes puffing behind them. They stopped some twenty feet away, but glowered at Dickens, whispering back and forth.

"It seems your reputation is the one in some peril, Mr. Dickens," said Eleanor with a crinkle of her eyes.

The women swaggered straight for him.

"Indeed, I'm not a man, I'm an exhibit!"

In the blink of an eye, the first twin pulled a pair of scissors from her purse, charged forth, and snipped a clump of fur from his collar.

"What on earth?" he shouted.

"I may not like your books," she said, brandishing her fistful of fur, "but I am a collector nonetheless!"

The lady turned on her heel with her nose in the air, while her sister lifted her heavy skirts, raised a black laced boot, and kicked his shin with a patent toe as hard as she could. Eleanor gasped. Dickens grimaced and clutched his leg.

"Good Lord, madam!"

"That is for our dear, sweet Little Nell!" she said, wagging a finger in his face. "Who did not deserve to die!"

The sisters marched away, victorious. Dickens hopped on one leg, wincing.

"Are you all right?" asked Eleanor, somewhere between concern and amusement.

"Well! I've been mauled by my readers before, but never so maimed as this."

Eleanor shook her head, trying not to chortle outright. "I'm sorry. It's only that I remember feeling the same, when I read every number of *Curiosity Shop*, and then came to it, and didn't know, couldn't believe, that you would kill off poor Little Nell. But I never dreamed of kicking you."

"Well, I'm grateful for that, at least," he said, regaining his footing. "But how shall I escape all the others?"

22

In a small room backstage at the Folly, squeezed and cluttered with tumbled angel wings, swords, crowns, hats, helmets, and odd bits of painted scenery, Dickens sat at a dressing table before a trifold mirror, staring at himself. This was Eleanor's theater, her domain, her costumer's room, and here he was, surrendering his welfare to her best instincts. She had struck on an idea after witnessing the twin ladies' frontal assault, followed by listening to him bemoan the slings and arrows of life as Charles Dickens. Giving no clue at all, she instructed, even dared him to follow her, ask no questions, and simply trust her.

"What do you see?" she asked, throwing the heavy curtains open to let in the light.

The brass mirror dared him to look. It stood confidently on four sturdy peg feet, and despite a hairline crack in the middle part, its folding wings were beveled and cloudless. But it was she who filled the reflection, standing behind him in a gray wool dress. The window poured a halo around her, making her eyes into moonstones now, shimmering feldspar, translucent pale blue, then lavender, then another color altogether, or no color at all. Only clarity. He found it hard to look away.

"What do you see in *you*?" she repeated, arching a brow.

Dickens flapped his mouth shut, cleared his throat, and obeyed. Turning to his own reflection in the glass, he furrowed his forehead, winced, pouted, and frowned, trying on faces, testing his own feelings. A mirror had always been, for him, a working tool—the place he often found his characters, their attributes, tics, and nuances. How low could a man's brow go? How wide a smile? Was the head all pushed to one side, the ears pinned back, or the cheeks puffed out like a blowfish? Where did a mood sit on a poor man's face that had known too much sun, where delicacy on a young girl's who'd seen none?

It was an accepted rule of his house that he wasn't to be disturbed when at work in his study, unless the children were ill. Then he would carry the afflicted child to his sofa to be doted on and watch him work. He wasn't aware, until Mamie told him, how often he would leap from his chair and rush to the gilt mirror that hung beside their little portraits, contorting his face in all directions, sometimes talking to himself rapidly in a low voice, then back to his desk. Up and down, up and down, writing frantically while the features were fresh in his mind. He inhabited the creatures of his pen in every detail, and they lived in him.

But now a dreary version of himself gazed back.

"What do *you* see?" he asked her.

She put a thumb on her chin and scrutinized his face in every detail. "I see a man who feels set upon."

"That's it," he said. "So hemmed in by people who want a bit or a piece or a pence of him—that he's exhausted from want of air."

"A beleaguered man."

"Who wants to be left alone."

"Yes. I see him, too," she said, with a hand so lightly on his shoulder that he couldn't feel it through his coat. "Now close your eyes."

He hesitated. What a simple request, to shut one's eyes. Yet it had been so long since he'd trusted anyone through and through, at least without satisfying his own curiosity first, gaining assurances, wanting to suggest terms, if not dictate demands. In his earliest writing days, when he was only "Boz," agreements were made of handshakes and blind faith. Everything was complicated now, involving more people, more paper, more lawyers and grubbing, money-changing hands than he'd ever imagined. And still, he felt exposed and unprotected. But Eleanor engendered trust *and* faith, and seemed to want nothing in return. So he closed his eyes and waited.

The slide of a drawer opening, creak of a closet door, unlatching of a steamer trunk. Dickens guessed, from the clanks and dings and subtle whooshes of air, that she was rifling through props and costumes. Eleanor was humming to herself, soft and lilting, the singing voice he remembered from her stage debut. He liked the happy sound of her hands at work, with a periodic pause to exclaim some small victory under her breath. Whatever she was searching for, she was finding.

Soon his hat slid from his head, replaced with the stretch, wiggle, and tug of a headpiece over his scalp, all the way to his ears and down to his neck, his hair tucked underneath it.

"May I look?" he asked.

"No, not yet."

The flat of a hand, or something like it, pressed against his forehead and then the sides of his face.

"Now may I?" he pleaded, impatient.

"Hmm. Just one more thing."

A rummaging on the dressing table in front of him tickled his ear, the light jingle of tangled necklaces, the sorting of metal buttons, brooches, rings. He could see in his mind's eye a small open box spilling over with trinkets.

"Yes!" she said. "This will do the trick."

A pair of spectacles came to rest on the bridge of his nose, and the barest wind of her fingers looped them behind his ears.

"There," she said. "Now you may look."

Dickens opened his eyes slowly, fully expecting some version of himself thinly disguised. But there was an old man staring back at him, seventy at least, with a blotchy bald scalp at the top and prodigious tufts of unruly white hair sticking out at the sides. Thick woolly muttonchops stuck to his cheeks and jowls. The little gold-rimmed spectacles changed the nature of his nose entirely, which now seemed to have lived much longer than he had, the way old noses droop and hook. Wiry white eyebrows sat over the glasses like a pair of old terriers and sunk his eyes into a beady, hard gray. His skin seemed sallow in spots, where it wasn't mottled like marble. His forehead, maybe from the weight of the well-made wig, sported furrows like a field in winter. The whole face turned downward and mean, animated more by shadow than light. A scowl settled naturally on his lips.

"Uncanny," he said. "Why, I hardly know myself."

"Yet you're the same man on the inside."

He stood and leaned closer to inspect his reflection in the mirror, turning his head one way, then the other, admiring his clever new disguise. "But now able to walk the streets of London free from the critics, creditors, and hangers-on that plague my every hour!"

Eleanor returned his hat to his head. She stood back, pleased with the effect, but with a look of wanting perhaps one more thing. She put her hands at the plaited waist of her skirt and searched the room. Her eyes sparked when she spotted a silver claw-and-ball–handled cane leaning against the wall. She handed it to him with a flourish, like a knight's squire.

"Your cane, sir."

"Perfect," he said, hunching his shoulders into a full stoop when he took hold of it. The rosewood cane seemed to become part of him, a natural extension of his wizened frame. Taking his first rickety steps as the new old man he'd become, he hobbled across the room, then stopped and shook his cane.

"Oh, Miss Lovejoy," he said, cackling like a crotchety old griper. "This takes me back to my theatrical days!"

Carried away, he stepped grandly onto a hemming stool, spreading his arms wide. "Oh, to be young and on the stage, playing with fire, sitting on babies, falling off scaffolding . . . and all with no harm or injury, in fact, the coroner need never be called!"

Eleanor's eyes kindled to each word. She clapped and laughed.

"And applause, yes!" he exclaimed. "Because we have given every man, woman, and child an hour or two to forget the real world, and let them rejoin it with their sense of wonder restored. Never mind the press of people, the poking umbrellas, and irreconcilable cabs. We are all players in the great pantomime of life!"

"Bravo!" she shouted. "Bravo!"

Dickens took off his hat and bowed deeply, like a great tragedian basking in the admiration of the house. When he straightened up, a thought struck him with blunt force.

"Why, perhaps India's not a bad idea after all."

"India?" she asked with an inquisitive smile.

"India, indeed! A Shakespearean troupe!" He gestured with his cane across the room, as if an entire continent lay before him. "It is a vast, untapped market!" He pointed his cane at her emphatically. "And you, Miss Lovejoy! With your dazzling debut on the stage? Why not join our company as well, and at last have the actor's life you're meant for?"

Eleanor gazed up at him, playing along. She pressed her hands to her flushed cheeks, melodrama perfected. "India! But how ever will we live?"

"Ah. On love and art alone!"

"A rich diet, indeed!" she said. "But still, India's such a long way."

"But just imagine, will you?" he said, stepping off the stool toward her, his hat to his chest. "A sea of lovestruck admirers, all done in by the incomparable beauty and talents of one Miss Eleanor Lovejoy, the greatest actress ever to grace the Indian stage . . . or whatever it is we perform on in India."

She curtsied and laughed, bright fearless notes. Her whole being glowed like a chandelier with a thousand crystal facets. Stunned by her luminance, he stepped even closer, very quiet. Every detail in sharp focus. Twinkling eyes, downy hair at her temple, the soft-pointed chin. Eleanor didn't flinch, didn't blush. A sudden seriousness had come down on them like a curtain.

"But no one in all of India . . ." he whispered, "more done in than I."

Eleanor stumbled backward, catching herself on the edge of the dressing table. All the light drained from her face. Dickens had an instinct to reach out to her, offer a hand or an elbow to brace against. She turned sharply away, joined her palms together, and pressed them to her lips. He stepped back, too, having blundered where he had no business to. It was a whim, a fancy, a fool notion that had invaded his imagination before he had time to defend against it. His own brazenness mortified him, but it was too late to offer amends. There was no making a joke of it, no taking it back.

"I've said the wrong thing, Miss Lovejoy," he said, gripping the brim of his hat. "I'm so sorry."

Eleanor closed her eyes and lowered her chin, one hand against the scalloped trim of her collar. Her fingers trembled, whether from anger or repulsion, or even fear, he couldn't tell. He waited to be reproached, without moving or speaking. It was what he deserved. At last, she opened her eyes slowly and raised her gaze to his.

"No," she said. "India is a beautiful dream. But I am not at liberty . . . to dream."

Dickens nodded with sorry eyes. Sorry to have tripped, unthinking, into a moment that pierced their lighthearted bubble. Of course she was right. There was no liberty between them at all. He had not kept his marriage a secret, from her or from anyone else. And had no intention of betraying his wife any more than he already had. He didn't understand the kinship he felt toward her, or gratitude maybe, or some ineffable affinity of nature and qualities. Eleanor could never be more to him than this, but in her presence, "this" felt like everything.

"Nor am I," he said. "At liberty to dream."

"Of course," she said. "We are, neither of us—"

"Timothy, is it?" he blundered, before she could finish or he could think better of asking.

Eleanor startled. "You know him?"

"Of him, perhaps," he said, stuttering apologetically, once again embarrassed that he had snuck, uninvited, into the secret corners of her life. It wasn't like him to hunt and pry, and yet he couldn't help himself. Eleanor opened her mouth to explain, but Dickens shook his head and held his hand up to stop her. "No. I'm sorry. It's not my business at all. I don't want to know anything about him. Except . . . do you love him very much?"

"I do," she said, without hesitation, but considered her

next words with care. "Though I confess a certain distance between us."

Dickens knew what she meant. The distance between him and Catherine, as in all marriages, was sometimes an inch, but other times the great expanse between hill and valley, ocean and desert. It was Dante's dark forest, shrouded in shadow, the right path so often obscured. It was being together but feeling alone. Yes, he knew what she meant, and that was enough. He tugged and peeled off the bald wig and turned it in his hand.

"A door closes at times. Even between those who've loved well."

Eleanor bowed her head, saying nothing.

Dickens turned back to his own image in the mirror. Even without the wig, he seemed very old still. "I feel ridiculous."

"Don't, please. I couldn't bear it," she said, her voice hushed to a prayer. "You're like no one I've ever known. And were we free to love—"

"Yes, well, it was only a dream," he said. "Forgive me."

23

Humiliation makes its own haste. So Dickens thought as he fled the Folly, mortified by what he'd done. He pocketed the wig and spectacles and bolted across the little square to seek refuge at Furnival's Inn. He winced when he peeled away the pasted-on eyebrows, but his pain was well deserved. It was a keen embarrassment; there was no comfort for it, and no one to blame but himself. His head jutted forth in front of his legs, hands buried deep in the silk lining of his coat pockets. He felt a great brooding coming on, and wanted to race away from it as fast as he could.

"Charley! Wait!" a familiar voice called from behind.

Dickens didn't turn to acknowledge the voice or slow his pace one bit. He wanted it to recede, go away, give up. But his brother Fred soon appeared, trotting beside him, gasping for breath.

"How on earth did you find me, Fred? How does everyone find me?"

"I'm afraid I had to strong-arm Topping," said Fred. "I practically had to sit on him."

Dickens chuffed and quickened his step.

"It's just that I've been hoping to speak to you, Charley. You see, I've a new scheme."

"What a surprise."

"But am a bit shy of capital."

"Another surprise!"

"But this idea," said Fred hopefully, "you're going to love it. For it capitalizes on Christmas!"

Dickens halted his march, full stop. He turned to his brother, every muscle in his face like a rubber band pulled taut. "Have we not all capitalized on Christmas quite enough?"

"But it's a card, Charley. A holiday card. To send only at Christmastime!"

The veins in Dickens' neck pulsed at his collar. He jutted his nose close to his brother's face and lowered his voice two registers. "What is Christmastime to you, Fred, but a time for paying bills with no money?"

Fred retracted his weak chin into his green-and-red-checkered cravat, and stared at his shoes. Dickens expected the usual pity and regret to rise up inside him; instead, he had to resist slapping his brother's face. He'd been a good older brother, dependable and true, collected Fred from school when they were young, taken him in when a bachelor at Furnival's, then as a family man at Doughty Street, taken him even once to Italy, where Fred ran into difficulties swimming in the sea and had to be rescued by local fishermen. Dickens had, over the years, come to believe that his father and mother had brought up a large family with a small disposition for doing anything for themselves, himself excepted.

Fred was the least able among them. Dickens had begged favors to find him employment, which never lasted more than a few months. When Fred stumbled upon a wife for himself, he fell quickly into debt, using his older brother's good name at the bank. But when the bank came looking, it looked for him. Fred wasn't the only one. Relatives far and wide, if they were relatives at all—some so distant he hadn't heard of them—and even their friends traded on Charles Dickens' name, wrote for money, sent bills, sometimes begged. He had been ever generous despite his own mounting debts, but never more so than with Fred. He invited him to parties and dinners, often providing the additional service of wiping specks of food from his coat. And was forever ready to hear any scheme of his at all, sprinkling in ideas of his own—how to better it, sell it, give it a twist, make it sing. Fred had no lack of ideas, but was fickle and doomed, with no apparent chance of seeing anything through. Whatever Dickens had felt before, this was now clear. His brother was a luckless, feckless poor fish. And a bottom-feeder at that.

But hardest to comprehend was Fred's unrelenting good cheer.

"Good grief, Charley. Don't you believe Christmas begins in the heart?"

Dickens grumbled and huffed. "Let us not be childish, Fred. Christmas begins and ends in the purse. Now, good day!"

With that he stomped away, leaving his baffled brother behind him.

24

Back in his rooms, Dickens skipped supper and wrote furiously through the night. He woke in the morning at his writing table, his cheek pillowing on a stack of new pages. He rolled them up, tied them with a string, slapped water on his face, and put on his coat and hat. On the way out the door, he spotted the rosewood cane leaning against the wall and, above it on a little shelf, the headpiece, eyebrows, and spectacles Eleanor had given him. He could think of no better day to put it to the test.

The desk clerk took the key from his hand, screwed up his jagged nose, and squinted through his glasses at the old man before him.

"Excuse me, sir, but it's twopence for the museum! I didn't see ya go up!"

Dickens leaned in. "It's me. Scrooge."

The clerk raised his glasses onto his head to examine the face under the bald headpiece, the eyebrows, the clothes, the man. "I see the resemblance, sir. Ya sure it's you?"

"Who else would I be?"

"Well, I wouldn'ta known ya."

"Exactly the point. I am hiding from my 'admirers.'"

The clerk regarded the aspiring writer from No. 13 as if he were quite possibly losing his mind. "Oh, I don't think ya need to worry, Mr. Scrooge. I may not exactly be the readin' public, but I 'eard a most people, and I ain't never 'eard a you."

"Which is just the way I like it!" said Dickens, planting his hat onto his great bald head and marching out.

The warmish weather seemed to set all of London on edge, or all of him; he couldn't tell which. It did *not* deter an abundance of Christmas trumpery and gimcrack all around—holly sprigs and evergreen garlands, flickering candles and faux-snow flocking. Holiday broadsides were now in open warfare, covering each square foot of bare brick, one pasted sloppily over the other, touting RIMMEL'S IMPERIAL MOSCOVITE PERFUME & TOILET VINEGAR; COCOA & CHOCOLATE (DELICIOUSNESS OF FLAVOR UNEXCELLED); *A CHRISTMAS PANTOMIME FEATURING DICK WHITTINGTON AND HIS CAT*, and just in time for the holiday, BALDWIN'S NERVOUS PILLS (CURES IRRITABILITY, MELANCHOLY & INSOMNIA)! Hanging boughs were tied with garish red bows. It was clear to Dickens that mistletoe and its brethren were being employed to merry-up the town and encourage the buying and selling of things that no one needed but could not live without. If this was Christmas in a new age of commerce and leisure, he wanted none of it.

Suffused with a sense of purpose, namely, to show Forster the pages clutched in his hand, he passed through town quickly, long determined strides, his cane galloping beside him. He crossed streets as necessary to avoid bell ringers and carolers in particular, with growing confidence his incognito appearance would protect him from any variety of pest. To be certain of it, he skirted the Strand to stay out of the fashionable main, and plunged into the twisted streets tucked behind it, the quickest shortcut to where Forster would be lunching, as he did every day, at precisely twelve o'clock. Dickens turned onto raucous Holywell Street, once notorious as a rag fair for secondhand clothing, now a bustling bazaar of book and broadside sellers. Gables of crooked timber-framed buildings lurched over the street; books were stuffed into sooty windows, filling every last crack, or spilled onto trestle tables outside. A few of the shops were legitimate, but most traded in indecency, cribbing, and the splicing, rearranging, and gluing together of books in any way that might sell them.

Dickens kept his gaze trained as near to the horizon, and as far away from the cheapjacks, mongers, and peddlers, as he could. He especially wanted no part of the hawkers, every ten steps, pushing their frivolous catchpennies—nothing but fabricated stories designed for ignorant people willing to be gulled of their coins for the likes of *The She He Barman of Southwark* or *The Pig-Faced Lady of Manchester Square*. But midway down Holywell, something in the periphery caught his eye—a bookseller's bulging bay window jammed tight with familiar titles, in fact, he thought, his own. He edged closer to it with the vague hope that this might signal a sudden revival of his reputation. Putting his scroll of pages in his left pocket, he leaned against the glass to get a good close look. They were books, indeed, but not his at all. Instead, volumes stacked end to end: *Oliver Twits*, *Nicky Nickleberry*, and *The Pickwicks in Paris*, all by the "The Inimitable Baz!"

The overeager bookseller himself popped out of the shop with a newspaper under his arm. He had the long neck and pointy nose of a weasel. "Any help required, sir?"

"What are these?" Dickens demanded, his bushy white eyebrows arrowing angrily into one.

"Books, sir," said the man, clueless.

"Yes, I see that. But look, that one." Dickens tapped the glass with his cane. "The Pickwicks do not go to Paris!"

"Oh, but they do, sir. And have a grand time of it. And are thinking of quitting Paris for Italy!"

"I—I—I—" His tongue tripped over his own outrage. "Dickens did not write that. These are p-p-plagiarisms. Piracies!"

"And selling like hot cross buns," said the bookseller, quite pleased with the fact.

"But this isn't right at all. It's—wrong!"

"Only Dickens' due, sir." He unfolded his newspaper and flicked a front-page headline. "Fancy him nickin' *Oliver Twist* off the one who drawed it."

"Cruikshank?"

"Says so right here."

The seller turned the paper around to prove it. There, occupying a good portion of the space above the fold, was an unflattering sketch of Charles Dickens as rogue and wrongdoer next to one of George Cruikshank looking utterly beatific. Over them, a tall headline in black-letter script: "A TWISTED TALE!"

"Says all the good parts was his idea," said the seller, "stolen right out from under him."

"Slander!"

The bookseller studied the sketch in the paper and the old man before him, back and forth. He cocked his head to have a better look when one of Dickens' pasted-on eyebrows loosened and dropped lower than the other. "You look a bit like him, sir. But I thought Dickens a much younger man."

Dickens plucked the paper from his hand. "Well, I know him. And he would never stand for this. Why, he would get an injunction to stop all you wretched people lining your vermin-eaten pockets with money that was rightfully his!"

"Sir, if Dickens had not the imagination to send the Pickwicks to Paris, pity on him and good for the one who did."

Dickens pressed his dangling eyebrow flat against his forehead. "Bah! Humbug!" he bellowed, pivoting away.

His protest had gone off like a blast inside him, scattering debris to the very tips of his nerves. He felt hot on the outside but chilly within. Ice floes coursed through his veins. Walking was his only hope, and finding Forster, whose job it was to save him. But no sooner had he turned the corner when he spotted a stout-bodied evangelical woman in a dull beige bonnet and dress sitting on a step holding a sign: NOVEL READING CAUSES VIOLENCE! His simmering fit of pique now let loose all restraint. Dickens planted himself in front of her, harrumphed, grabbed the sign, threw it on the ground, and stomped on it three times.

"You devil man! Are you mad?" The woman stood in a righteous fury, drew back her purse, and clobbered him full in the face, sending his hat and spectacles flying into the filthy street. Not yet satisfied, she grabbed for a tuft of his white hair and yanked as hard as she could, when the wig came off in her hand. She screamed with shock at the sight of his scalp in her fist. Dickens clutched at the fire on his head. Leaning down to reclaim his crooked spectacles and tarnished hat, he snatched the wig from her hand.

"You see, madam," he said, pounding his cane and puffing his *p*'s with a rush of hot air, "without the wig, I am much improved! But were I to pull on your hair, you would remain a pug-faced, pigheaded, petty evangelical who knows not one whit about the causes of anything!"

The woman dropped her jaw, her underchin ballooning like a frog. Satisfied he had won the last word, Dickens marched away. But he had lost control and didn't like it. Eleanor had been right. He felt beleaguered by an army of people who wished him nothing but ill. It was clear he could mask himself, but that didn't change the outer world, which seemed evermore to be against him at every turn. Offenses in all directions. If he could just get to Forster, the sooner, the better. So when a gray-suited man fell in step behind him, he did his best to ignore it. But with some irregular effort, the man soon caught up.

"Excuse me, Mr. Dickens?" he said in a mild, obsequious tone.

Dickens turned sharply. "Yes! No! Well, what is it you want?"

The man pulled a folded paper from his pocket and handed it off. The author, still being an author, took out a pencil and roughly scrawled his autograph, grunting under his breath. He pressed it into the man's hand. "There you are. Now leave me alone."

"Oh, but it's for you, sir." The man handed it back. "A writ to appear in Her Majesty's High Court of Chancery in the suit alleged against you."

"Cruikshank?"

"No, sir. It's Magistrate Laing himself."

Dickens unfolded the writ, stupefied. "Judge Laing is su-ing *me*?"

"Yer a popular man, Mr. Dickens!"

25

The Whig & Pen was wood-paneled and wainscoted, air thick with the smell of tobacco and spirits and the pompous wit and sniggering gossip of grown men. In a corner nearest the door, with the best possible view of people coming and going, William Thackeray held forth at his usual table with young Wilkie Collins and a few highbrow hangers-on. Forster dined by himself three tables away, back turned, nose buried in his newspaper. Dickens, restored to his full disguise—if a bit slapdash—stormed into the room, smacking the writ against his palm. He aimed straight for Forster, with no choice but to go by way of Thackeray, who kept one eye trained on this curious new arrival, without missing a beat of his own loud harangue.

"Everyone knows I'm having a great fight at the top of the tree with Dickens, who knows my books are a protest against his mawkish sentimentality. For if mine are true, his must be false!"

When contemptuous laughter ensued among Thackeray's devotees, Dickens shot daggers at them over his shoulder, but he had one mission and must not be distracted. He bellied up to Forster's table and flung the writ in front of him, narrowly missing the plate of boiled beef.

"How could you let this happen?" he demanded in a low whisper.

Forster bent the corner of his paper and peered over his glasses to where the writ lay, between him and his food. An old man stood over him in a lopsided wig, bushy white eyebrows, and twisted glasses. But the fur-collared coat gave him away.

"Incredible! Is that you?"

"Shhh!" Dickens laid his cane against the table and plopped into a seat. "It *is* I, and, quite frankly, more myself than I ever have been." He tore off a piece of bread, gnawing it like a lion with a bone. "Yet not myself at all. Did you know Magistrate Laing is suing me?"

"Oh, that," said Forster, wiping his mouth with a napkin tucked in at his collar. "Yes, well. Claims he's the model for your Magistrate Fang. In *Twist*."

"But Fang *is* Laing! Every writer works from some point of his own experience."

"That's all well, Boz, but did you have to mention his bald head and red cheeks, and his 'drinking rather more than he should'?"

"But I've seen him! Drunk on the bench! Drunk and falling off the bench!"

"We'll fight it, of course," Forster assured him, folding his newspaper and surveying his friend's strange garb. "Why are you dressed like that? And what's wrong with your eyeglasses?"

Dickens tore the banged-up spectacles from his face, bent them into shape, and put them back on. "Never mind that now," he said, peering around Forster's head to Thackeray, who was staring back at them, always intent on knowing who dined with whom and why. "Let's go. Too many eyes and ears, and nosy noses."

Forster pierced his last chunk of beef, stabbed a potato with a carrot on top, swirled it once to mop up the plate's juices, and swallowed the lot. He wiped his mouth and stood, threw down his napkin, and followed Dickens toward the door. They were steps from Thackeray's table when Collins attempted a rebuttal.

"Still, Thackeray, you must admire Dickens' ability with characters."

Dickens grabbed at Forster's elbow to slow him. This would be worth a listen.

"Yes!" said Thackeray. "Why, whenever Dickens doesn't know what to do, he simply throws another one on the fire!"

Another self-satisfied chortle erupted from the circle of syco-phants. Dickens narrowed his eyes, headed straight for them, stuck out his tongue, puffed his cheeks, and blew a wide spray of spittle across the table right over their half-eaten chops. The men stared at their mutton in stunned disbelief. Jaws fell. Ker-chiefs were drawn. Faces dabbed.

Dickens turned calmly and pressed through the door.

"That man is no member here!" shouted Thackeray with a wag of his signet-ringed finger.

Forster stopped in front of them, the color of claret all the way to his collar. "That man is in a club all his own, to which you will never find admittance! No driveling, sniveling bloviators allowed!"

On the street outside, buffeted by seasonal buyers and sellers, Dickens pulled the crumpled page of newsprint from his pocket and plastered it against Forster's chest.

"And Cruikshank! Saying *Twist* was his?"

"So I've heard." Forster unwrinkled the paper and frowned.

"But it's a fiction! A comedy—"

"He has hired a solicitor."

"Tragedy!" cried Dickens. "Good Lord. He can't possibly win, can he?"

"No. But he can cost you plenty."

"Then I shall sue him in turn! Both of them!"

"A chancery suit is a life sentence no matter which end you are on."

"I am on the *butt* end, I assure you. Forster, you must put a stop to it."

"I'll do my part, but it will cost money, lots and lots of it, so you, too, must—"

"Finish the Christmas book."

"Our victory depends on it."

Dickens sighed and scratched his wig. He pulled the rolled pages from his pocket and held them out, an offering.

"Not finished. But promising nonetheless."

26

In a crowded tavern in Shaft Alley, Forster rubbed his hands together as he read, working them like dough. He huddled over the pages, throwing his full weight into the task. Dickens leaned back in his chair, the better to have a clear view past the low shelf of Forster's forehead. If Forster raised one brow, so, too, did he. If he grimaced, bit his lip. If he shook his head, Dickens suffered an unendurable agony.

"You are furrowing your forehead, John."

Forster grunted, not looking up.

"And before that you sighed, though I did not mention it."

"May I not finish?"

Dickens flounced about in his seat, twirled a spoon in his fingers. He peered out over the swilling crowd, suddenly aware that no one—not one soul—seemed the least bit interested in his presence, or, in fact, had any awareness of him at all. He had spent the morning being accosted, but now sensed the thrilling prospect of his own anonymity. Was his cover finally having its effect? Perhaps one man, two tables away, was staring at him, but he seemed most interested in the juncture where his leathery wig met his scalp. Dickens gave him an evil eye punctuated by his barbed brows, which frightened the man's gaze away.

Finally, Forster turned over the last page. He restacked the pages neatly and gazed at the ceiling, tapping his fleshy fingertips together, thinking, thinking. Dickens held his breath.

"Well," said Forster, "it is . . . interesting."

"Yes. It is, isn't it?"

"But when does the Christmas bit start?"

"Soon, I'm sure."

"It's just . . . a tad grim for what's meant to be . . . a cheerful time of year."

"What do you mean?"

"Well, your Scrooge is a dreadful man."

"Not so dreadful."

"And this getup of yours, why, your Ebenezer fellow looks exactly as you do now."

"I inspired myself!"

"To write a recluse? Who hates his neighbors, bemoans his friends, and despises his relatives?"

"They're hateful people. They hound him for money. The poor man is tormented by his tribe of dependents, who all want a bit or a piece of him and cannot make a single step in the world without his aid!"

The decibel of their discussion rose above the ambient chattering and clinking of cups, attracting the attention of several customers. Forster leaned in to whisper.

"But he's plotting the murder of Fred? The hapless distant cousin?"

"The cousin isn't hapless. He's . . . malevolent!"

"But your man doesn't actually kill him, does he?"

"At the pace I'm going, he'll be dead by Thursday morning."

Forster looked at him, nonplussed. "But at Christmastime?"

Dickens slammed down his tankard and stood abruptly, sweeping his pages from the table. "Christmas need not always end in eggnog and sugarplums!" He rolled the pages back up, in fact tighter than before. "Though perhaps I will reconsider the murder."

He adjusted his hat on top of his bald wig, grabbed his cane, and marched to the door, where he turned back with one last roar, rattling the rosewood stick overhead. "In fact, a *lawsuit* seems more in keeping with the spirit of the season!"

And with that, he pushed outside into thundering rain.

"Charles! Stop!"

Forster chased Dickens four city blocks and around three corners, raindrops pummeling his face. About to give up ever catching him, he found Dickens standing bewildered in front of Mudie's, water pouring off the back of his hat. The shop was dark inside and out, surrounded by a crude scaffolding. It couldn't have been more than two weeks since he'd been here, but its large glass panes were already cracked and grimy, a memorial to neglect. The storefronts on either side were the same, as if the whole block had gone dead overnight, now a mere ghost of a place.

"Good Lord, John!" he squalled, trying to drown out the rain. "Is Mudie's gone out of business?"

"I certainly hope not." Forster gasped and puffed, skimming the sweat and rain off his lip with a thumb. "They've just placed an order for five hundred of your Christmas book!"

Dickens drew back. "Five hundred in one shop? But how can they afford to—"

"A small . . . discount."

"How small?"

"Thirty percent," Forster spat out, as if the quicker he said it, the less it would bite.

"Thirty percent? But they'll drive all other shops out of the literary market!"

"It will certainly separate the goats from the sheep—"

"Writers told what to write. Readers told what to read. People who do whatever you do . . . told what to do!" Dickens waved his arms like a windmill gone mad. "And once again, everyone making money on me but me!"

The rain renewed its assault, on again, off again, slanting and slashing away at them both. Forster strained his smashed bull-dog face out of his collar, rivulets running down his jowls. "A percentage of something is a good deal more than a percentage of nothing. Which is what we shall have if you do not finish this blasted book!"

"I am knocking on the door, I assure you."

"Mind you," said Forster, cheeks flapping in the air, "your relatives' creditors are at *my* door; your publishers at my throat. Christmas Eve is closing in, my friend. Two weeks! That means having it to the printer in one!"

The raw truth of Forster's calculation snapped at Dickens like a whip. He had lost track of time, day and night, hours. There was no way to get from the middle to the end in one week, but nor was there turning back. He was in too deep now; the book must be written. He pulled off his hat and wig, rubbed his rimpled forehead, and hung his chin. Rain dripped off his limping curls.

"I know it's true, what you say," he said, flinging his hair back from his forehead. "But I'm in a most disheveled state, John. And fear I've lost my muse."

"Your muse?"

At the mere mention of Eleanor, the rain thinned and stopped in a span of seconds. Dickens, wet as a dog, took it as another sign. Signs everywhere. Why, if a rainbow now appeared in the cloud-heavy sky, it would be her doing, her presence in his life, her influence.

"Miss Lovejoy. Who made me want to write again. Why, I feel it was she who led me to Furnival's Inn."

"*She* led you?" Forster wiped his face hard with a waterlogged kerchief.

"Not meaning to in any way."

"Or in every way? Let me guess, she has stolen your heart."

"She has a husband."

"And you a wife!"

"Who has all but done with me!"

Dickens wanted his friend to feel his despair. But Forster's fists were in tight, knuckled balls; his eyes bulged out of their sockets.

"Think, Boz! It may not be your heart at all she's intent upon stealing. This woman 'works' at your old theater, and 'lives' near your old lodgings? The coincidence is almost more than one can bear. And this husband of hers. Are you quite sure he exists?"

"She is somewhat mysterious—"

"Because she and her husband or paramour, or whatever he is, plot against you!"

"Why would they?"

"Plagiarisms! Parodies! Piracies! Just imagine what it would be worth to them to know what the great 'Inimitable Boz' is writing. So they can sell it to someone who will sell it to someone who will imitate *you*! Why, everyone wants to know."

"Not Miss Lovejoy. She cares nothing for the book. Hasn't even asked."

"Of course not! Why must you be so naive? I've no doubt of it. The woman is a temptress and a thief."

"She's an innocent! It was she who disguised me. And my whereabouts remain a great secret."

"Don't be a fool!" Forster snorted. "*She* knows where to find you!"

Dickens jabbed a finger into the breast of his friend's frock coat. It was a pent-up kind of pointing, full of old furies and new wrongs. "Eleanor Lovejoy is not my problem, Forster! It is these lawsuits, of which it is your job to rid me!"

Forster brushed Dickens' finger away, grinding his teeth. "Which I can only do once you've done with the book! With or without your silly 'muse'!"

Dickens recoiled. To hear Eleanor spoken of this way, as a conspirator, a plotter against him, a seductress, brought a bitter taste to his mouth. But Forster's disdain for his "muse" was most hurtful of all. It meant he didn't believe in it, in *him*, in the magic of words that came out of air and things and people and tiny shifts of mood and feeling, the street, the gaslight, the gossamer of all life, the high, the low, the things you reach for but cannot touch, the finely webbed shadow of meaning, bearing down, ephemeral and inescapable all at once, the things that cannot be said that demand to be said, that would never be said without him, not the way he said them.

His work was a fight for all this. Whatever else was between them, he'd thought this was why Forster loved him.

"Fine," he said coldly, his lower lip a tightrope. "Tell Chapman and Hall I'll finish the book in time for *their* profitable Christmas trade. And yours, of course."

Forster pulled at his chafing cravat, grunting like a boar.

"And as for my relatives at your door," said Dickens, "I'll take care of them myself!"

In a show of defiance he filled his lungs with a willful breath and strode away, his molten core hardening by the second. He knew Forster would be watching him, standing his ground, wanting the triumph of the last word, not entirely understanding what had passed between them. The sudden escalation, the fall.

Ever true to himself, Forster called after him. "Mind your secret's kept! And beware this Lovejoy woman!"

Dickens turned, walking backward, to see him wagging a sausage finger.

"I shall prove you wrong about her!"

In Printing House Square, Blackfriars, every day of the week (Sunday excepted) *The Times* was printed and distributed throughout the civilized world, its whirring machines throwing off six thousand sheets of eight pages an hour. On that particular day, in the front office, an awestruck apprentice nearly fainted on seeing the man who occupied the space before him, in fact not so much occupied as colonized, colonized as owned. Dickens had taken off the wig, but tufts of feathery hair plumed from his pocket. The false eyebrows and spectacles were not by themselves enough cover. In newspaper circles, Charles Dickens— former law reporter, parliamentary reporter, plain reporter twice over—was legend.

The apprentice could not believe his good luck. "In this paper, sir? This very one?"

"In every one! Across the land!"

"Well, we've a nice spot you might like 'tween the shaving soap and the diuretic—"

"I do not want a spot. I want a whole page!"

"A whole page, sir?"

"Yes. Now, read it back."

The apprentice cleared his throat, as if preparing his stage debut. "'I, Charles Dickens—'"

"Louder!" said Dickens, pounding his cane on the wood floor. "And with more feeling!"

The apprentice straightened up, ribs jutting out like a ship's bow, and took a nervous gulp of air. "'I, Charles Dickens, declare publicly that as of this day and for all time to come I am no longer responsible for the debts incurred by my relatives, or relatives of my relatives, or friends of my relatives, or anyone but me. Signed, Charles John Huffam Dickens.'"

27

The Folly was the next stop on Dickens' warpath. Outside, tall letters on a placard announced WILLIAM MACREADY IN *HAMLET*—SET TO MUSIC! The once-prosperous theater now seemed to change hands every other week, with an alternating whirl of entertainments meant to satisfy a fickle public, all proclaimed "the greatest hit of the season." When drama didn't suffice, melodrama was offered, then pantomimes and mock nautical battles, mixed in with the occasional dog drama, lion tamer, or rope-walker. A plot was fine, but even here, in this snug box of a theater, novelty and spectacle were preferred.

In the pre-pandemonium of the evening's performance, Dickens found Macready in his shabby dressing room, and begged him a favor. Half dressed for his Hamlet, in a doublet of ruined velvet, furs, and leather, Macready now stood, vaguely thumbing through an old cloth bound ledger worn away at the edges. Dickens cleaved to his friend's shoulder, trying to keep him on task. But the actor railed away, gesturing, as he did onstage or not, for dramatic effect.

"The critics simply build us up that they might then describe in some detail the very moment in which we fall from the heavens, where they themselves have installed us, and land, *splat*, on our faces, naked and writhing and useless."

"Bad reviews?"

"The worst." Macready turned to his old friend, frowning. "To care or not to care. That is more to the point."

Dickens softened, forgetting for a moment why he'd come. He recalled the night of their first and only joint review, so long ago. Forster had introduced them; Dickens straightaway offered to write a play for Macready, his hero, the eminent tragedian of Drury Lane and all England. But the critics had pounced upon opening night, calling it "an unfortunate little farce that ought to hurry its way into obscurity." To salve their wounds, the playwright and actor conspired to empty a punch bowl of spiced smoking bishop, just the two of them, and pledged drunkenly to be devoted to each other from that moment on, without reservation. If anyone would understand his current state, Macready would.

"Perhaps the page before. I have to know whether she works here."

Macready flipped a page and ran a disinterested finger down the column of names and dates and wages. "It's not really my department."

"Yes. But I knew you'd at least try. For me."

"Of course I will. Lovejoy, you say?"

"Surely you know her. A quite particular purple cloak? A seamstress? In costumes."

"Hmm . . . rings a bell. Though the young women come and go, you know."

Fidgety and bored of the task, he glanced back at Dickens and noticed the white wig blossoming from his friend's coat pocket. Macready snatched it up. "I wore this wig when I gave my Lear! The critics loved my Lear!"

"Yes. It was Eleanor who gave it to me, in fact, devised my disguise that I might walk, unknown, through the streets of London."

"Unknown? Why whatever for?"

Dickens took the wig back and turned it in his hand. "I have, I'm afraid, tired of being Charles Dickens."

"Mmm. I think I see," said Macready, at last finding a chord sympathetic to his own misery, a loathing for his own profession. "But I can assure you there is not a single critic in all of India. For critics are slack-spined and cannot stand up to the heat!"

Dickens smiled wearily.

"Although they've a mind to put up a Christmas show here," said Macready. "Rumblings, in any case. Not quite to a script yet, but a money-spinner for sure. So they say. Shouldn't delay India but a few weeks. A month at most."

"Yes, of course. But, please, Macready . . ." Dickens' hopes were dwindling. "Her lips are like Burmese rubies, her eyes, Kashmirian sapphires."

"Good God, man. A bad case, have you?"

"I only need to know whether she's deceived me. If you say you do not know her, then my case is lost."

Macready nodded, moved by the shared plight of floundering men. Reinvigorated to the cause, he turned another page, tracing down the column. "Here she is! I've found her!" His finger moved along the line as he read. "Eleanor Lovejoy. Seven shillings and eight pence. Paid the week of November fourteenth—"

"Yes!" Dickens leaned over Macready's shoulder. "I knew Forster was wrong!"

"—last year."

"Last year?" Dickens looked closer.

"It's the first entry I can find. November the fourteenth, last year."

"Perhaps another name, a maiden name—"

"Most women who marry leave the theater at once. Are you quite sure she still works here?"

Dickens was reeling. He didn't want to believe it, but here, finally, was a hard, cold fact written in rusty brown ink. He looked at his old friend with sunken eyes.

"I am sure of nothing."

28

The night was fraught with demons. They came and went in his dreams, frightened and rattled him. Loomed over his bed, led him by the hand, made him look at things he'd rather not see, including a door knocker with an ugly man's face in it, distorted and mean. When he rustled to waking, relieved to have escaped one phantom, he fell asleep again only to be accosted by another. He woke up hot and twisted in his dressing gown, or shivering with cold.

Pelting rain through the night had kept him from his usual walking remedy, but as soon as it stopped, Dickens got up, dressed down to every detail of his costume, and set out to shift his mood and shake the spirits that haunted him. The more he walked, the more his false garb became him. He carried himself like an angry old man, hunched back and puckered face, buffeting anyone who dared into his path. He pounded his cane with each step, even once shaking it at a beggar who tottered in his direction with bleary eyes and an outstretched hand. Head down, trudging through the holiday throng, he grumbled to himself, lips moving fast. Soon shoppers, carolers, even dogs crossed the street to avoid the madman walking their way.

Dickens was glad of it. He was mad at Forster for doubting Eleanor, mad at himself for not—mad at the world for some nagging wrong it had done him.

When at last he looked up, he found himself barreling toward Mr. Bumble, who stood beneath a ladder outside his shop, supervising the hanging of yet more holly and boughs. Bumble turned but seemed not to notice him. Dickens jagged into the street just in case, unaware of an omnibus bearing down fast. A sharp tug on the tail of his coat saved him at the last second, sending his already aggrieved hat flying into the muddy road. It was Bumble himself who leaned over to fetch it, slapped off a clump of dirt, and handed it back.

"There you are, Mr. Dickens, good as new."

"You must be mistaken," he said, putting his hat on and pulling it low. "I'm not Dickens."

"Of course you are. And nearly flattened by a bus, at that. Why, you must be in a terrible hurry." Bumble looked his costume up and down. "Father Christmas, is it? A theatrical benefit, no doubt, for the Ragged School." Bumble pulled out his red notebook and black pencil. "In fact, now that I have you safe and sound, I would be remiss not to remind you of our holiday fund for Field Lane. What shall I put you down for?" He licked the sharp pencil tip.

Dickens readjusted his white tufts of hair. "Don't put me down at all."

"Ah! You wish to remain anonymous this year?"

"Are there no workhouses?" Dickens' face splotched red.

"Workhouses?" Bumble tried to make sense of it. "Ah! Well acted, sir," he said, playing along, though clearly with no idea what his part in the charade might be. "'Tis the season."

Dickens took stock of the scene around them, Christmas traps and trimmings everywhere. Bumble's Toy Shop itself dripped with faux-icicles and flocked evergreens. Customers in and out, towers of gold-wrapped packages, that annoying, cloying jingle bell over the door. He had never seen it quite this way before, the bald excess, the bold overembellishment, but it was clear to him now—the nothingness of all things. And how those things were peddled and hawked this time of year to willing victims who lined up for the pleasure of it, in fact fought for first place so they might be bilked and fleeced before all others. No one bothered to wait for a blast of seasonal cold air to put them in the proper mood; acquiring was all that was necessary to call it up, whatever the mood was, which even he had forgotten.

His face burned red, newfound jowls shivering with fury. "Yes, 'tis the season. So you'd all remind us at every turn. Spend, spend, buy, buy, give, give. Well, I am bled dry. We are all bled dry! By the lot of you!" He poked Bumble's notebook with staccato jabs. "You may put me down for nothing!"

And with that, he turned for the muddied street, looked both ways, eyes wide open, and crossed to the other side.

29

Dickens couldn't write and didn't want to. There was a stewy mess inside him. He'd suffered one blow after another, but not even the pair of lawsuits eclipsed the painful truth that the ledger at the Folly had revealed. He felt chagrined and abashed. What if Forster had been right all along? A clever young woman had laid a trap for him, which he'd fallen into, no, leapt into, headfirst and feet flying. But if it was a trap, why would she admit to being married? Perhaps she was more clever than either he or Forster could conceive, and there was more of her plot to come. He had wanted only her kindness and company. Eleanor had repaid him with pretending. She had worked in the theater once, that was clear, knew her way about, the ins and outs, where things were found, and hidden. It was a perfect ruse.

He recalled the day she'd first disguised him, the wig, the cane, how at ease she seemed. An actor, indeed. And if she no longer worked there, and had a husband but no means, or means but no morals, of course she would know that knowing what Charles Dickens was writing would be gold. At first he tried not to think of her at all, but she was lodged in his brain, inescapable. No amount of imaging forth on any other subject could make Eleanor Lovejoy go away.

Finally, under cloak of darkness, he slipped away from Furnival's late at night, wearing his own head and hair, to disappear into the tangle of fog-filled streets. He hoped to lose her once and for all, or at least lose himself. The day hung heavy on his spirit and London reflected his gloom in spectacular fashion. A heavy cloud floated overhead like a coalfield. Smoke from chimney pots rained down with specks of soot as big as snowflakes. The wicked emanation from wavering gas flames blurred the city, which seemed a wretched caricature of itself, daubed in charcoal and lampblack. It gouged out the eyes and jaundiced the cheeks of dog-tired dolly-mops and whores. Puff-faced drunkards staggered into foul streets and blind alleys, punching the air looking for fights, or stumbled into shadowy doorways to join with the beggars and thieves who snored and choked. A late pie-man trundled home with his sad, limping donkey pulling a broken cart. Two cabs clattered by, then none.

The longer Dickens walked, the more he wanted to be alone. The last embers of waking life were an irritant, rubbing against his nerves. He was glad the theaters were dark and lifeless, that the last public houses were turning out their lights. He welcomed the ghostly quiet. When he reached the middle of London Bridge, he gripped its balustrade. The skin on his gloveless hands looked waxen and strange under the dim yellow lamplight, like a carapace growing thick and hard. Even without the wig and brows, he felt old and tired of the world. The gritty fog circled and pounced. Even the Thames beneath him roiled like a cauldron, then disappeared in the ether.

Dickens looked toward Southwark, and though he couldn't see five steps ahead, some greater darkness called him there and showed him the way. He knew it already. Though he hadn't walked it in years, his boots remembered how to go, turning out of Angel Court onto the paved stones leading to Bermondsey. South of King, east of Borough High Street, north of Mermaid Court. There it was still, Marshalsea Prison rising from the brume like the menacing specter of ruined lives. It was a grim, forbidding barrack with insurmountable brick walls, a spiked wicket on top, and metal doors bristling with rivets and bolts, a memorial to vice and misfortune, human stupidity and cruelty. Of all the useless prisons in London, squalid and teeming with broken people—killers, arsonists, robbers, smugglers, and debtors most of all—Marshalsea was the worst of the lot, an extortion racket run for the profit of private gaolers who lined their pockets with garnish and chummage from pathetic debtors who had no defense against them.

The prison was empty now, closed just a year, with blackened holes for windows and dead air for sound. Dickens stood before it, eyes cold and flinty. His fists, deep in his pockets, clenched with each slow, spiteful beat of his heart. An implausibly warm wind on his face made him think of hell—or purgatory, even better. Closed or not, this was a prison in perpetuity, a forever place of no release.

Never had Dickens known the desire to despise his fellow man, but here it was, in front of him now.

With nothing more to show for his long night-wandering, and no desire for daylight as it encroached by small degrees, he turned back the way he'd come, head low and heavy, eyes set on the ground beneath his feet, blind to everything else. He wanted no commerce with the few working people straggling into the streets, sought no succor from the first breakfast-sellers. He wanted exile, and sleep, perhaps, but not to dream.

Charles Dickens wanted to forget.

30

John Dickens stood at the window of No. 13 Furnival's Inn with a newspaper folded under an arm of his coat and his hat in his hand. Charles Dickens walked in without a word, only half surprised to find his father standing there. He'd always had a way of tracking him, with a ferreter's instinct; the son felt at times like prey. But the back of his father's ill-fitting coat was sad and pitiable, a match for the groveling look on his white-whiskered face when he turned to greet his son, who hung up his hat with a sigh. This capped the night just right.

"Hello, Charley."

"Father." His ears pulled tight at the sound of his father's voice. "How did you find me? "

"Why, I deduced the fact! Concealing your whereabouts from your publishers, eh?"

Dickens removed his coat slowly. He threw it on the back of a chair and waited, expressionless, letting the silence stand between them.

"I spoke to Topping," his father confessed.

"You're a clever man, Father."

"But you. How clever *you* are!" John Dickens wobbled between his good leg and his bad. The tremor in his hands was visible as he removed the newspaper from under his elbow and unfolded it. His son could see that its edges were worn to paper fur, pages coffee-stained and creased from too much handling, as if it had been read and reread, folded, pocketed, pulled out, and read again. He knew what was coming. *The Times* was open to his very large advertisement, as expected.

"What a wonderful jest, Charley, just the sort of humorous waggery we've come to expect—"

"It is not waggery, Father." Dickens fixed him with a deadcold stare.

The shoulders of John Dickens' coat sagged. His arms dropped heavily to his side. "But we've always relied upon one another, you and I."

"Have we?"

"Of course." He took a cautious step toward his son. "In fact, just now there's a piddling sum that's come due—"

"And have I not always given you whatever you asked? Handouts, loans, allowances. For years and years, without question."

"And have I not always had every intention of discharging my pecuniary liabilities, despite the humiliation I've suffered—"

"Stop!" Dickens yelled, louder than he'd meant to. He drew close to his father, his eyes red-ringed with fatigue. He was done taking care of him. The piddling, niggling, trifling sums. Too many years of it, too little of being cared for back. He was beside himself with resentment, pig iron in a blast furnace, hard but brittle.

"Can you not see the humiliation *I* have suffered, being trapped in servitude to my own father's debts and failures?"

His nostrils flaring, he held his father's gaze as long as he could. John Dickens hung his head. He clutched his hat with quaking hands and cleared his gravel throat. "Why so near to Christmas would you elect to break your father's heart?"

"I remember another Christmas, when I saw clearly that I would have to make my own way in the world, without my father."

"Wh-whatever do you mean?"

"You know exactly what I mean. If you don't recall it as vividly as I do, I should worry for your memory. Or your conscience."

John Dickens stood very still, eyes rheumy and red-ringed, too. The lines down his cheeks seemed like crevasses. His whole face was a ruin. "But I am your father, Charley. Perhaps not a father to be proud of, but not one to be ashamed of, either."

Dickens pressed his lips together, but said nothing. No longer able to bear the sight of the shrunken man before him, he stared at his own boots. John Dickens folded the newspaper with great care and placed it on the writing table, a last attempt at dignity. He shuffled to the door and paused, wrapping his knotty fingers around the knob. He turned to his son, tears skimming his eyes. "Never forget that I was always proud to call you my son."

Dickens turned away, crossed a hand to his shoulder, and rested his chin there, until the door shut behind him. He closed his eyes to wait for his father's clunking steps, the creak of uneven stairs. When the quiet returned, he took a gulp of air and walked to the window, leaning his forehead against it. Below, his father came into view, hobbling down a sliver of street into the thick fog of bare morning, smaller and less sure-footed than Dickens could ever recall.

There was so much hard feeling he wished would fall away.

31

The fog refused to let the city loose from its grip for two nights and three days. By day it was a foul, brown-colored fog that threw monstrous shadows on the craggy rooftops visible from Dickens' rooms. It was just the right weather to power his quill. He laid three fires and burned through them all, down to nothing but silvery ash. He slept in fits and starts upright in a chair, ate a few crusts of bread and some cheese. When there was nothing left to burn in the hearth, he threw a wool blanket over his shoulders, put on a pair of fingerless gloves, and wrote even faster. From the moment his father left, he'd collected all his disappointment and anger, like kindling to fuel his own *feu de misère*—a bonfire of agonies. He wrote it all down, made it part of his tale. Turn it outward, that's what he'd do, give it back to the world that gave it to him. If he couldn't obliterate his memories, he would put them all to good use, find in them the fodder he needed to finish the book, and forever be done with the hangers-on and will-you-pays.

Page by page, the plot congealed. The longer he wrote, the

more the sight of his father dimmed, Fred faded away, and even Eleanor became strange to him. He did use a dash of her, mixed with a dram of Maria, in the service of Belle—Scrooge's own once-betrothed, who had trampled his feelings and turned his heart cruel. Dickens considered her demise by consumption. The murder of the unsuspecting distant cousin played like a violin, with poisoned ginger in the Christmas punch. The birth of a long, bitter lawsuit in its aftermath was tempered, as it must be to appease Forster, with a cheery holiday ball near the end. The requisite foil to his skinflint Scrooge he called Fezziwig, whom he made a happy, foppish man in a big Welsh wig dancing under a mistletoe. Mr. Cratchit would be spared for now, though Jacob Marley, he had not forgotten, was dead from the start.

When the clock tower in the square struck midnight on the third day, he laid down his pen, pleased with his progress. The writing had cured him, he was sure. No need to rehash or revisit anything in the past. The mere chime of a silly old clock need not remind him of Eleanor or anyone else. It marked the end of a day and the start of a new one, that was all. And with only one chapter left to go, a reward for his hard work was in order. And so Dickens ventured out in full disguise, in search of a late supper.

The square was shrouded in the same sooty, choking fog that had grabbed on to the city days before and wouldn't let go. The air was thick and wet; it smelled of burning coal, horse dung, and roast chestnuts. Dickens started across, his will strong; he could taste the pork chop already. But each step whittled his will away, like the sharp blade of a knife. By the time he reached the tower itself, he couldn't taste the chop at all. The Folly broke through the veil of fog like an apparition. It seemed so close, just beyond where he ought to turn. The last theater patrons were climbing into cabs, the rest scurried for the Strand. A few jobbing actors lingered by the stage door. Macready might be long gone. Would it do any harm to anyone if he simply waited to see whether Eleanor emerged? One final piece of proof. A nail in her coffin.

Dickens skulked in a darkened alcove with a clear view of the stage door. His calculus was plain: if she didn't appear, there could be no shred of doubt that Macready was right, and Forster more right than he. She had lured him to the theater and pretended to work there, but only as it suited her sinister needs.

When a janitor came out to turn down the gas lamp, the theater fell into darkness, and Dickens with it. Feeling a fool to have detoured at all, he was about to step from the shadows when the stage door cracked open and Eleanor stepped out, all alone. Furtively, he watched her pad across the square. She was headed, no doubt, straight for home.

Dickens followed her without a thought. He told himself he wasn't spying, simply seeing her safely to her door, but this new development did have the added benefit of proving that Forster had falsely accused her and Macready had simply been wrong. He knew Forster meant to protect him, and Macready had had other things on his mind. Both could be forgiven. But his hope was that Eleanor worked and lived where she'd said, thus hiding nothing from him. It would exonerate her, and even if he was wrongfully prying once again, surely that was a cause for good.

She turned down her narrow street. He was forty steps behind, he judged, trying to keep her in view through the miasma. Each step closer to her lodgings was an argument for her innocence. He thought of trying to catch up to her, toss it off to coincidence, ask after her well-being, wish her good night. But when he turned the corner himself, his heart fluttered and sank. Eleanor had passed the door of her own thin house without even a sideways glance. Whatever her business, its urgency drove her on, first around one corner, then another, down two alleys, across a mews. Dickens kept his distance, and only once ducked into the nook of a building when she looked over her shoulder, then pulled up the hood of her cloak as if to hide her face, which shone like a lighthouse beacon. He watched her scurry down a stone-staired snicket that led to a lower street. Wherever this path was taking her, there was no doubt she knew it well.

When Dickens stepped back into the street to follow her, footsteps rustled behind him; it was hard to tell in the dense muffling smog. When he stopped, they stopped. Or did they? Perhaps the stealth of spying had fueled his imagination, and they were his own footsteps echoing back to him in the brick-lined street. He clocked three warehouses, a pin, a needle, one cutlery, before he stopped again to look back. The fog seemed to wrap its furry fingers around him, strangling his vision and blurring the night.

Creeping down the snicket himself, he never let his eyes lose the hem of the purple mantle sweeping behind her. But the hem was all he had. The fog enveloped her, too, as if protecting her from him, giving her cover. It was a great effort to stay close enough without being detected. His heart raced, his feet hurried. He no longer knew where he was, every direction obscured. When he stopped to listen for her footsteps, he couldn't tell whether they were ahead or behind him, or even there at all.

When the dampened sound of an iron gate groaned open somewhere in front of him, he tiptoed toward it, feeling his way like a blind man. He found it twenty steps ahead—rusted finials, one side of the gate pulling away from its crumbling brick post and rotted hinges. He slipped through the narrow cleft where the cobbles under his feet became gravel and dirt, then mounds of raw earth. Somewhere in the soupy air a shovel hit dirt—gouge-burrow-heave—again and again. He stumbled on a flat sandstone slab sitting crooked in the ground. He put his hand on what must be a grave marker, with carved letters, worn away by time and weather. There were ten others near it that seemed to float in the brume—old obelisks, crosses, and busts, some toppled in the sunken earth that had given way to the decay of long-buried coffins below. Dickens moved from one to the next, from carved skulls, snakes, and cherubs to shattered urns covered in moss and dead leaves, worn away, desolate, and neglected. And only white blankness beyond.

Suddenly the gate creaked behind him. Dickens flinched and drew a quick gulp of air, trying to silence his own hammering heart. He had lost Eleanor. Lost all sense of which way was which. But he trudged on to find decrepit headstones giving way to close-lying heaps of earth, coffin-shaped, with rotted wood tablets, cairns of rough stone, or initials traced in pebbles and shells to mark the poorer graves. There was no church that he could see. Poor graveyards like this were born of the Great Fire, when dead bodies took up the sockets where a church once stood. And sometimes bodies on top of those.

When he spied Eleanor again she was standing, statue-still, ten times the distance between his nose and his outstretched arm. Dickens ducked behind a barrel-trunked tree not a second before she peered out past the hem of her hood, looking right and left, as if she, too, felt followed. He removed his hat and pressed his back to the mottled bark of the ancient, leafless plane tree. Through the very spectacles she'd given him, he watched her kneel before a slab-of-wood footboard. The fog lifted and swirled around the cloak that settled in folds at her feet. She lowered her hood and bowed her head in a silent prayer, then leaned close to touch her lips to the simple marker. He waited while she lingered there, shoulders huddled over the ground.

When she stood, it was an effort, slow and deliberate, to pull herself away. She raised her hood, refastened the cloak at her neck, and turned back the way she'd come.

Dickens sucked in his breath, flat against the tree, waiting for her to pass. A swish of her skirts, the moan of the rusty gate. He exhaled relief; then strangeness all around. Even the grave digger's spade had stopped. Only the dead were left, and ghastly silence. He stepped to the footboard and knelt, as she had, laying his hat on the ground beside him. The marker was home-made, rough and uneven, the work of loving hands and a sorry heart. A dried laurel bouquet rested against it, the very one he'd bought her days before. Under it, in letters carved by a dull knife, the name of the poor grave's inhabitant: TIMOTHY LOVEJOY.

Dickens ran his fingers along the crude lettering, confused. What could it mean—her Timothy Lovejoy, dead and buried? Was this the man Forster had accused of conspiring against him, lying cold in the ground?

A chill ran from his neck to his toes. He pushed himself to standing, searching the air for an answer, but the fog closed in on his lungs, suffocating him. The tufted mounds all around seemed to undulate, as if they would devour him whole, pull him into a grave of his own. He had an instinct to flee, but didn't know which way. Dickens hugged his arms to his chest, pale as death, and swallowed hard. He shut his eyes to steel himself, lifted one leaden foot, stepping backward, then the other. Two more steps in the sodden earth, when he stumbled over a figure in the dark!

"Who is it?" Dickens yelled, grabbing at its clothes. It was a boy, he could tell by the sprig of an arm, the puny wrist now gripped in his hand. He was small and wiry but determined as a fisting cur, struggling to escape. A spare patch of moonlight swept over his brown eyes and thick lashes. It was the small ragged boy from the doorway in Covent Garden, who'd darted into the crowd when he approached.

"It was you! You followed me here!" He fought to keep hold of the slippery boy. "I know you!"

The boy writhed and grunted.

"Tell me who you are!" Dickens demanded.

The boy shook his head, trying to wriggle his wrist free. An open sketchbook dropped from his hand. He lunged for it, slipping from his captor's grasp. Dickens grabbed his shin, tripping him, at the same time reaching to snatch the book away. But the boy clutched at it fiercely, straining and pulling, a stronger will than his own. A single page tore away in Dickens' hand. The ragamuffin grabbed Dickens' hat from the ground, clambered to standing, and bolted into the fog, hurdling over gravestones, quick as a rabbit pursued by a fox.

Dickens looked at the hastily drawn sketch in his hand. He could just make out the figure of an old man in a dismal graveyard, surrounded by leaning, irregular markers, a pale bald head with white swatches of hair, and muttonchops on a ghostly face with wild, sunken eyes. It was the frightening specter of a bitter, crazed old man.

The thin whine of the rusted gate startled him. He folded the sketch roughly and slipped it into his pocket, retracing his steps out of the graveyard, back onto the street, chasing the faint patter of boots on cobblestone, and a street boy, breathing hard. The boy was small and quick, but no match for Dickens' own long legs.

"Give me back my hat, you thief!" he yelled.

The boy climbed to the top of the snicket, and stopped to stuff the sketchbook into the belt of his pants. His lungs fanned like bellows. Dickens scaled the stairs by twos, closing in, when the boy started off again, scudding into a dark alleyway just ahead. This wasn't the way he'd come. The streets were empty; he'd lost his bearings. There was nothing to do but keep his quarry in sight, follow the sound of his steps, anything to catch him. Dickens was soon back on his heels, gaining ground, when the waif saw him bearing down and put on more speed. This boy would be hard to catch, Dickens thought, redoubling his own effort.

The boy ducked into another alley, racing to the next crossing. But when he turned back to look for his pursuer he stumbled over a pile of garbage in the narrow passage. He clawed, slipping and sliding, through the rotten food and oily paper, dropped the hat, and picked it up again, crawling back to his feet. When Dickens rounded the corner, he saw him stalled under a gas lamp in the next street up, grabbing at his ankle, hopping on one foot. He sprinted toward the boy, who watched in horror.

"I'll get you, you little scapegrace!"

He was three fathoms away when a carriage appeared from nowhere, horses rearing and snorting, nearly trampling the boy as he skittered under their raised hooves pawing at the fog. Dickens couldn't see him until the carriage passed. The boy was limping as fast as he could, scampering past the Folly and on to the clock-tower square. He was headed for the little street straight across. It was Eleanor's street; there could be no doubt of it. Dickens doubled his pace to take the corner himself. The ragged boy stood, frantic, jiggling the doorknob of the lodging house.

Dickens growled at him. "Stop!"

The boy's chest heaved in sharp, short breaths. He kicked the door three times with his good leg and surely all the strength he had left, at last opening it. With his pursuer just steps away, he slipped inside and slammed it hard behind him.

Dickens banged on the door, rattling the knob, yelling at

full decibels. "Let me in! Let me in at once, you wretched, good-for-nothing guttersnipe!"

He pounded harder; the door held firm. He drew back his own leg to kick it, when the door screaked open. Eleanor stood on the other side of it like a pillar. Dickens pushed past her in a rage, flying up the narrow staircase and through the open door of her room. He didn't see the boy anywhere, but spun around to find Eleanor right behind him, holding his top hat, eyes blazing.

"So! I've found you out at last! Where is he?"

"Hiding from you!"

Dickens followed her gaze to the bedstead. The worn heels of the boy's brogans peeked out from the end. "And well he should hide! I caught him in the shadows, spying on me!" He stepped closer, inches from her face. "But you know that already, of course. That decrepit graveyard is your meeting place."

Eleanor stood her ground, unafraid. "You followed me to the graveyard?"

"The boy followed *me*! He's one of those street urchins, is he not? The ones who accosted me coming out of *this* very house."

"You've been in my house?"

"And a good thing it is, too. Or I would not have uncovered this sinister plot! You. Pretending to work at the theater!"

"Yet you think nothing of spying on *me*?"

"Are you their 'Fagin,' is that it? A kidsman running your own band of boys who filch and steal for you? Hat snatchers, pocket pickers, sneak thieves! You've had them stalking my every move!"

Eleanor stepped toward him, and held out his hat with a stiff arm. She spoke slowly, lips quivering with anger. "It is *you* who haunt *our* doorstep! I cannot but turn around and there you are!"

"That's different!" said Dickens, snagging the hat from her hand. "However foolish it was, I . . . admired you."

"He admires *you*! And if he follows you, it's only because your stories have meant a great deal to him. Why, all the boys and girls talk your fun in the streets. He's only as they are."

"Then let him second your story. Tell him I demand to speak to him!"

"He does not speak."

"No, of course he wouldn't, would he? For then he'd have to tell me the truth about you."

Eleanor set her jaw, giving no ground.

"Perhaps he would write it for me," Dickens snarled.

"He doesn't write. He draws."

Dickens fumbled for the sketch from his pocket and waved it in her face. "Yes! He has drawn me as a ghost in a graveyard!"

She grabbed the drawing from his hand, scoffing. "A fair likeness, I think. Look at you! You've scared him out of his wits! Timothy is but a boy!"

Dickens wanted to snap back, but hearing "Timothy" stopped him short. He looked at the sullied hat in his hand and shook his head, as if to jiggle his own thinking free.

"Timothy? *He* is your Timothy Lovejoy?"

"Named for his father," she said in a whisper, "who died when he was small."

Dickens turned the hat like a wheel. His mind went round and round, too, up to the ceiling and down to the bed. He rubbed his head to take it in, but it wasn't his head, not his own hair, it was the wig she'd given him. Suddenly conscious of his appearance, he peeled away the muttonchops and pulled the headpiece off in one gesture. From where he stood, he could see the boy's shoes quaking with fear.

"I—I don't know what to say." He put a splayed hand on his matted head of hair. "This is quite a shock."

Eleanor glowered at him, eyes like cast iron. Dickens understood, berated himself for suspecting the boy. He had let jealousy get in the way of clear thinking. What a fool he'd been to be threatened by a child. Once again, his own imagination had betrayed him.

"I didn't mean to scare the boy."

Eleanor crossed her arms over her chest like a shield. "He doesn't speak, but he hears. You could say something to reassure him that you mean him no harm."

Dickens pulled on an earlobe and knit his brows. "I'm not, I think, just now . . . very good with children."

Eleanor angled her head toward the bed, insistent. Dickens moved to the other side of it and crouched down, where he could see the full length of the boy, shuddering under the bed beside the old leather trunk, hands covering his ears, but his eyes as wide as two pound coins. He took off his glasses, pulled the eyebrows away, and came face-to-face with the frightened boy, trying hard to think what to say.

"Timothy, you are . . . a very fast runner." He stood abruptly, duty discharged.

Eleanor narrowed her eyes.

"Perhaps I should go," he said. "I've not been myself, these last days. I scared away my own family, and now I've scared away yours." He lowered his chin. "Forgive me for behaving badly."

He searched her eyes, desperately wanting some sort of reassurance himself. But there was none there. It was irredeemable, driving a young boy away from his own father's grave. Forgiveness was too much to ask. He started for the door, but turned when his hand reached the knob. "Timothy hurt his ankle, I think. Might I look in on him? Perhaps tomorrow?"

Eleanor crossed her arms at her waist and pinched the elbows of her gray muslin sleeves. Dickens had not seen her angry before, and he was struck by the raw power in it, the fierce line of her jaw, the blue fire in her eyes. He waited, wanted for it to pass, to be subsumed by her goodness. He hoped.

Finally, she looked at him. And without any hint of forgiveness, any inkling of ceding ground, she nodded.

32

Even a grown man can be an orphan.

The bald wig was wadded up and stuffed deep in Dickens'
pocket, but he felt older than his years, older than he ever had
before, irreparably alone, with no one left to blame. He wandered into the small hours of the night with a ponderous gait,
treading the way his feet knew to go when his heart was too
heavy to care. His own melancholy mapped his route. He wasn't
surprised, then, to find himself outside Bumble's Toy Shop in
the sad gas-glow of near-morning. His reflection in the paned
window was a fright even to him—hollowed eyes and sunken
cheeks, lips tapered to a sharp frown. But past his own image,
behind the glass, an exuberance of toys came into soft focus. The
little *Théâtre Française*, the one Katey had admired, stood proudly
between two articulated boy puppets on wooden sticks and a
pull-horse made of papier-mâché and coarse wool, with leather
ears and saddle, black-button eyes, and a real horsehair tail.

But at the center of it all was the prize of the lot. A dollhouse with four open floors, in the German style with a blue slate roof, sat on a high table bathed in the glow of pink dawn behind him, which shot its little paned windows through with the glorious light of new morning. Dickens pressed his face against the glass to take in every detail. There was an attic nursery, with a painted crib and cupboard, a Punch and Judy theater, a full-masted wooden sailboat, and a rolling toy sheep. Three floors below was a busy kitchen with checkerboard tile and pointed lace curtains. But the true jewel of the house, like its own heart center, was a fine drawing room with vined wallpaper, a Turkish rug, a Biedermeier desk, and striped taffeta tacked at the top of its windows for drapes. A tall Christmas tree with ornaments graced the middle of the room, around which the little family of bisque dolls, each no bigger than the palm of his hand, stood: the master and mistress of the house, three children, a baby, two dogs, and a Doreen of their own.

Dickens lowered his head with a shallow sigh. He wondered whether his children were asleep in their Scottish beds under downy quilts, dreaming of their Christmas wishes. He imagined Catherine sleeping peacefully, their newborn in a rocking cradle beside her. He'd had no word from her; Topping surely would have found him if there had been. And he had nothing of worth to report to her in turn. He was no better than when she'd left, in fact worse—a tumbled down version of himself, whom he hardly recognized at all. Catherine had been right about him, but he didn't know how to fix it. And he couldn't return home, or ask them to come back, until he did. All he could think to do was weave back into the skein of streets in hopes of untangling himself.

But all the roads, even the little ones, smelled of Christmas. Markets at every turn, like dense evergreen forests of holly, laurel, and fir, springing up in front of him, blocking his way. Each one doing its best to mark the advent of the great, irrepressible annual fact. Dickens soon found himself following his nose and the clatter of wheels on all sides. He fell into the stream of carts and wagons pouring into Covent Garden, where hawkers and hucksters croaked hoarsely, tuning their voices for the long day's performance ahead. "Mackereel all alive, fine silver mackereel, six a shillin'," and "Mizzletoe, penny a pinch!"

The four coffee-sellers he liked best were all there, oilcloth-covered spring barrows in separate corners of the piazza, two with tables, two with trestle and board, the one who cut his coffee with chicory, the other who used saccharine root, the man with the best ham sandwich, the woman with the sweetest cake. Wanting some small taste of human fellowship, even if he didn't deserve any at all, Dickens chose the shiny green truck with polished cans of hot coffee and tea mounted with brass plates. He took his coffee in a mug, wrapped his long fingers around it for warmth, and was suddenly aware of the whisper of a light cold wind on his neck and visible patches of blue sky above.

Even the fog was rethinking itself.

When the early coachmen crowded under a balustraded gallery, Dickens shouldered in among them to watch a plucky magician in polka-dotted lederhosen, braces, a ballet blouse, and yellow tights, all topped with a starry blue velvet cape. A portable table, draped in red satin, displayed all manner of apparatus: a pack of cards, sticks and string balls, a wand, linking rings, three thimbles, a knotted silk kerchief, and a top hat, which soon found its way to the conjurer's head. His diminutive assistant, with a little crutch under his arm—possibly to spur compassion when the hat was passed for the nobbings—shifted props and kept things moving. The bleary-eyed drivers, sucking their morning coffees, seemed dazzled by a simple *sautez-le-coup* with the cards.

Dickens knew the deception well, but he smiled nonetheless, not for the brilliance of its execution—it was on the sloppy end of magic tricks—but for the truth at the bottom of every illusion, every fiction, every lie: our own great desire to believe.

33

"And my, oh, my, if you could have seen me turn the watches into tea caddies and burn handkerchiefs without hurting them—you would never forget it as long as you live!" Dickens stood on a plain wooden stool in Eleanor's lodging wearing the lederhosen, blouse, and star-spangly blue cape he'd purchased from the magician at Covent Garden, who had parted happily with all of it when a punishing rain interrupted the proceedings and his peevish assistant promptly quit. Before he'd wanted to write, Dickens wanted to act, but before that to be a conjurer, which he'd practiced since he was a boy himself, on whomever he could find to watch. He fancied himself an unparalleled necromancer, and had been delighted when Jane Carlyle, after the Christmas party last year, said that he was the best she'd ever seen, and acknowledged having paid to see many. He could make playing cards burst into flame, transport a watch into the middle of a loaf of bread, and cook a steaming-hot plum pudding in a gentleman's top hat. Forster was often his accomplice in the early days. It had started when the two eager conspirators purchased the entire stock of a magician's supply store that was going out of business and put on amateur shows at home and at parties. Adults were astonished, but children, any children, were the best audience by far.

Now he was holding forth at his flamboyant best, but it was no use. Timothy sat at the table alone; Eleanor wasn't there. He had let Dickens in reluctantly, and returned straight to his post, chin resting in one hand, the other clutching a stump of pencil, which he rubbed busily across the paper. His eyes were cast down, focused on his sketch and nothing else.

Dickens was undeterred. "Why, I once transformed a bran box into a guinea pig, pulled a plum pudding from an empty pan, and sent coins flying through the air, without benefit of human hands!"

Timothy shot him a brief but skeptical glance.

"Ah, I detect an unbeliever in our midst." Dickens held out a gold sovereign in the palm of his white-gloved hand. He waved a thin wand over it and closed his eyes while chanting, "Albri-kira-mumma-tousha-cocus-co-shiver-de-freek!" He repeated the incantation twice, opening his right eye enough to catch Timothy watching out of his left. With one last circle of his wand, he shouted, "Presto-quick-begone!"

Timothy gasped. The coin had disappeared from the gloved hand, not a trace of it anywhere, while the other hand, fingers unfurled one by one, was empty, too! Dickens had his attention now. He stepped off the stool toward Timothy, even as the boy leaned away.

"Wherever could it have gone?" Dickens asked, opening both his hands again for proof, with not a thing up either sleeve. He swept his hand lightly near the boy's ear with enough ostentation to make his point, and produced the coin with a flourish. It gleamed in the palm of his hand like a treasure. Timothy looked at it in disbelief.

"Go on," Dickens said. "It's real."

Timothy took the coin from Dickens' palm. It glinted gold in his lead-marked fingers. He turned it over twice, as if he'd never held anything so dear.

"It ought to be yours, I think."

Timothy shook his head.

"After all, that's where I found it," he said, pointing to the boy's ear. "And there's no one else here to claim it but you." He knelt, eye to eye, and gently closed the boy's fingers over the coin. "I promised your mother I'd look in on you."

Timothy tilted his head, dubious. The same way his mother had done the night before.

"I don't blame her for not being here. After my inexcusable behavior. But really, I feel sure she'd approve of my checking on that ankle of yours."

Timothy cast his eyes down, crossed his ankles, and tucked his dirty brogans under the chair.

"Just the one," said Dickens. "Very gently, I promise you."

The boy scratched his uneven shrub of brown hair, put down his pencil, and turned his small frame to face his visitor. It seemed to take all his bravery. Dickens admired how he lifted the afflicted leg a few inches off the floor, his foot dangling from a swollen ankle, without making a face. Dickens took the boy's floppy shoe in his hand and slipped it off, as gently as he could. It was weather-beaten, with yawning seams and no laces, too big for the tiny, sockless foot inside. Timothy gripped the edges of his chair as Dickens moved his ankle ever so slightly to one side, then the other, trying to keep the boy's mind on anything else.

"You know, I have a daughter who doesn't speak. Well, not

much, anyway. Mamie is her name. I call her my 'Mild Glo'ster,' named after the cheese, her favorite. And also for her shyness. Have you ever tasted a Gloucester?"

Timothy shrugged a shoulder. It seemed enough of a yes that Dickens carried on. "But nobody's fooled by her not saying much. Mamie's a deep thinker."

Rolling the ankle gently, he kept his gaze on the boy's smudged, freckled face and found him listening closely, not wincing at all. "Well, I don't think it broken. Should heal on its own." He set the boy's foot on the floor. Timothy tucked it back under the chair, and tugged at a loose thread on his sweater. He was pulling back into himself, no doubt. Why, he might never have been to a doctor, and here he was, having to trust a man who'd menaced him through the streets of London, chased him all the way home. Dickens surveyed his fresh store of magical tricks, but nothing was just the right medicine. Instead, he stood and retrieved the assistant's crutch, and held it out for Timothy's approval.

"I was lucky enough to procure this from a man only a little taller than you, who assured me he was quite done with it. He offered me the additional benefit of a magician's saw, so I've cut it down to fit just right, I think." Dickens watched Timothy consider the crutch. "Only for a few days, while your ankle heals."

The boy stood, with some effort, on his good foot. He fit the crutch awkwardly under his arm and hopped a step or two. He looked back at Dickens for encouragement, the way a small child does who's just learning to walk.

"You'll be running races in no time." Dickens willed a smile for the boy's benefit, but how slight he seemed, more air than substance, not tethered to the world enough. He'd seen it at the ragged schools, where there were rough-and-tumble boys, throwing headlong into daily battle with hulls so hard, nothing could crack them. Then there were boys who hung back, at the edges of everything, wide- and glassy-eyed, too hungry to say so, too timid to fight. He guessed Timothy to be nine or ten, but no bigger than a seven-year-old. There was a shy sweetness about him, despite the bravura, or necessity, of wearing a man's clothes, perhaps his own father's. Dickens felt genuinely for the boy, and guilt for whatever pain he'd caused. At least the boy had a mother, who could provide some small measure of protection, or love. At least he had Eleanor.

Timothy managed one turn of the room, but even that seemed to tire him.

"Perhaps you should rest. Plenty of time to practice later." Dickens helped the boy to his chair and laid the crutch against a wall. He thought he should go. He was an unwelcome intruder in their lives. Still, he was not accustomed to leaving children alone to fend for themselves. Timothy was just a boy. Dickens didn't know where Eleanor was, but without her, the room seemed cold and bare.

He threw the last lumps of coal he could find on what was left of the fire and poked at it, trying to coax a little more flame, some modicum of warmth. He took the threadbare quilt from the bed and spread it on the floor near the hearth, then offered his elbow to Timothy, who leaned on it to limp closer. The boy lay down and curled into himself, like a snail in its shell, arms tight to his little chest, bone-tired and shivering. He was asleep within seconds.

Dickens removed his own wool coat with satin lining and fur lapels and laid it over the boy, tucking it in at the sides, careful not to wake him. It was then that a simple locket on a brass chain slipped from inside Timothy's shirt and fell open on the floor. He picked it up between his fingers to close it, but couldn't resist a glimpse at the oval frame on one side holding a tiny, detailed pencil sketch of a younger Eleanor—a serious girl who gazed kindly at the world with hopeful eyes. In the other side, a lock of her hair under glass.

"What a lucky boy you are," he whispered, "to be loved by such a one as she."

Dickens closed the locket and tucked it back inside the boy's collar. Timothy puffed a sigh and fell deeper into sleep. His exhaustion was palpable. Dickens wanted to put his hand on the boy's hair; to touch it, smooth it, the way he did with his own children as a way of giving them comfort, and getting some, too. But he felt unworthy of the tender touch between parent and child, and didn't dare disturb him. He sighed himself, long and sad.

"I will haunt your doorstep no more."

34

Never mind necessity, melancholy is the mother of invention.

Dickens sat at his wobbly writing table at Furnival's, dispatched and forgotten by the world, but full of words to say so. He was dog-tired, with a blanket around his shoulders, a thick stack of pages, and an inkpot bled nearly dry. He had written straight through the rest of the day and well into night, when he found himself at a natural stopping place, an apt end to his brooding tale. He paused to stare into the hearth, where his own fire had burned to nothing, and found there the final words of his Christmas book.

When he crossed the final *t*, there was a quiet knock at the door. He wasn't sure of the time, but the clock tower had long ago declared midnight. It must be very late indeed, and none but the clerk, his father, and Forster knew him to be here. Expecting one of the three, and surprised to find himself even hoping so, he took up his pages and opened the door. But he found Eleanor Lovejoy instead. Her hood shadowed her face, giving him no clue to her state of mind. Ire or indifference, he imagined both. Still, his heart swelled in his ribs, pushed at the buttons of his waistcoat. He opened his mouth to welcome her, but had a sudden feeling of having used up all the words he knew.

"I took a chance that I'd find you here," she said.

"But how did you—?"

"You mentioned it yourself."

"Did I? Never mind. It doesn't matter how you found me. You did." He stepped aside with an awkward wave of his arm, pages tight in his grip. "Come in, please." Eleanor stepped out of the hall only as far as the dim-lit threshold. Her eyes darted about the room, unsure. Dickens understood. A young woman, even a widow, should be careful what company she keeps, though he didn't take her as someone who cared one whit what anyone thought. She drew a breath and stepped all the way inside, then turned to him, lowering the hood of her cloak. The one lamp in the room threw velvet light across her face. Her cheeks were the color of claret, as if she'd hurried all the way, cold and hot at the same time.

"I only came to say thank you . . . for your kindness to my son."

His chest burst with relief. "It was a small thing."

"But he felt cared for."

"Did Timothy tell you that?"

"In his way," she said, looking out the window, as if the mystery of her son's silence lived there.

"I didn't blame you for not wanting to see me again," he said. "In fact, assumed that's why you stayed away. Why, I wouldn't blame you at all if you'd come to despise me."

Eleanor threaded and twisted her fingerless-gloved hands, worrying her way to an answer. Dickens followed her gaze outside, where some small change in the weather had split a seam in the fog. The clock tower where they'd first met peeped over steep roofs in a navy-blue night, as if saying hello. It seemed to hold up the bright winter moon all by itself. And she seemed to find in it the thing she wanted to say.

"I stayed away because I've come . . . to care deeply for you."

So unexpected was her declaration, not of love, but of some abiding sympathy between them, that his loneliness fell away in an instant. A tingling rushed down his spine.

"Please, won't you stay?"

She smiled a little at the corners of her mouth, but shook her head. He could see she was tired, but couldn't bear to lose her good graces, not again. Or her presence. He looked at the pages still clutched in his hand.

"What about hearing my tale?"

35

Charles Dickens was an enthusiastic reader of his own work. Even Thomas Carlyle, not the least of his critics, said he was better than any Macready in the world, a whole tragic, comic, heroic theater under one hat. Macready himself agreed. From the time he started his own little theater troupe at the age of nine, Dickens had never needed more than an audience of one to inspire a full-throated performance of the play of the moment. But his own words, his own work, he could deliver with the force of a hammer blow, or the airiness of a falling feather.

Eleanor sat in the "missus" chair near the now-glowing fire, hands clasped in her lap, listening with every part of her being. Dickens stood in front of her, acting it out as he read, each character, all the lines, bringing everything he could to sell it. He wanted her to feel each shiver, sense the murder coming and the chilling terror until the cathartic ball near the end. She was still throughout, an inscrutable look on her face.

He reached the last page, the last line, and paused to fill his lungs as if an opera singer about to reach for his highest note.

Every word aspirated, each equal to the other. "And Scrooge's heart, though frozen . . . began to melt." He returned the page to the bottom of the stack and bowed his head, moved by his own reading. "The end."

"Hmm," Eleanor said, eyes closed. Small, indecipherable movements of her head suggested she was recounting the story's high points to herself in quick succession. A nod, a tilt, a raised brow. At last she opened her eyes, elbows planted on the arms of the chair. She rested her chin in one hand, thinking hard, for what seemed a very long time, an era in itself. The wait was excruciating.

"Well?" he asked when he could stand her silence no longer.

Eleanor leaned forward and pressed her hands together. "That is quite a book, Mr. Dickens."

"Yes. And quite to the point, I think. "

"Though perhaps not quite to the point of Christmas."

"Well, but, you see—"

"He's a cold, unfeeling, disagreeable man, your Scrooge."

"There's the melting heart at the end."

"It's just . . . so long waiting for the end."

"Oh, my. Perhaps the name doesn't quite capture him. What about Screege? Scrumble?"

"I suppose," she said with a shrug. "If it will aid the cause of Christmas."

"Any old hack could beef up the Christmas bits. But I refuse to overdo."

"Then I suppose you are done." She rose abruptly from the chair.

Dickens stood in front of her, full of restless energy. "Exactly. I deliver it to the printers tomorrow, first thing. At last done with the tyranny of deadlines and pages and word counts, in short, the sufferings and torments of those who are bound to the life of the pen. It will be a new life."

She half smiled, retrieving her cloak from the back of the chair. "A new life in India?"

The firelight danced in her eyes, shaped at the edges with a sadness he was just beginning to see. It softened his bearing, brought his own thoughtfulness to the fore. He hugged the stack of pages to his chest.

"I did always long to know worlds beyond my own. Had I, as a young man, ventured far enough to discover those boundless riches, I may have had no need to write."

Eleanor fastened the cloak at her neck and looked him square in the eye. "How sad to think you might not have found your Oliver Twist. Your Nickleby. Your dear Little Nell."

Her sincerity was her sword. It thrust straight through him. He swallowed hard and stepped closer to her, now just inches away. She didn't step back this time, nor avert her gaze. Neither of them breathed.

"Far sadder to think I might never have found you," he said, lost in the marine depths of her eyes, so bottomless and clear.

She blushed and looked down. The not-touching between them was as conspicuous as if they had full-embraced. They both stood, deep in their own thoughts, not daring to move.

At last, Eleanor raised the hood of her cloak. "I should go."

"Of course," he said, nodding. "As you wish."

There was no need to say more; it was their tacit agreement. Dickens was touched by the ease of understanding between them. So few words said so many. He followed her to the door, a reluctant procession. She turned to him one last time, eyes glistening.

"I do wish it were otherwise."

As did he. As does anyone, he knew, who has a moment of

true feeling without encumbrances, that cannot be got another way. That has no history, no list of injuries and faults. Someone to see only the best in us. For the worst parts are written on our skin in iron gall ink, indelible, and recited on a regular basis, by whoever knows us best. But a few simple, kind words, even from a near-stranger, can say everything else. And that in itself must be a prize.

Was his own heart beginning to melt? He didn't know. Eleanor had given him his Scrooge, unintentional as it was, but it was his book now, his journey. She didn't care for the book, perhaps, but she cared for him, and that was enough.

"May I walk you home?"

Eleanor shook her head. She was a self-contained woman who had never asked anything of him, perhaps of anyone.

"It will be dawn soon enough," she said.

He put his hand on the knob, reluctant to open it and let her go. "A new beginning, I suppose."

She hesitated. "A new beginning. Yes."

He bowed his head and opened the door to let her pass. But she stopped in the threshold and turned, bright with curiosity. "What will you call the book?"

"Hmm," he said, leaning his head against the doorframe. "I haven't a title yet. But you shall be the first to hear it when I do."

Her eyes crinkled at the corners. "I should like that very much."

He hugged his stack of pages to his chest and watched her slip down the stairs without a sound. Not even a creak of the stairs, so light was her step. When she was consumed by the dark, he went back in, closed the door, and rested against it. An ember popped in the hearth. He walked over to coax one last flame, a little warmth, now that he was alone again. He pulled the wool blanket back onto his shoulders and stared into the fire. "*A Christmas Log*," he said. "That will do fine."

He took his pen from his desk, dipped it into the inkpot, and scribbled the book's title, and his own name, its author. Glad to be done with it, he sat in the chair where Eleanor had listened so patiently and placed the manuscript on the small pedestal table at his elbow. He unbuttoned his waistcoat, folded his hands behind his head, and watched the fire burn to its last white ember and expire.

Dickens slept through to morning, dead to the world. He woke from a swirling dream, still in the chair, blanket twisted around his neck and chest. He untangled himself, sat forward with a lazy yawn and a stretch of his long legs. He rubbed his eyes, rolled his shoulders. It was a slow coming-to-consciousness, re-calling Eleanor's presence just hours ago, how happy he'd been to read to her at all. The book was done and now had only to be delivered to his publishers, who would ever after haunt him no more. With the blanket around his shoulders, he splashed water on his face and considered whether to find coffee on his way there, or back. He dried his hands on a towel so he wouldn't get his pages wet, and reached for the manuscript on the pedestal table.

It wasn't there.

His eyes darted around the room, over every visible surface. The table, the mantel, on the floor—it could have fallen, or maybe he knocked it down in the dream. He kneaded his forehead, trying to work loose some thought of what he might have done with it. Sat in the chair, closing his eyes to relive the moment in his mind. He could see it clearly. Placing the pages on the little scallop-edged table with his right hand, sleeve rolled up on his forearm, unbuttoning his waistcoat, the fire, and then sleep.

When he pushed himself up, the chair fell back and hit the floor. Even the blanket dropped like a corpse. Frantic, he raced around the room, opening drawers, checking coat pockets, on his hands and knees to search under the bed. But the pages were nowhere to be found. Not a single one. *The Christmas Log* was gone. Gone!

Dickens flung open the door and scuttled sideways down the narrow staircase to find the clerk snoring away, head on the counter, drooling into the crook of his elbow. He rang the little bell impatiently—*ding-ding-ding-ding-ding*—but had to shake him by the forearm before the young man finally groaned and lifted his heavy head.

"Wake! Up!" Dickens shouted.

The clerk wiped his mouth with the heel of his hand and opened one eye to find the roomer from No. 13 hovering over him. "Oh, top o' the mornin', sir."

"No, not top. Not top at all. Bottom all around. Something terrible's happened. I need you to wake up this instant!"

The clerk breathed on his spectacles, wiped them on his dirty shirt, and perched them on his nose. "There, then, now I can 'ear."

"Then listen very carefully." Dickens enunciated each word, with wild eyes. "A young woman in a purple cloak came down from my room quite late last night. Did you see anyone go up after her? Anyone at all?"

"There's comin's and goin's all night, Mr. Scrooge. Every night. Lots o' girls."

"I must know who has been in my rooms!"

The clerk scratched his greasy hair, as if thinking were an effort so early in the day. "Well, there's them that follows you, sir. Those street urchins always 'angin' about, askin' to go up—"

"The little boy?"

"No, these ones are big, sir. A whole gang o' them. Got fuzz on their lips and everythin'."

"I know just who you mean! Those boys have been in my rooms?"

"Oh, no, sir. Cuz they won't pay, so I don't lets 'em."

"But you've let others? Into my rooms?"

"I told ya, sir. It's a sideline."

Dickens reached across the desk, grabbed the clerk's shoulders, and shook him. "Good Lord, man, are you mad?"

The clerk righted himself and readjusted his glasses on his nose. "Pot callin' the kettle black, if you ask me, sir."

Dickens released the poor, clueless clerk. He ran his fingers through his drooping curls. "I'm sorry, I—I . . ."

"Never mind, sir. I've been shaken before. Git used to it, one does. Don't do me no 'arm."

"It's just that, well, you were fast asleep. They could have snuck in, couldn't they?"

"I s'pose, sir."

"I simply have to find them. The street boys. Do you know where I might?"

"In the street, I guess. Where d'ya always find 'em?"

Dickens pressed his fingers to his perspiring temples. His mind was zigzagging around the city, plotting his search, with no idea where to start. Without another word, he dashed out of the inn, looking left, then right. It was a dark morning with a raw, heavy fog. The shops were still shut up; there was hardly a soul yet about. When a single hansom cab trundled toward him, he bolted into the street, waving his arms at the snorting horses, but the driver didn't slow at all. Dickens sprang out of the way at the last second and raced after it, legs pumping. He banged on its side, called and yelled for it to stop, until it outpaced him, took a sharp corner, and disappeared.

He took off at a run, into the mass of streets and courts as they filled with city dwellers setting out to start their day. From

Leather Lane to Smithfield, Spitalfields to Leadenhall, he
asked anyone who would listen.

"Tattered clothes and dirty faces!" said a cabbage seller at
Exmouth Market. "But there's a 'undred like 'em every mornin',
multiplyin' like rats by noon."

It was the same answer everywhere he went, from sweepers at
street crossings to gangs of boys trundling their hoops, or racing
after omnibuses. He asked beggars crouched on stone steps, near
stalls and shop doors, each wanting his own halfpenny for nothing useful at all. He lurked in an alley near the still-shuttered
Mudie's, scanning the crowd of ladies and gentlemen in hopes
of a glimpse of one of them tailing a pocket to pick. But it was
as if the boys he sought had sprung out of his own imagination
to vex him and then disappeared. London teemed with carica-
tures just like them—wretched ruffians everywhere, all made of
the same dull, ragged cloth, and now seeming indistinguishable.

By late afternoon he had run out of places to look and the will
to carry on.

"What do you mean, gone?" asked Forster, watching Dickens
pace in front of him, collar unbuttoned, nerves shredded.

"Disappeared. Vanished. Evanesced."

"Stolen!" said Forster, pounding his desk.

Dickens shook his head and shrugged all at once. He cupped
the back of his neck. "Perhaps."

Forster pounded the desk three more times for good measure
and stood in a blustering fury. "But it was to be delivered to the
printers this very morning. It should have been there hours ago!
And Christmas is but days away. You have the reading—"

"Believe me, I am well aware—"

"It was that Lovejoy woman!"

"You're wrong!"

"Was she with you?"

"Well, yes. But she wouldn't."

Forster scoffed. He rounded the corner of his desk to come face-to-face with his friend. "She's not some character in one your books. Do not sentimentalize her."

Dickens slitted his eyes; his lips curled toward his teeth. "Eleanor did not take my book."

"She's an actress. But one step from the whorehouse!"

"She's a seamstress. But one step from the poorhouse!"

"Why must you be so blind?" Forster spat back.

"I think I see quite clearly that I wouldn't be in this situation were it not for you."

"Rubbish!"

"You sold my soul to Chapman and Hall, but I am the one paying the debt!"

"I never imagined *Chuzzlewit* would be the titanic failure it has been!"

Dickens tapped his finger hard on the breast of Forster's coat, punctuating each beat of his rant. "Let me tell you something about titanic failures, my friend, because I am surrounded by them, present company *included*. Everyone, as far as I can tell, depends upon *me* for their living. And yet if I have but one moment's peace, with a beautiful being who depends upon me not but feeds my soul, I am to be faulted, and she slandered!"

Forster huffed and crossed his arms on his belly, shoulders cinched to his ears. "The girl stole the book. Whether you choose to believe it or not."

"What I choose is an end to our friendship, beginning this very moment!"

"Not a moment too soon for me!" yelled Forster.

Dickens fled, letting the door slam behind him. It was a dramatic exit, full of fury and grit, but when he launched into the crowded street he had no idea which way to turn. It was dusk in his spirit, dusk all over. The sky drained of light, rushing toward darkness. He plunged his hands into his pockets and retraced his steps. There was only one place left to look for his lost book, and no way around it. He was coatless, gloomy, and ground down, his chin tucked into his chest. Even the Folly, when he passed it, was deserted and dreary, but for a lone worker dragging away the HAMLET sign out front to replace it with another. Everything was finished.

When he arrived at Eleanor's lodging, he peered into the window, but the blackness blinded him. He knocked lightly on the ramshackle door. Knocked on it hard. Leaned his forehead against it, lips moving silently, praying for a clue, a sign, redemption. But nothing came, and no one. The door itself now seemed determined to stay shut against him. How wrong he'd been about so many things. All that was good felt lost to him.

"Please, Eleanor," he whispered. "Let it not be you."

36

Bang! Bang! Bang!

Dickens woke with a start, at first not sure where he was or what he was hearing. He had dreamed he was home in his own bed, but it was Furnival's still, dingy and colder. *Bang! Bang! Bang!* He pulled the blanket around his shoulders and stumbled toward the clatter at the door—eager pounding mixed with excitable shouting.

"They're 'ere, sir! Downstairs!" a familiar voice yelled.

He swung the door open to find the desk clerk jumping out of his skin.

"I swears it, sir. This very minute!"

"Who do you mean?"

"Them street boys. Demandin' to talk to ya straightaway!"

Dickens flung the blanket from his shoulders, coming to quick attention. "Holding my book for ransom, no doubt! I shall put a stop to it at once!"

Without a thought to his own wrinkled clothes and disheveled hair, he pulled on his boots and pushed past the clerk, skittering down the stairs at top speed. He wanted his book back, that was sure, but, even more, some assurance Eleanor hadn't taken it. Livid as he was, it was a relief to find all five ragged boys like a phalanx at the bottom of the stairs—this surely was proof enough—and their captain right out front, blocking his way. It was him against them.

"Aha!" he pounced. "I knew it was you!"

The clerk had followed him down and now stood on the last stair, eyes as big around as his spectacles. The captain took off his hat and flattened his hair with a lick of his hand.

"Mornin', sir—"

"Dogging my step at every turn! Spying on me!"

"Sorry?"

"Don't play innocent with me, you rapscallion, you. It's one thing to pick my pocket, but to sink so low as to steal my story! And now to blackmail me for it? Is that your game?"

The captain cocked his head and looked back to check whether one of his merry band had any clue. There was a round of shabby-coated shrugs. He turned back to Dickens. "'S not like that, sir. See, we're not in the story-stealin' business—"

"I don't believe you for one moment!" Dickens roared, grabbing the captain by the uppermost lapel of his three coats. "Where is my story?"

With as much genteel restraint as he could muster, the captain separated his lapel from Dickens' furious grasp. He flattened his hair one more time and cleared his throat. "We didn't take yer story, sir. But we think we know where ya might find it."

"I don't understand," said Dickens, hands clapped to his shirt-waist, searching their faces. But they all looked away, avoiding his gaze. All except the captain, who didn't blink. "The Folly, sir, in the little square not far from 'ere," he said, pointing vaguely. "We can take you there."

Dickens pulled on his chin, tugged at a button on his shirt. Despite every part of him not wanting to believe the boy, he did. "I know it already," he said, hanging his head.

How often in his writing life he'd wanted to fight for what was rightly his. The more fame, the more fighting. He'd never shrunk from it, not once, and Forster was more of a bulldog than he, always out at the end of his leash, snarling for a brawl. But he didn't have anyone now; he'd run everyone away. No one to shield him from this, whatever it was. Still, he had to know.

He fastened his waistcoat like armor, and without saying anything slipped past the boys into the fog-thick morning, straight for the clock-tower square. He found a small mob crowding the stage door of the theater, nearly obscuring the sign out front, announcing to the world: AUDITION TODAY! *A CHRISTMAS BOG: THE MUSICAL!* BY CHAZ PICKENS.

Dickens trudged closer, pushed into the throng of actors, singers, jugglers, and want-to-be's, all determined to get inside. "Let me through!" he yelled.

"Back o' the line!" shouted a young actor, pushing back. "We were 'ere first."

"But I am the author!" Dickens shouted, at which they parted for him like the Red Sea.

No sooner had he rushed inside than the ragged boys were right behind, shoving their way in. "Friends of the author!" their captain yelled, which seemed to do nicely as well.

Inside, Dickens stormed down the tunnel-like backstage hall. All the doors looked the same. He opened each one willy-nilly, anything with a knob. But no Eleanor, not anyone at all. At last, he barged into the room with the tumbled wings, swords, and bits of scenery. Still, no sign of her.

Suddenly he was aware of voices not far away. "What's my motivation fer killin' the cousin?" he heard someone ask. Inching closer, Dickens found himself standing in the wings with a clear view of an actor standing alone, center stage, under a gaslight, a few pages in hand—a sloppy white mop of a wig perched on his head.

"He seems hardly to deserve it," said the actor.

Dickens had heard enough. He bolted from the wings onto the stage and ripped the pages from the actor's hand. Slicing the air with them, he turned to the stage manager, seven rows back in the lower gallery. "What is the meaning of this?"

The stage manager's mouth drew open, but he seemed unable to speak.

"And who is this 'Chaz Pickens'?" Dickens rapped the pages with the back of his knuckles.

Another actor, next up for a turn on the stage, held up his copy of the audition sides and made a sour face. "He's no Charles Dickens, that's fer sure!"

Dickens scowled and grunted. He crossed his arms, awaiting an answer.

The stage manager, in full panic, seemed to cast his eyes about until they settled on a poor old man hunched over his broom, sweeping the gallery floor. "There!" he said, pointing. "*He* is the author!"

"The sweeper?"

"Yes! Mr. Pickens. A genius with a pen!"

The sweeper, who seemed the sort of man so rarely noticed at all, waved vaguely in Dickens' direction, playing along.

Dickens stomped his foot. "This isn't genius! It's plagiarism! The fruit of my pilfered manuscript!" He flipped through the three pages. "And in less than one day?"

"Only the one scene, sir, and we haven't quite worked out the music," the stage manager explained, "but it is the Christmas rush, you know—"

"It must have been someone who's plotted this all along. I demand to know who gave you my book!"

The stage manager was on his feet, arms akimbo.

"Was it . . . Miss Lovejoy?" Dickens asked, unable to bear the sound of her betrayal on his own lips.

"No, no! I don't know a Lovejoy. You've got it all wrong," said the stage manager, stepping sideways toward the aisle, no doubt plotting his escape.

"Which part of this dodgery have I misunderstood?"

"I wouldn't call it d-d-dodgery," stuttered the manager, frozen in the aisle, ready to flee.

Dickens stomped his foot again, impatient, when he spotted the purple velvet cloak flaring past the open door at the upper end of the gallery. "There's the thief!" he shouted, leaping from the stage. The manager ducked and cowered as he passed; all other eyes followed Dickens' raging flight up the aisle.

He arrived at the threshold just as Eleanor reached for the outer door. "Running away, are we?"

Eleanor stopped and turned, unyielding. "Yes. For I cannot bear your accusations one minute more."

"You would deny that you have wholly deceived me?"

"No," she said, with a subtle shake of her head.

"And for your own purposes?"

"Yes. But not the purpose you think."

Dickens threw back his head, trying to conceive of some way, any way, he could have misconstrued this course of events. But Forster's voice thundered in his head. He stepped closer, facing her squarely. The pages shook in his hand. "I think I am a fool. To have allowed you into my heart. To have thought you the one person who wanted nothing from me."

Dickens closed his eyes, trying to shut out the pain. He couldn't stand the sight of her, of himself, of any of it. Eleanor, face full of regret, lifted her trembling hand from inside her cloak and reached her long, delicate fingers toward his face, stopping just shy of his cheek, when suddenly, from inside the theater—

"'Ere's the one who done it!" a voice yelled from the stage.

Dickens opened his eyes and glanced back and forth from Eleanor to the gallery door, torn. He detected concern in her countenance, but didn't know whether it was for *her* well-being or his. If he walked away she would flee.

"'Ere's yer thief!" the voice said again. Dickens couldn't resist the commotion inside. He stepped back into the gallery, standing at the far end of the aisle with a clear view of the stage. There, donning helmets and armor themselves, the gang of boys surrounded a cowering figure, swords drawn. He couldn't make out who it was, but the captain's sword glinted at a man's neck, as two others held him down.

"This is 'im," the captain shouted. "The one that took yer story. We saw 'im comin' outta Furnival's early this morning with it under his arm, I swears."

Dickens took a heavy step down the aisle, then another, another, as if pushing against a fierce wind. Resistance, inside and out. If not Eleanor, if not these ragged boys, then who would deceive him so? When he neared the stage, the captain stepped aside, still clutching the man's snuff-colored coat. And there, hunkered and quavering, was John Dickens, watching his son walk toward him.

The captain pulled the crumpled old man to standing and let the sword fall to his side. Dickens stopped, unable to take another step. It was impossible to look away. Here, in the great palace of the suspension of disbelief, was a shattering truth right in front of him.

"I can explain, son," said his father in a small, creaking voice.

"Do not," Dickens whispered.

John Dickens hung his head, gripping his hat in his liver-spotted hands. His quiver of words had fallen away. His skin was the color of his coat, all pale, naked shame. The stage manager, the sweeper, the actors all watched without a single twitch of a muscle. Even the ragged boys slipped off their helmets and held them to their chests, heads bowed.

Dickens' eyes flashed sorrow, despair, disdain, but he had nothing to say. He rubbed his forehead and turned to walk slowly up the cant of the aisle, like steps on a high mountain, each one harder than the last. When he crossed the threshold where Eleanor stood watching, he could hardly muster the strength to say, "Forgive me."

At which he took his heavy heart and pushed outside into a city shrouded in grief.

37

Warren's Blacking Warehouse stood, just barely, at 30 Hungerford Stairs, where it seemed to tumble and lean into the blackness of the broody Thames. Dickens stood before it, clutching the collar of his shirt tight around his throat. He had come straight here, shot like an arrow tracing its arc to his own beginnings. It must have been afternoon, but it felt like night. It was always night at Hungerford Stairs. It had been all his life.

He stared at the warehouse's falling roof, into its jagged broken windows, like glass teeth, watched rats scurry in and out. His breath made rolling white plumes in the sudden cold—as if the factory itself had changed the weather. His own eyes were black sockets, brow heavy and weary of the world, which now found its center, the darkest center of his own being, right here at a place that should never have been.

Lost in a spiral of self-pity, he wasn't aware of Eleanor's presence until she stepped beside him without a word. He couldn't bear to look at her.

"You told me my past would catch me soon enough," he said at last, staring at his boots.

"I remember."

"Seeing him there, cowering on the stage, he looked so small to me, and scared—the way he looked the day, that day—" His voice faltered. It was as if speaking it aloud made the moment real again, alive in the unbearable present.

"What day?" Eleanor asked.

The words stuck in his throat, trapping long-buried demons. "I was just eleven. It was nearly Christmas. My father came and took me out of school, and told me it would be my last day there, because the next day . . . he would enter Marshalsea."

"Many people have gone to debtors' prison," she said, lowering the hood of her cloak.

"But took their families with them." Dickens searched the sky for some logic to it. "My brothers and sister, my mother. He took all of them, every one. I begged him to take me with him. But I alone was to secure their release. By working here."

He nodded toward the decaying warehouse looming over them, over everything. He pointed to a third-floor window. "I sat in that very window, week after week—a mere boy—working ten hours a day putting labels on pots of boot polish for six shillings a week. Eating one stale pastry a day and nothing else, frantic to save enough money to rescue him. But I felt thrown away, all alone in the world."

His Adam's apple bobbed in his throat as he plumbed hard for the words to explain. It was a rotted well inside him, and undisturbed for so long. He wiped his nose on his sleeve, then plunged his cold hands into his pockets.

"I shall never forget," he said, voice cracking as if he were still that young boy, "that Christmas Eve, just before the iron doors of Marshalsea Prison closed between my father and me. He held me close to him, and we cried, both of us, swearing loyalty and undying affection. But I knew somewhere deep inside . . . that he had broken my heart forever."

Eleanor lowered her eyes.

"It's been my dark secret all these years. Of that moment between my father and me, until now, no word has ever passed my lips. Nor his, I'm sure."

"Of course not, Charles."

"What kind of man would leave his son?"

"A lost man," she said.

He wiped his sniffling nose again and half nodded.

"But can you not see," she said, "that in that moment, his heart was broken as well?"

Dickens squeezed his eyes shut, trying to see what she did. He shook his head.

"For the second saddest thing in the world after a child who's been abandoned," said Eleanor, "is the parent who abandons him."

Dickens glanced at the Thames, a dark, unstoppable current. Life rolling over him and away, shifting the dross at the bottom, remaking the banks, but always, always receding for the mudlarks, who dredged for its ruined leavings. He was powerless against it.

"Perhaps I'm the one who's lost," he said.

"We are all lost, all broken," said Eleanor. "Trying desperately to be whole again."

He nodded and shook his head, both at once. It was true, and sad. But unspeakable, even now.

She let his silence stand. Watched him cross a hand to his shoulder and rest his chin there. Waited while he stared again at his muddy boots. When he met her gaze, finally, he couldn't think what else to say.

"Why didn't you ask for your book back?" she asked.

"I don't know." He shrugged.

"Perhaps it wasn't the Christmas book you meant to write after all."

His shoulders caved toward each other in surrender, defeat. "I have no other Christmas book within me."

She nodded, her voice quiet as a prayer. "But every book you've ever written is a book about Christmas. About the feeling we must have for one another, without which we *are* lost."

Eleanor stepped closer. Their faces were at near angles, her mouth by his ear, voice thin and trembling, each word an effort.

"When my husband died, your books were all he left us, all he had. Yet I think them the very thing that saved me, and my son."

Dickens gripped the back of his neck. A tear ran down the length of his nose and fell to the ground. He wiped his face roughly.

"I read them aloud to cheer him, each of your stories, again and again. And found from the very first page of the very first book the strangest sensation that I did know you, and that you knew me, and Timothy, too. All of us. No matter our faults, our weaknesses, our station in life. That you felt the greatest tender-ness for us."

Dickens looked into her eyes, shining with tears of their own.

"And your books made me think of my own family, and *our* Christmases past. How we had no money, yet felt rich as kings. We danced and made merry into the wee hours," she continued, eyes lighting at the memory. "All the worries of the year seemed to vanish with the first snow, for then we'd gather 'round the hearth and tell stories, all ending happily . . ." Her voice caught in her throat—a melancholy so powerful she had to pause to let it pass. "And the colder it was, the nearer we were to each other, and to the truth of Christmas. The truth of your books . . . That despite what is cold and dark in the world, perhaps it is a loving place after all."

They were both sniffling now, lost in their own memories, and each other's. She wiped her tears with the palm of her thin crocheted glove; he, with the sleeve of his shirt. One sighed and then smiled; the other whimpered and laughed. Moonlight cut through the fog to dance on the tips of the river's whitecapped waves. It made a circle of light on the spot where they stood. They turned their faces to the sky, where a few stars burst through to assure them they were not alone.

"If I could believe," he said, "standing here, that I'm that writer still—"

"You were that writer long ago, even here; and that very boy, the writer you became."

"A boy who loved Christmas, with all his heart."

She stepped to his side, gazing upon his past with him. "Then let the specter of your memory be the spark of your imagination."

He turned to her wondrous eyes, where lived the moon and the stars and forgiveness and hope.

"Perhaps I could try . . ."

Part III

38

Some days are blessed with a feeling of newness from the start. Dickens blinked open his eyes the next morning at Furnival's Inn to find an undeniable lightness in his heart. He wiggled his toes into slippers and walked to the window to see if London felt the same. The fog, at last, was in full retreat, rolling away in curls and wisps to make space for a clear winter sky. A light frost settled on the rooftops outside, whose narrow chimneys puffed with the warm fires of humble lives.

Still in his nightshirt and stocking cap, he pulled on a robe and lit a fire, sat at his writing table, and pulled out a single sheet of paper, struck by the pure possibility of its blankness. The lost book was forgotten; here was a fresh beginning, a second chance. He filled his lungs and closed his eyes, surprised to find his mental museum just where he'd left it, corridors stacked high, shelves overflowing. When he opened them, he dipped his pen into the blue inkpot with precision and purpose. Then Charles Dickens began to write.

He wrote without coffee, without breakfast, without washing

up. Without any sense of day or night passing outside—neither noon nor three nor eight o'clock, nor two more rounds of each. He slept in tiny snatches, and woke still writing in his head, the quill often clutched in his hand.

Jacob Marley was dead to begin with, still dead as a door-nail, but now he would mark a path to his old partner's salva-tion. Dickens' own spirit awakened, too, his mind on fire. It was fueled anew by Scrooge, Fred, Fezziwig, and Cratchit; an old love who'd been lost, doors that close and open, and the ghosts of one's own past, inescapable as they seem; and Christmases that once were and are, and might be again. Now he knew who and what they all were and why, almost beyond thought, in the fullness of his reborn heart.

When he came within a stone's throw of finishing, Dickens couldn't bear to say good-bye to his story. He had written fast before, but never like this. He washed his face, dressed, and can-tered all the way to Eleanor's lodging house, where he knocked on the door with a cheery *rap-rap-rap*, his manuscript held to the breast of his coat.

"I've nearly done!" he declared, when she greeted him at the door.

"How happy that makes me."

"But found I no longer wanted to be alone," he added, mak-ing his appeal.

"Then I welcome your company," she said, stepping aside to let him in, "but Timothy is his own master."

"What? He's yet to forgive me harassing him through the streets like a madman and accosting him in his own house?"

"He has his own way with the world."

Dickens nodded. She led him upstairs, where a fire in their small hearth bathed everything in warm light. Timothy sat at the modest table, drawing in his sketchbook with the last possible stump of black pencil. Eleanor said nothing, but gave Dickens a nod of gentle encouragement. He crept toward the table and crouched to the boy's level, still holding his stack of new pages. Timothy kept his eyes fixed on his drawing.

"I wonder if I might share your table with you, Timothy?"

The boy pressed harder with his pencil, saying nothing.

"I can see that you're hard at work. But I promise to be quiet as a mouse. Why, you shall hardly know I'm here."

Timothy shrugged a shoulder. Dickens took it as invitation enough. He enacted a relieved sigh and walked to the other side of the square table, just big enough for two. "Well, if you insist," he said, making a show of sitting in the other pine chair, which wobbled on a broken leg and threatened to topple altogether. "I see what you mean. That won't do at all."

He stood and carried the little tufted armchair to the table. He settled into it as if it were the finest seat known to man. "How right you are. Yes, this chair does me very well. It fits just as a chair should fit. And arms! How fortunate a chair to have arms. And legs as well! If only it had a head, I should think it would do the writing for me!"

Still nothing from Timothy, more rough lines and rubbed shadings. Dickens placed his elbows on the table, folded his hands under his chin, and watched the boy draw with quick sharp strokes. He studied the tossed scruff of hair, the soft lines of the boy's face that hadn't yet claimed its true jaw, freckles here and there, a smudge of lead, a smidge of dirt. He felt an exquisite sympathy for the boy, but didn't know entirely why. He was poor, but he was loved.

Eleanor blinked her approval. *Keep trying*, her eyes told him. So he turned back to Timothy. "You know, there's a young boy in my new story. Who takes somewhat after you."

Timothy tucked his chin into his sweater until its rough woolly edge tickled the tip of his nose. Dickens squinted and screwed up his lips to make an exaggerated point of examining the boy's features. He rubbed his chin. "Oh, my. Now I see that I've stolen you whole cloth. My Tiny Tim is you."

The boy pulled his chin from his sweater.

"Oh, you don't mind, do you? I tried other names—Thomas, Theodore, Thaddeus—but nothing suited him quite like your name. He's small, like you. But large in presence."

Timothy looked at Dickens, but not straight in the eye. Eleanor nodded again, urging their visitor on.

"In fact, if you hadn't nearly trampled me in the churchyard, I'd have had no new book at all!"

The boy blushed. The dimple on his left cheek dented enough to suggest there might be a smile somewhere to be had.

"And that drawing of yours, of me like a ghost in the graveyard? Inspired again! So I threw in a spirit for good measure. What do you think of that sort of thing, Timothy? Are you yea or nay for it?"

Timothy shrugged again.

"What harm can come of a ghost?" Eleanor added, speaking for them both.

"I'm so glad you approve," he told Timothy. "I've in fact thrown in a few."

"The more, the merrier!" said Eleanor, amused.

Timothy smiled at last, a small crescent moon. The boy was a copy of her, in all good ways and measurements—the proportionate forehead to chin, the fine round cheeks, the rosebud mouth, the way his eyes did all the work for his face, showed gladness, worry, relief. They shone together, mother and son, reflected in each other's light. The indelible link between parent and child moved him greatly.

He leaned over the table and cocked his head to look at the

drawing, albeit upside down. He could make out the beginnings
of a family—a large family—around a simple table. He pointed
to one of the children.

"That one there, the tall girl. That could be my Mamie."

Timothy put his pencil down.

"Looks like it from here, anyway." Dickens watched the boy
study his own sketch for a good while, as if trying to see what he
saw. He made a gesture of reaching toward it. "May I?" he asked.

The boy bit his bottom lip and then, with small, smudged
fingers, slid the sketch across. Dickens took it and turned it
right side up. He studied it long and hard. "Hmm. Oh, no.
Now that I see it up close she's far more like my Katey, with
those fat sausage curls . . ."

The boy scooted back his chair and, with the help of the little
crutch, limped to the other side. Dickens pointed to a young boy
in the drawing. "Oh, but this one. This one here is Walter, only
Walter would have lots more freckles, and a dimple like yours,
only on the right cheek, just a little higher."

Timothy rested a hand on his shoulder and leaned a little
against him. It was a small gesture, as natural and unthinking as
could be. How often his own children had done the same, that
simple tenderness. He looked at Eleanor, who seemed to see it,
too. Dickens carried on, not wanting to lose the moment.
"Whereas Frank would have mussy hair and a sucking candy in
his mouth, and sticky fingers, always sticky fingers . . ."

His voice trailed away. He was suddenly overcome with
missing his own children, each one in turn. But how grateful he
was for Timothy's light touch on his shoulder. He patted the boy's
hand, just that, so as not to scare him away with sentiment. But
he could barely speak, trying to hide a hundred feelings. "Sticky,
sticky fingers . . ."

It was somehow enough. Dickens and the boy soon settled at

the table, one on each side, like old working partners. When Eleanor announced she had to go to the theater, she asked Dickens if he would stay to watch over him until she returned, and he was glad to accept. When she left, Timothy barely looked up. He sketched on, front and back of each sheet, right to the edges, until his stump of pencil ground to black dust. Dickens wrote until his hand hurt, then wrote some more. When night fell, Timothy lit a small candle for him, then wrapped Dickens' borrowed coat around his own little shoulders and curled on the floor near the fire.

Dickens carried the tufted armchair back to its place by the hearth; it might be a comfort to the boy to sit near him. He had a thick sheaf of pages on his lap, and thought to read back through them. But he was soon asleep himself, head dropped to one side, mouth open. He stirred once, not quite sure where he was. But when he found Timothy resting against his calf, asleep, head on his knee, everything came back. He watched the reassuring rise and fall of the boy's sparrow chest in his too-big shirt. How he missed the soft breath of sleeping children.

When Eleanor returned, she thanked him with her eyes and took his place in the chair. Picking up his things, Dickens found, tucked beneath his manuscript, the boy's finished sketch: a family at Christmastime, all the children so like his own, with Timothy there, too, enjoying a feast with a bulging roast turkey at the center, big enough to feed them all. They were a poor family, but beamed with happiness, rich as kings.

What a gift it was. Dickens held the drawing to his chest, aware that Eleanor was softly humming a carol to her son, her hand hovering over his crop of hair so as not to wake him. It was an old song, from childhood—a hymn that had long ago found a special place at Christmas, then lost it, then been resurrected, though hardly anyone could remember what it was called; its words were always half forgotten, mostly mumbled or rearranged. Still, no one ever forgot the lovely tune. Eleanor sang in a whisper, slower than he remembered it, but his ears perked to her dulcet notes. He hugged his pages and gazed out at the waxing gibbous moon, humming along to himself.

Then, filled with the dearness of her simple carol, he bade mother and son a silent good-bye, and left, alone, to finish where he'd begun.

39

Dickens couldn't sleep, didn't want to. The end was too near, close enough to touch. With Timothy's sketch occupying a proud place to the right of his ink and nibs, he wrote feverishly through the next afternoon, racing for the end of it, the final stave, now that the last of the three spirits had shown Scrooge his own grave, and dwindled to a bedpost. Ebenezer Scrooge was waking to a new world, a new self, tears still wet on his face. For a miserable pinchpenny who had long made a business out of men, he now knew that his business was all mankind. Dickens wept and laughed and wept again.

"Yes! and the bedpost was his own. The bed was his own, the room was his own. Best and happiest of all, the Time before him was his own, to make amends in! 'I will live in the Past, the Present, and the Future!' Scrooge repeated, as he scrambled out of bed."

Dickens felt restored as he hadn't in days, weeks, was it months, could it be years? He wrote churches that rang with lusty peals, made the air outside Scrooge's window fogless and jovial, his fellows blithe and good-humored. His streets and people, children and beggars, houses and windows gave his once-miser so much happiness, he thought they both might burst. And burst they did.

"I don't know what to do!' cried Scrooge, laughing and crying in the same breath . . . 'I am as light as a feather, I am as happy as an angel, I am as merry as a schoolboy. I am as giddy as a drunken man.'"

Eating a stale crust of bread, Dickens wrote a fine surprise for "nephew Fred" with Uncle Scrooge knocking at his Christmas door and nearly shaking his arm right off. The turkey for the Cratchits would be twice the size of Tiny Tim, and the boy would live, he would, and be loved. As for Bob Cratchit himself, Dickens made Scrooge determined to catch him late coming to the office the next day, and when he did, pounced on him, only to double his salary and pledge help for his family, whatever was needed, all to be decided over a Christmas bowl of smoking bishop.

Dickens' pen lost speed. He had arrived at the finish, lingering over the final few words of his book. He had put all phantoms to rest forever except for the spirit that infused his being and radiated outward. It had no end. It lived in the wispy feather of his quill, the wavy grain of the pale birch desk, the abalone dusk outside. The world was whole and had every color in it.

Then, with great care and purpose, he dipped his quill and, while at it, wiped his own wet cheek with the heel of his hand, clear-eyed, to write the final words of his Christmas book.

Dickens laid down his pen. There was a frisson in finishing, a rush of great feeling for the life of his characters, all the Cratchits and Fezziwigs, Fred and his wife, and Scrooge most of all. He didn't want to say good-bye; he wanted to keep them close, where he might watch over them. But he knew that the end of his book was a beginning of their life without him, and he must let them be born into the world, and welcomed, as he felt sure they would be. Still, how grateful he was to have known them at all.

He stacked the pages edge to edge, corner to corner, humming the carol Eleanor had sung to her son. It popped into his head just then; he closed his eyes and tilted his face to the ceiling to stretch the moment a little further, to let the song sing to him. How glad he was that carols were the thing again, after being stamped out by the Puritans two centuries ago. They'd survived in the hearts of the people, sung in secret, but had returned, of late, to their rightful place in church choirs, on the streets, house to house. Village tunes were commandeered, new carols written, old ones revived. Songs of pent-up praise and joy on the lips of every man and woman, no matter their class; all the children, well dressed and ragged, knew the words.

A knock at the door. Dickens opened his eyes, pushed back his chair, and stood, full of new life. He picked up the stack of pages and reached for his coat. "Yes, come in! Come in!" he shouted cheerily through the door, more into his coat than out of it.

The desk clerk poked his head inside. "Pardon, Mr. Scrooge, we've some payin' customers for the museum," he said, hardly believing it himself. "All the way from Ireland!"

Dickens buttoned his last button and waved them in. "Of course! I was just going out."

The Irishman and his wife shuffled in behind the clerk, as if entering hallowed space. Dickens guessed they were a pair nearing the winter of their years together. They were the sort who begin their couple-hood quite distinct from one another, but grow into one—the same fleshy jowls and ruddy cheeks, spidery veins on their noses, craggy laugh lines emanating from the drooping corners of their eyes, as if they'd shared all the same jokes in all the same measure, and had done for years. The man stood, taking in the room.

"Please," said Dickens, gesturing. "Nothing sacred here. Look anywhere you like. It's just as he left it. So they say!"

Dickens winked to the clerk as he said it. The Irishwoman leaned in to scrutinize his face, nagging the sleeve of her husband's coat until he looked, too, at the full fact of the man standing before them. The wife pinched her husband's arm.

"Beg pardon, sir," said the Irishman, taking a small step toward him, "but . . . you're not 'im, are ye? Boz 'imself?"

The desk clerk exploded with a giggle, nudging and pointing at his tenant. "Charles Dickens? Don't 'e wish!"

But the Irish couple held their breath, awaiting his answer.

"I am," he said, surprised to hear himself say it. "I am Charles Dickens."

The desk clerk's jaw slacked open. He looked at Dickens, took off his glasses, and squinted. The woman's hands flew to either side of her round face. The man slid his hat from his head and crushed it to his heart.

"Ooh, I not ounly want to thank ye fer yer books, sir . . . but fer the light you've been in me 'ouse (and God love yer face!) this many a year!"

Dickens tilted his head in a smallish bow, with the sort of humility he hoped would mark a place in the Irish couple's memory for the rest of their years, as they'd just done for him. And then, with his hat on his head, on his own hair, own forehead and face, and his new book under his arm, he left Furnival's Inn to find the muse that had led him back to it and, doing so, led him back to himself.

40

The night was an embroidery of stars on a taffeta sky so blue it bled all the black away. No more drab-colored December fringed with fog. The eve of Christmas week burst into the world, clear and dry, the streets one continuous blaze of ornament and show. Even the lesser thoroughfares were crowded late with holiday people all dreaming of the celebration to come. Shops sat in their best trim under bright gaslights turned all the way up, with evergreen plumage four stories high, like a great forest canopy. There were great pyramids of currants and raisins; brown russet apples and golden bobs, Ribston Pippins and huge winter pears; towers of jams, jellies, and bonbons; solid walls of sardines, potted meats, bottled pickles, drummed figs. Every third-rate inn and public house still pushed its "never-too-late goose-and-brandy club." Even the gin shops had brushed up and varnished over their dirty paint on the outside and decorated their insides with hopeful smatterings of red and green. Over grappling horses' hooves, roaring drivers, and chaffering dealers, rose the harmonies of an oboe, French horn, and flute, warbling a pastoral Christmas tune.

All of London seemed set upon suffering gladly a sprinkle of brotherly this and that, but cheer most of all.

Dickens walked with Eleanor at his side and drank it all in. The throngs dwindled and fell away, but they wandered on, soon feeling themselves the last two people awake. He felt a steady calm in her presence, the utter absence of his customary restlessness. His stride was an easy match for hers. There was no question of keeping up or falling behind; it was shoulder to shoulder, soul to soul, the whole time. He told of his bright hopes for the new story, rolled tightly and tucked in his pocket, how he looked forward to delivering it to the printers in the morning, but wanted her to be the first to hear it, and Timothy, too. Eleanor spoke dearly of her late husband, how good a man he was, a patient father, how he taught his son to read, how much books had meant to him. *Twist* had been his favorite until *Nickleby* came along, but it was *The Old Curiosity Shop* that nursed him through his first bout of illness, until Little Nell, whom he loved dearly, met her own demise, which propelled him, determined, from his sickbed for another three months. But they were glad months, and not to be traded for all the gold in the world.

The weather grew colder with each passing hour. Eleanor pulled her mantle more closely around her; Dickens clutched at the collar of his coat. They wended their way through rich London and poor, where inside, families gathered around the warm glow of candles and hearths, no doubt telling stories of their own. When they stopped on Waterloo Bridge to watch moonlight skitter down the Thames, there were no words between them, no thoughts at all, only contentment.

It was nearly midnight when they came full circle to the little square where they'd begun their long perambulation. Their steps slowed in unison, as if resisting return. But Eleanor stopped short of the clock tower where they'd first met. She lowered the hood of her cloak and gazed with wonder into the sky, now a gray wool blanket above them.

"Snow," she said, touching her fingers to her cheeks.

Dickens turned his chin upward, too, to find flakes floating down like feathers on the air. "Snow," he repeated, taking off his hat and closing his eyes.

They let it land on their faces and melt on their gloves, tiny crystals of intricate perfection that couldn't be kept or held, in an instant gone. Dickens thought of his children, and how long they'd waited for a moment like this. He knew Catherine would have read to them by now, listened to their prayers, and tucked them into their beds with kisses on their little foreheads. How gentle her kisses were, like lullabies in themselves. He hated them being so far away, but there was nothing for it but to hope they'd all awake to snow in Scotland, and be happy.

Eleanor seemed to know what he was thinking, and he soon found himself describing each of his children in great detail, from head to toe, leaving nothing out—not a flamboyance, a freckle, a foible. She listened closely and laughed like a bell, peppering him with questions, wanting to know what made Mamie so quiet, and Katey so sure of herself, and what sort of candy was Frank's favorite. All the while the snow fell faster and with more determination; the flakes seemed to grow wings and dance in every direction before flitting down to settle in a skiff on the ground around them, beautiful and quiet.

Finally, Eleanor pulled the velvet hood of her cloak over her snow-sprinkled hair to resume her now-brief journey home. Dickens kept close to her side as they continued on under the watchful gaze of the clock tower's shining face. She looked back over her shoulder once, as if to bid the little square good night, and wish the clock sweet dreams.

"Don't worry," he told her. "I'll give my regards when I pass back this way."

Her eyes flashed under her hood; he thought he caught a soft sideways smile. When they reached her door, they stopped and turned to each other. He pulled the manuscript from his pocket.

"It would be a great honor to read it to you, Eleanor, if you'd hear it."

She turned to the dark window of her lodging house, rubbing her brow with the back of her hand. He sensed her reluctance, not ambivalence at all, but some worry or weariness had overcome her. A shadow fell across her face. How suddenly tired she seemed.

"Time's run away from me. Timothy will be fast asleep, and I do want him to hear it."

"Then it will wait, of course," he said, touching the pages to his chin. "I promise you."

Eleanor cocked her chin as if to find a better angle to study him. Her eyes shimmered, almost transparent. Even in the darkness, they shone with their own brilliant light. He felt her gaze strongly, knew there were snowflakes on his brows and lashes, in his hair, and imagined he looked like an old man again. But she had only kindness in her eyes. It was as if she saw all the way inside him, the boy he once was, the man he wanted so much to be. It was strange to feel known by someone he'd met only a short time ago, who seemed to grasp his sum and parts. He was a man filled with flaws who meant to have a heart as big as the world.

"It seems as if the book has rewritten itself," she said.

"I think, more, the book has rewritten me."

She looked away, her voice fluttering. "That is a happy ending, indeed."

"Please," he said, stepping a little closer, "do not talk of endings."

She nodded, blinking away tears.

"You've given me a great gift, Eleanor. And I cannot think what, in return, would mean half as much."

A tear pooled at the rim of her eye and fell, tracing a path down the pale rose of her cheek. "Let the book be my Christmas present," she whispered. "And your friendship with my son."

Dickens nodded. "If you cry, I'll cry, too."

"It's only from happiness," she said, wiping the tear away.

He looked out over the white-kissed cobbles as far as he could see, that softened the world around them. "Happiness, yes," he said, misty-eyed, too.

She watched his intense gaze, so far away. "What are you thinking of?" she asked.

"Of India."

"India," she repeated, each syllable a poem.

"I should miss the snow, I think." His voice caught. "But, oh, how I would miss my wife and family."

Eleanor nodded, a complete understanding between them. "India was a wonderful dream," she said. "But this is more wonderful."

"It is," he said, almost unable to bear the bittersweetness. "A wonderful life."

He knew, as she must have, too, that this was their unspoken good-bye.

"I shall hear it, Charles. Your story."

"Of course you shall. Good and early, before the printers get their hands on it," he said, lightly tapping the rolled pages three times to the left breast of his coat, where his heart was. They lingered in each other's gaze, not wanting to break it, if only to take the moment in for all it was. And then, saying nothing more, Eleanor Lovejoy slipped inside.

Dickens looked up to the window above, waiting for the reassuring glow of a lighted candle. When it came, satisfied that Eleanor was safe in her room with her son, he put his hat on his head, the pages in his pocket, filled his lungs with winter air, and turned to follow his own frosty breath swirling away.

One, two, three . . . Ah, the clock tower, proclaiming midnight. It boomed and echoed, a loud, sonorous peal rising above the snow-muffled air and filling his ears. He smiled at the sound of it, stopping at the juncture where Eleanor's narrow street met the square to look up at the wise old clock face and wait for each bold clang—a declaration, a beginning, an end. The face seemed to look down on him, too.

Four, five, six . . . He thought of Eleanor hearing each chime, too. How easy it was to image her forth, leaning over her sleeping son to brush away a lock of brown hair. He could almost hear her humming the carol, and whispering "sweet dreams" in Timothy's ear. And then, so vivid and clear, he saw her bend over the single burning candle on the table, filling her lungs and cheeks with air. *Seven, eight* . . .

Something made him turn back toward Eleanor's window to make sure it was true. *Nine, ten* . . . The candlelight seemed to flicker and grow, illuminating even the street outside, making magic of snowfall. *Eleven* . . . The light shuddered and fell. Eleanor had blown the candle out, just as he'd imagined. In a breath, darkness.

Twelve . . . The last chime rang through the square, longer than the others, rattling his ribs. He waited for the echo to finish its round. The circle complete. Then he started back across the square to retrace their shared trodden path in the whiteness before him. A few steps on, he looked down, expecting their footprints side by side in the fresh-fallen snow. There was one set of footprints, the precise length and width of his boot, but *one* set, not two. Dickens stopped short and stared at the ground. It made no sense. He took off his hat and dropped to his knees, brushing the snow away, searching, as if he'd find her lighter footprints buried somewhere underneath. But where she'd walked beside him just moments ago, there was nothing. Nothing but fine virgin snow.

He looked up at the clock tower. Its face had gone dim, its stature dwarfed by the night sky. Clouds purled above it, pale gray-and-white marble against deep blue satin, tumbling upward as if parting to clear a path to the heavens, lit by the moon, which shot the night through with rays of silver light. And still, gossamer flakes drifting down.

Dickens snapped his head back toward Eleanor's street. The snow glistened in front of him, lighting a path to her door. He took off as fast as his slipping feet would allow, back to her lodging house. *Bang, bang, bang!*

"Let me in! Eleanor! Timothy! Please!" he yelled, hitting the door until his hand hurt, then pounding with the other, then slapping it with both. "Please! I beg you! Let me in!"

A door that had ceded its will to him now stubbornly refused. He leaned a shoulder against it, pushing with all his strength, until it gave way beneath the weight of his body. He stumbled inside, rushed up the narrow stairs and into the darkened room. His eyes darted all around, with not enough light to see, when a sharp blade of moonlight swept across Timothy's face. He huddled in the farthest corner, wrapped in Dickens' old fur-lapel coat, shivering with fear.

"Where is she?" Dickens demanded, tossing aside his hat.

Timothy tucked his knees to his chin, covered his ears, and

pinched his eyes closed. Dickens grabbed his wrists and dragged him to standing. "Where is your mother?"

The boy shook his head side to side. Dickens pulled him close by the coat's lapel. The boy's body tensed like a board, gripped with terror.

"Why will you not tell me? Where is Eleanor?" he shouted, eyes wild like a man who's lost his mind.

At last, Dickens felt the boy surrender, every muscle wilt, too exhausted to resist anymore. Timothy opened his eyes, tears clinging to his lashes.

"D-d-d-dead, sir," he said in a small, rusty voice. "A y-year this very night."

Dickens sucked in, but there was no air to breathe. It was a kick in the gut, a battering ram to the heart. He released the boy. His manuscript tipped out of his pocket, pages scattering at his feet. With knotted hands he gripped two fistfuls of his own hair and pulled hard, as if that might stop his mind whirling. It wasn't possible. How could it be? He was with her but moments ago. Close enough to reach out and touch. He crumpled to his knees, body folding against itself, and pressed his palms hard against his eyes, willing the truth away. *Make it stop,* he wanted to say, *bring her back.*

"Please, please, please," he said.

Timothy blinked, tears splashing onto the floor. Seeing them, Dickens looked up, blurry-eyed, as the boy wiped his face with a tattered sleeve, but the tears came too fast, in fully formed drops rolling down his cheeks. And he knew, with sudden and complete awareness, that his own grief was nothing. The boy's mother was dead, and he'd just spoken of it, perhaps spoken any words at all, for the first time since she had passed. A year ago this very night.

"Oh, Timothy," he said. "Forgive me."

Timothy looked away, still quaking, his arms tight to his chest. Dickens glanced around the room, but it wasn't as he knew it at all. It was a sad, dreary place. Dirty windows with rags stuffed in craggy holes, torn lace curtains, blank squares on the walls where the saints had been, a lumpy horsehair mattress, both arms of the threadbare chair broken away and gone. A lifeless hearth. Everything was changed. Her presence, whatever it was— phantom, spirit, figment, wraith—had transformed it. And now she was gone.

Desperate for any proof of her, he pivoted to the bedstead, where the small leather trunk still sat, staring back at him. Dickens lunged for it, leaning on his elbows to pull it out by its worn leather handles. He blew the dust away and threw it open, relieved, even grateful, to see the neatly tied numbers, red ribbons intact. The *Pickwicks*, the *Sketches*, the *Curiosity Shops*, all there.

He held one in each hand and turned to the boy. "But these books, Timothy, these are real!" He was asking more than telling, even if the boy didn't understand.

"She made me crisscross promise I wouldn't sell 'em, sir. I wouldn'ta done anyway. 'S all I've left of her."

Dickens dropped the numbers in the trunk and inched closer to the boy, still on his knees. "But I've been here, haven't I? With you?"

The boy nodded.

"And we sat by the fire? Into the night?" He pointed to the hearth, still trying to make sense of it. "You slept with your head on my knee—"

"To hear you breathe, sir," said Timothy, running a dirty sleeve across his nose. "'Twas a comfort to me."

"But you live here, by yourself?"

"Promised her, too, I wouldn't sleep in the street. I sells my sketches, sir. Yours sell the best of any."

"But who would let a boy, all alone—"

"It's only the money they cares about, sir. Nuffin' else."

Dickens nodded, still reeling on the inside. He took out a kerchief and gently wiped the boy's tears, awash in the guilt of his own selfish despair.

"Y'knew her, did ya, sir?"

He paused, masking his own sadness. "I did."

"Sometimes I feel she's still 'ere with me. Even though I know—"

"Yes," he said, clearing his throat of tears. "I'm sure of it."

Dickens stood and held the damp kerchief to his lips. He couldn't stand the sight of the grim room, so empty of Eleanor, or the thought of her son being without her. But the moon pulled his gaze to the window, where the skiff of snow graced the rooftops and streets, giving off a pure white light. It was her light, everywhere.

"Will ya be goin' now, sir?" Timothy asked, pinching the elbows of the coat sleeves.

Dickens shifted from one foot to another. He looked at his manuscript on the floor, pages askew, but still of a piece. He leaned down to pick them up, straightened them into a stack as best he could. And, in that moment, recalled what Eleanor had said to him just before they parted, her cheeks paled almost to nothing, as if the life was draining from her.

"Let the book be my Christmas present . . ."

Dickens pressed his lips together, willed his chin to stop

quivering. "Actually, Timothy, I believe your mother wanted . . ." He struggled to say the words. "That is, I was hoping to find, this very night . . . someone to hear my tale."

The boy looked at him with great dark lashes and wet, gleaming eyes.

"And I believe that person might be you."

41

"Stave One . . . Marley's Ghost . . ."

Dickens paused to find the word "ghost" stuck in his throat. Images flickered in his head. The billowing purple cloak, eyes that changed with each tilt of her gaze and became every blue that ever was, or no color at all; how she'd been everywhere, and nowhere, appearing and disappearing, knowing just where to find him, but never, never once had he seen her speak to anyone but him, no one else seemed to see or hear *her*. And the clock tower that had heralded their first meeting and their last—oh, the clock tower! Now dark and done.

"What harm can come of a ghost?" she'd asked, here, in this very room. But it wasn't a question at all. It was the answer. The great mystery of Eleanor Lovejoy.

How real she'd seemed, and if not, at least as true as anything he'd ever known. Maybe she'd sprung from his imagination, his own roiling conscience, but it didn't matter now. She *had* led him to Furnival's, made him write again, followed him to the blacking warehouse and the ghosts of his own past, perhaps even inspired the spirits that would grow Scrooge's heart, and his own. And all for the sake of her son. But the boy was nestled at his feet by a blazing fire—right now, right here—as real as any boy. This was where she'd wanted him all along. This, her wish for her son.

"Marley was dead: to begin with. There is no doubt whatever about that . . ."

With every molecule of his being, every expression and feeling he'd ever known, Dickens gave each word to Timothy what each word—and the spirit of his mother—had given him.

"The register of his burial was signed by the clergyman, the clerk, the undertaker, and the chief mourner. Scrooge signed it: and Scrooge's name was good upon 'Change, for anything he chose to put his hand to . . ."

Night pulled to morning. Timothy was gone when Dickens awoke in the broken chair. He looked outside, where the season's first snow was now a soft white quilt, making the city all one thing, lovely and pristine. He scavenged a stump of pencil and left a note on a scratch of paper telling the boy to pack what things he wanted, whenever he was ready, and come to Furnival's Inn. If he wasn't there, the clerk would show him to No. 13.

"Old Marley was as dead as a door-nail . . ."

Back in his rooms, Dickens sat at the writing table, wrote his title page—it was clear to him exactly what he would call it—and penned a short preface to his readers, an afterthought, two simple lines, and signed them. Then came a long letter to his darling Catherine telling everything as best he could, leaving nothing out. He placed it in an envelope finished with a red seal and stamp, and addressed it to Scotland. He tied a string around his manuscript, and set out to rejoin the world.

"Oh! But he was a tight-fisted hand at the grindstone, Scrooge! a squeezing, wrenching, grasping, scraping, clutching, covetous, old sinner! . . ."

Dickens plunked the manuscript onto the counter at the printing office, pressing it flat with his hand. A young apprentice picked it up, astonished at what he held in his grasp.

"*A Christmas Carol?*" he asked, reading the front page.

"I think it strikes just the right note, don't you?"

The apprentice wagged his chin in awe. Dickens then instructed him, in short order, that he wanted a handsome production, salmon-cloth on the outside, eight illustrations on the inside, a gold wreath around the title, gold on the spine; in fact, gilt on the edge of every page! But the price should be just five shillings apiece so people could buy it. And if Chapman and Hall wouldn't pay for it, he would, out of his own pocket. It wasn't a long book, it was a short book, and if they set seven typesetters to work through the next two days and nights, it would be on bookshelves three days shy of Christmas. And run six thousand copies, he said, at which the apprentice gripped the edge of the desk to steady himself.

"And might I entrust to you one last thing?" Dickens asked, handing him the red-sealed letter. "If you make certain that the very first copy boards the train for Scotland, with this letter, I would be eternally grateful."

The apprentice took the letter gladly, having memorized every word of his mission down to the last possible detail. Dickens shook his hand and wished him a happy Christmas.

"*The cold within him froze his old features, nipped his pointed nose, shrivelled his cheek, stiffened his gait; made his eyes red, his thin lips blue; and spoke out shrewdly in his grating voice . . .*"

And so it was, two days and two nights later, the book ran on two shiny new cylinder presses all the way from Germany, with Hall looking sternly on and Chapman mopping his brow.

"*A frosty rime was on his head, and on his eyebrows, and his wiry chin. He carried his own low temperature always about with him; he iced his office in the dog-days; and didn't thaw it one degree at Christ-mas . . ."*

Slender volumes in festive green wrappers flew off the shelves of every bookshop within two hundred miles. People lined up, clamored, borrowed, and pleaded to hear it.

"No beggars implored him to bestow a trifle, no children asked him what it was o'clock, no man or woman ever once in all his life inquired the way to such and such a place, of Scrooge . . ."

Silence in a courtroom at the Old Bailey one morning found even Magistrate Laing himself, stone-cold sober, reading a fresh copy on the bench while a jury waited, holding its collective breath as the head juror read aloud to them.

"Once upon a time—of all the good days in the year, on Christmas eve—old Scrooge sat busy in his counting-house. It was cold, bleak, biting weather: foggy withal . . ."

At home, Thackeray's daughters took excited turns with the book, reading to each other, while their father sat in his think-ing chair, tugging at his brows.

"'Bah!' said Scrooge, 'Humbug! . . . Out upon merry Christmas! What's Christmas time to you but a time for paying bills without money . . .'"

Ill-clad illiterates squeezed together on benches in a spruced-up gin shop to hear it. The men crushed their hats in their hands; women worried the cloth of their skirts, hanging on each new word.

"'At this festive season of the year, Mr. Scrooge,' said the gentleman, taking up a pen, 'it is more than usually desirable that we should make some slight provision for the Poor and destitute, who suffer greatly at the present time . . .'"

The five ragged boys sat front and center. Their three-coated captain bit his lip and gazed upward, closing his eyes to listen better with his ears.

"*'Are there no prisons?' asked Scrooge . . .*"

At Furnival's, the desk clerk leaned over his very own copy, the first book he'd ever owned and already his proudest possession, which was given him by the resident of No. 13, who signed it and tied it with a bow. The clerk's glasses were thick with steam and fright. His finger moved along the text word by word, each one read with great deliberation.

"*. . . it came on through the heavy door, and passed into the room before his eyes. And upon its coming in, the dying flame leaped up, as though it cried, 'I know him; Marley's ghost! . . .'*"

At Artillery Place, Maria Beadnell, in a high-collared silk nightdress and lace cap, sat in a canopied bed beside her beloved Henry, older and weaker, taking their morning tea. Open on her tray was a note signed, "Affectionately yours, C.D." and a check scrawled with his name. She held the book with one hand, her husband's hand with the other, and read to him, content.

"*'You may be an undigested bit of beef, a blot of mustard, a crumb of cheese, a fragment of an underdone potato. There's more of gravy than of grave about you, whatever you are! . . .'*"

In his elegant dining room at Lincoln's Inn Fields, John Forster sat at one end of his long table, cutting his boiled beef crisscross hard, trying not to care as Mary sat at the other end, reading out loud.

"*'I wear the chain I forged in life,' replied the Ghost. 'I made it link by link, and yard by yard; I girded it on of my own free will, and of my own free will I wore it . . .'*"

Forster chewed fast, then slow, then stopped altogether, setting his fork and knife on his plate, as quiet as church, so as not to miss a word.

"*'Business!' cried the Ghost, wringing its hands again. 'Mankind was my business. The common welfare was my business; charity, mercy, forbearance, benevolence, were, all, my business . . .'*"

Far away in Scotland, Katey, Mamie, Charley, Walter, and Frank sat at Catherine's knee or on her lap, or leaned against one another's shoulders on a nearby settee, as she read to them with eyes full of feeling. Her husband's letter lay by her elbow, with a look of having been read many times.

"... *They were not a handsome family; they were not well dressed; their shoes were far from being water-proof; their clothes were scanty. . . . But, they were happy, grateful, pleased with one another, and contented with the time. . . .*"

Catherine paused to consider her own children, their eager eyes and apple cheeks. She put one hand on her newborn, fast asleep beside her, to feel his tiny beating heart.

Little Frank tugged at her hem to read on.

42

On Christmas Eve day at Furnival's Inn, Dickens had two tablespoons of rum with fresh cream for breakfast, a pint of champagne for tea, and two hours later a raw egg beaten into a tumbler of sherry with a biscuit on the side. The desk clerk made sure of it. Topping brought him his full evening dress with plaited shirt-frill and white neckerchief, punctuated by a snappy buttonhole and purple waistcoat, at his master's request, and before leaving fortified him with a cup of beef tea. Dickens couldn't bring himself to ask whether there'd been news of his family; Topping would have said so straightaway. But when he reached into his pocket on the way out the door, he found Katey's list of their Christmas wishes, folded neatly into a square. He knew he had Topping to thank for putting it there; it was just the thing to set him right for reading.

It was a fine afternoon under a pearl winter sky as a great throng of merry Londoners outside the new hall at Long Acre poured past a placard—CHARLES DICKENS READS *A CHRISTMAS CAROL*! PROCEEDS BENEFIT THE FIELD LANE RAGGED SCHOOL!—having been earnestly requested to be in their places by ten minutes to four o'clock, and please, all top hats and bonnets to be removed upon entering.

Inside, the hall and galleries filled quickly; those who couldn't sit stood at the back, shoulder to shoulder, glad for their small square of space. The stage was set. A deep maroon backdrop, a row of gaslights, and a fine Turkish carpet, on which sat a reading desk specially built in two days for just this occasion, according to specifications drawn by the author himself. It was straight up and down, nothing fussy about it except for a trim of gold fringe, a small box on top where he could rest an elbow, and a pitcher of water and a glass on a small side wing. Dickens waited, unseen, for a quiet to settle on the crowd, but heard only rowdy applause and loud murmurs.

He peered around a heavy gold curtain to see rows upon rows of hatless heads, eager faces, people leaning out of the galleries, nearly hanging from the rafters. How he wished his family were here, but at least he had Timothy, right in front where he'd installed him, hair combed half-heartedly to the side, brogans dangling off his chair. It gave him strength.

Dickens was waiting for a quiet inside himself, but every atom in his body took a turn at somersaults. He was like a child at Christmastime himself, palpable excitement, his own long list of impossible wishes. He wanted everyone to feel what he did, see with his eyes. He wanted to deal a sledgehammer blow for the poor, wanted to lift the thin veil that separates one person from another and in its place raise the flag of fellow feeling, selflessness, charity, and return Christmas to the little child whose story had begun it. But he knew, too, for the first time, what had always been true—that he wanted them to love *him*. In some shadow-corner of his being, he was the eleven-year-old at Warren's Blacking even now, a boy all alone in the world, who wanted only to be seen and cared for. If they might only treasure the part of him that Eleanor had reawakened.

And so, with hands pressed together in gratitude, Dickens at last emerged from the wings to wild clapping, the waving of kerchiefs, the stomping of winter boots. A great calm came over him when he took his place at the reading desk. He blinked his eyes at Timothy, who blinked back; set his white gloves and cloud of silk kerchief on the side wing, opened his book and pressed it to his chest. The preface he knew by heart.

"I have endeavoured in this Ghostly little book, to raise the Ghost of an Idea, which shall not put my readers out of humour with themselves, with each other, with the season, or with me. May it haunt your houses pleasantly, and no one wish to lay it. For I am, ever your faithful friend and servant, Charles Dickens."

He bowed his head. A muted thrill, a shudder of anticipation, swept through the crowd until, at long last, came the silence that begged to be filled. Dickens said a little prayer to the gaslights above, cleared his throat, took in a breath all the way to his toes, and began.

"A Christmas Carol . . . Stave One . . . Marley's Ghost . . ."

And without a single prop or a snippet of costume, he did fill it, peopling the entire hall with his extended family of characters, who became intimate companions to everyone present. From the first stave to the last spirit, he was all his creations at once. For Scrooge, he became the old man that Eleanor had made him, with a croaking voice and a pinched, sneering face, neck drawn in or thrust out of his collar like a big old turtle. For Fezziwig's party, he danced his fingers on the podium in a mad display of two-fingered hops, arabesques, and pirouettes. He was timid Bob Cratchit, kind nephew Fred, the beaming moonface of his long-lost fiancée. For Tiny Tim, he was Timothy, in every detail. With a wave of his hand, a drumming of fingers, a flutter of his kerchief, he was one person and then another, man or woman, young or old, rich or poor. The audience seemed to fall into a kind of universal trance. No fidgeting, no rustling. Even a dropped pin might have caused an uproar of annoyance.

"'Spirit,' said Scrooge, with an interest he had never felt before, 'tell me if Tiny Tim will live.' 'I see a vacant seat,' replied the Ghost, 'in the poor chimney-corner, and a crutch without an owner, carefully preserved. If these shadows remain unaltered by the Future, the child will die . . .'"

Dickens told the story as if his life—as if all life—depended on it. Everything he had felt, hoped, lost, and regained came together in that moment. It was a crisp, startling, rattling tale. But it was all heart, or nothing.

". . . every man among them hummed a Christmas tune, or had a Christmas thought, or spoke below his breath to his companion of some bygone Christmas day . . ."

Well-dressed men perched at the edge of their seats. Hardened carpenters cried and trembled. Macready was undisguisedly sobbing. Women, young and old, dabbed their eyes, or all-out wept, gripping each other's hands.

"He became as good a friend, as good a master, and as good a man, as the good old city knew, or any other good old city, town, or borough, in the good old world . . ."

Dickens looked at Timothy, and something in the boy, of Eleanor, nearly toppled him. He had to look away, somewhere, down at his book, though he didn't need it anymore. The words were inside him.

"Some people laughed to see the alteration in him, but he let them laugh, and little heeded them; for he was wise enough to know that nothing ever happened on this globe, for good, at which some people *did not have their fill of laughter in the outset. . . . His own heart laughed, and that was quite enough for him . . ."*

His voice stalled in his throat. Dickens paused to press the kerchief to his lips so no one would see them straight-out quivering. He put a finger on the text where he'd left off, but his hand was shaking, too. When he gazed out, it seemed that no one was breathing. Their eyes were upon him—two thousand pairs—sunken, crooked, squinty, kindly, wistful, glad, red-rimmed, clear whites, deep blues. Across the sea of faces he found such varieties of beauty, and felt a rush of inexplicable tenderness for each of them, awe for their own lives and loves, disappointments and frailties, but hopes, most of all hopes. Eleanor had been right. No matter their faults or weaknesses, their station in life, he felt only kinship. And that they knew him, too, offered their tenderness in return.

He could tell in the way they waited for him, not Charles Dickens the author but the man, just a man, trying to gather himself to finish what he'd begun.

"And it was always said of him that he knew how to keep Christmas well, if any man alive possessed the knowledge . . ."

He stopped again, filling his chest with air.

"May that be truly said of us, and all of us! . . . And so, as Tiny Tim observed . . ."

And then, somewhere between a bellow and a whisper, a godsend and a cheer, he found the strength to say—

"God Bless Us, Every One."

Dickens pressed his eyes shut against tears. Tears everywhere, Timothy in his seat, Macready a mess, the Carlyles holding each other, Hall dabbing his eyes, Chapman all but blubbering. The theater was bone-still and quiet but for the whimpers, sniffles, and sobs; two thousand souls struck dumb as if each had been lifted high enough to look down upon his or her own life and find it not wanting, but giving. And then a thundercrack of applause. It started at the back and grew to a booming crescendo as it rumbled toward him across the hall. People leapt to their feet, clapping, voices calling out, each on top of the other, "Bravo! Bravo!"

Dickens took it all in with a hand on his heart. Men stomped their feet as if to say, *Give us one word more, we will hear it!* Women called out, too, and would have listened again, from the very first word. Each turned to the person next to them, in front and behind, still applauding, but for each other now, and the great gift of being alive.

Dickens bowed, long and low. His heart was thundering inside him, too, louder than all the clapping, which seemed not to subside at all. He needed the moment. It was as if he'd come to the crest of a great mountain peak and, though panting and spent, could see all the world. And how vivid a view. Even the Turkish carpet under his boots was every color imaginable, an alchemy of alum, copper, and chrome mixed with madder root, indigo, poppy, and sage. What magic there was all around him. Words were inadequate, but all he had. He didn't know where they came from or why, but it was how we told one another what the world was and might be. Who we were, and might become. It was the only magic he had. Everything else was faith.

He felt blessed and grateful.

He rose, clasping his hands together, and tucked his chin to his chest. When he lifted his gaze, he looked for Timothy. The first person to hear the story; it was his story, too. But the seat was empty. The one small, safe place in the world he'd reserved for the boy couldn't hold him. Dickens looked to the right and left, up the aisle, across and down again. Panic swelled inside him. He leapt off the stage in a rush toward the door, intercepted by a throng of well-wishers.

"Ah, Mr. Dickens, what a book it is!"

"I've a Tiny Tim myself, sir."

"Ooh, I shall never think of Christmas in the same way again!"

Macready was too tear-stricken to speak. Thomas Carlyle bellowed over ten heads, "Boz, I'm going to buy a turkey this minute! For everyone I know!"

Chapman and Hall brought up the rear, bubbling like champagne. "Charles!" said Hall, clapping him on the back. "Six thousand sold the first day!"

"There's to be a second printing before New Year!" added Chapman.

Dickens looked past them, where the small slip of a boy disappeared through a door at the top of the hall. He wanted to lunge for him, but found an ocean of bobbing admirers blocking his way. "Forgive me," he said, pushing through the crowd.

He broke out of the hall, out of the building, and onto the street like a madman escaped from Bedlam, but there was no sign of the boy at all. Only bell ringers, muffin men, shoppers, and carolers, bustling to the last possible hour of Christmas Eve. But no Timothy. He careened down the street, legs pumping, across a small quarter of the city, down the snicket, up the cobbles, all the way to the rusted churchyard gate, standing ajar. He stepped through the threshold and followed a set of small footprints in the snow that ended where Timothy sat on the ground, knees pulled to his chest, head buried in his folded arms. Even in the twilight, Dickens recognized the marker for his father's grave. But next to it, by the boy's feet, was an even smaller wooden marker, hand-carved with rough, simple letters, that read: *Eleanor Lovejoy, 1815–1842.*

Dickens sat beside him on the cold ground and waited, saying nothing. He watched Timothy heave in quiet sobs, his shoulder blades like little bird wings arrowing out of his coat. He put a hand lightly on the back of the boy's collar and let him cry. Finally, Timothy raised his face, wiping it roughly with a sleeve.

"Hearin' yer story this time," he said between sniffles and gasps, "I thought I might never know Christmas again."

The boy dropped his head into his hands, threading his mop of hair through his fingers. Dickens turned to the sky above, dotted with faint stars, clouds skimming the moon. "I remember a time when I felt the same," he said.

Timothy lifted his face, all snot and tears. Dickens handed him a kerchief and sighed, pulling Katey's list from his pocket. He unfolded it with great care.

"This is a list of my children's Christmas wishes. They work so hard on it, year-round, all that thinking and hoping and imagining. But you see here, at the bottom, they've left room for one more wish."

Dickens offered the list to the boy, but he didn't take it. "Do you have your pencil?"

Timothy shook his head. Dickens pulled one from his own pocket. "Well, then mine will have to do." He held them out, prepared to wait all night.

Timothy took them from Dickens' hand. He pressed the paper against the grave marker, scratching out a few simple words in a slow, careful hand. Then gave it back. There was just enough light for Dickens to read it.

"Oh, dear," he said. "I'm afraid that wish won't do at all. You see, that one is already taken—"

Timothy looked at him, crestfallen.

"By me," Dickens said, standing. "So will you, Timothy? Have Christmas with me?"

The boy turned his head to look up at Dickens. "Will Mamie be there, sir? And the others?"

Dickens lowered his head and shook it lightly. "I'm afraid we are, both of us, orphans this year. But if you'll share it with me, that would be Christmas enough."

He reached his arm down and opened his palm to the boy, who stood slowly, circles of snow about his knees, and considered Dickens' outstretched hand. Timothy wiped his eyes one last time with the back of his fingerless gloves, and took it.

A yes.

43

If ever Charles Dickens met a fine December morning, the sort that sparkles and chatters of things hoped for and blessings to come, here it was now. He and Timothy left Furnival's Inn for the last time, wishing the desk clerk good cheer and great happiness. Hand in hand, they ambled toward the first flush of Christmas Day, pausing at the corner of what's-long-forgotten and all-things-possible to watch their shared city yawn to life. The sharp scent of evergreen mingled in their noses with a blast of fish and the wafting aroma of a fresh-baked Christmas pudding.

Church bells pealed. The streets thickened with hansom cabs, omnibuses, costermongers, and muffin men. Eager children gripped their mothers' hands, standing in long queues at the butcher's shop, the poulterer's, the baker's, the grocer's, all counting the minutes to the long-awaited Christmas feast. A light wind had snow-kissed the cobbled streets of the city, and what had been smog and soot just days before gave way to a soft winter light that tamed all it touched. The metropolis seemed to sigh with one breath, beat as one holy heart. Even birds caroled overhead. Dickens' own icy breath floated like glitter on the air.

"Merry Christmas! Good day to you! Merry, merry everything!" he called to passersby with a tip of his hat, or said quietly as he paused to press a coin into every beggar's hand, even crossing the street to reach them. Timothy called out, too, in his newly regained voice, a little echo beside him. People of all classes craned their necks to get another glimpse of the man who had awakened some long-lost Christmas spirit and the young ragged boy holding fast to his side.

Dickens peered into the window at Bumble's Toy Shop, relieved to see its proprietor still inside. He opened the door, happily anticipating the jingle overhead. Timothy stood on the threshold, gaping at the bell, afraid to step across. A thin furrow across the boy's forehead told Dickens he'd only ever been on the looking-in side of the store, never the looking-out. "It's all right, Timothy," he said, reaching to ring the bell again, by hand, to announce their entrance. "You're welcome here."

At the second jingle, Mr. Bumble looked up from his register, dismayed by the sight of the lately unpredictable Mr. Dickens, and with a street boy beside him.

"Mr. Dickens. I'm soon to close up shop for the rest of Christmas Day."

But his once-prized customer took off his hat and stepped toward him with a ready hand.

"Your fund for the Field Lane School, Mr. Bumble?"

"Done, sir."

Dickens took Bumble's hand in both of his. "Why, not done at all."

"I do not get your meaning," said Bumble, waiting for the other shoe to drop.

"Why, it cannot be done until it's been *doubled* . . . by me!"

Dickens leaned in to whisper, "I do not have it now, but am good for it, upon my word."

The sincerity on his face was unmistakable. Bumble twittered with glee and reached for his ledger to mark it down. Dickens dipped into his pocket and unfolded Katey's list, handing it off.

"And do you mind? If you've time. May I have these few last things for my children?"

"Of course, Mr. Dickens! I'll have them delivered this very afternoon."

"It may be they'll need to go to Scotland."

"As you wish. I am at your service."

"And is it too late for some presents for the boys at Field Lane?"

"Never too late, sir. Never!"

Bumble looked past Dickens to where Timothy ogled the shining blade and scabbard of a pirate sword.

"Is that one of them, sir?" he asked in a whisper. "The ragged boys?"

Dickens followed his gaze to Timothy, who had turned from the sword, wide-eyed, to the four-story German dollhouse at the center of everything, a little world unto itself. He was like every child in a toy shop, where hardships and fears fall away to make room for wonder.

"He's one of mine, Mr. Bumble. And he's to have anything his heart desires."

"Of course, sir. A merry Christmas to you both."

Back on the street, turning in to the bustling Strand, the two sang a Christmas tune, crowing like chanticleers.

"Oh, bring us a figgy pudding, oh, bring us a figgy pudding, oh, bring us a figgy pudding and a cup of good cheer . . ."

They quickly found their voices drowned out by a group of street boys, hats off, arranged like a little choir around a baker-boy cap on the ground in front of them teeming with coins. Despite the dirt and pimples on their cheeks, whiskers sprouting on their lips, they sang with round mouths and delicate harmonies.

". . . *Sleep in heavenly pe-eace. Sle-ep in heavenly peace.*"

Dickens knew them at once and stopped to applaud. Timothy the same. Their captain took a bow; the rest followed in turn.

"Oh, boys. I'm so happy to find you, for I never made good on my grievous mistake."

The three-coated captain stepped forward, hat to his chest. "We didn't want to steal yer story, Mr. Dickens. We wanted to be *in* it."

Dickens cocked his head, bemused.

"Thought if we made an impression of some sort, might get a mention."

"That's why you followed me? All over town?"

"Be famous then, sir. To get a part in a Dickens story. Everybody wants one."

"Well, not everybody."

"We're prepared to pay, sir. Been savin' up." He picked up the hat full of coins from the ground and whomped his nearest crony on the chest with it. The lieutenant produced a felted bag, pulled it open by strings, and dumped the jangling pennies into the hat with the others. The captain offered it to Dickens.

"I cannot take your money."

"Oh, dem what's parted from it don't miss it by now," said the captain. "The way we sees it, money comes and goes. Fame's what makes a name."

"But it's who you are that makes a name."

"It's 'ow many people read yer name, sir, and 'ow many times.

And you write the longest stories of anyone!" He winked at Timothy, who smiled shyly back.

"I'm sorry, boys. My story is done."

With a sigh and a shrug, the captain lowered the hatful of coins and scratched his bristle-haired head. "D'ya know a Mr. Thackeray, then? We 'eard 'e's got a long one."

"I shall mention it," Dickens said, offering his hand. "What is your name?"

The boy pumped Dickens' hand up and down. "David, sir . . . Copperfield!"

Dickens looked down at Timothy. Timothy looked at him.

"Good name!" he said to the young Copperfield, leaning in. "Never mind Thackeray. I shall put it in my own mental museum."

And having satisfied the captain that his fame was assured, Dickens and Timothy proceeded onward into the snow-lit evening, singing their carol.

"We won't go until we've got some, we won't go until we've got some, we won't go until we've got some, so bring some out here . . ."

The two carried on, singing and kicking up dustings of white powder as they went. Suddenly Dickens stopped, stunned by what lay before them. Four storefronts, from 30 all the way to 34 New Oxford Street, had been joined to make one: MUDIE'S BIG LIBRARY & BOOKSELLER—CHEAPEST BOOKS IN LONDON— TEN THOUSAND VOLUMES IN STOCK—GRAND OPENING! Buffeted by hordes of elegant shoppers flurrying in and out, they stepped closer. It was a vast emporium, two stories tall with acres of windows, Ionic pillars, railed galleries, and cases of books with bindings in every imaginable color, from sober blacks and browns to scarlet-red, pink, green, and even fashionable magenta! Men

in tails mingled with women in capacious muffs, all carrying
fresh-wrapped stacks of brand-new books.

"This place," asked Timothy, "what is it?"

"The Ghost of Christmas Future, I'm afraid. But never mind,
Timothy," he said, squeezing the boy's hand. "There's someone
I'd like you to meet."

Dickens knew the way well, around a corner, down two alleys, across a frozen dirt thoroughfare to a tavern, not of the
fancy variety. It was peopled with men, mostly, who found
their Christmas cheer at the bottom of a glass. John Dickens
sat at the bar, with a book gripped in one hand and a porter ale
in the other.

The son took off his hat and approached him. "Do you like
it?" he asked his father's back.

John Dickens started at the sound of his son's voice. He set
down his tankard and turned around to face him. As a man who
often spoke a surplus of words to obscure what was true, here he
found only a few.

"I think it your finest book."

"I'm glad. Because if you didn't like it, I should consider it a
failure."

"Whyever so?"

"Because you're my father. And a son wants his father to be
proud of him."

John Dickens stood from his seat and regarded the ground,
jostled some sawdust and a few peanut shells with his foot.
When he looked up, his eyes were damp.

"Oh, son. I only wish I'd been a better father. And a better
man."

"As does any father. And every man." He hesitated. "As do I."

A tipsy man approached, face-to-face with the younger Dickens, scrunching his eyes trying to focus. "Why, yer Charles

Dickens!" he said, as if he'd made the literary discovery of a lifetime.

Other patrons looked their way. Timothy, standing by the door, waited for his answer.

"Everyone knows that," he said, loud enough for all to hear. "But did you know . . . this man is my father!"

John Dickens held his shabby bowler to his heart, and beamed.

44

In the gloaming eve, Devonshire Terrace was quiet with new-fallen snow that sparkled like diamond shards scattered across the ground. The sky had cleared for the rise of the Christmas moon and enough twinkling stars to light everyone's merry way, if merry was the way they went. John Dickens gabbled away to Timothy, but his son lagged several steps behind. Neither the young boy nor the old man was aware of the trepidation Charles Dickens felt as he neared his own house, empty of the family he now longed for. He was determined not to show it.

"I myself am particularly partial to turkey, though likewise am game for a goose!" John Dickens declared to the boy. "What about one of each, wouldn't you think, Timothy?"

"Will it be enough, sir?" the boy asked.

Both Dickens men followed his gaze. They were halted at the gate of One Devonshire Terrace, where a large wreath glistened on the red varnished door. There was light inside, a warm glow from the hearth, a hubbub, revelry, people milling about, a tree—the Christmas tree! As sure as they stood there, as right as the snow, there was the Christmas soiree in all its glory!

"The party!" he said, reaching for the boy's hand. "Oh, Timothy! My family's home!"

They rushed inside to find the rousing annual party in progress. Macready was there, Thackeray and his daughters, Wilkie Collins, the Trollopes, the Carlyles, Chapman and Hall, the everkindhearted Fred and his wife, and so many more. The long table was set magnificently, with tiered stands, flowers, and candelabras, everything on Catherine's list and more: stuffed turkeys, a goose, oysters, mince pies, plum puddings, and Christmas cake, timbales, jellies and molds, punch bowls of eggnog and smoking bishop. In the foyer, a magnificent tree nearly two floors tall was strung with candies, fruits, nuts, and trinkets, and a hundred lighted candles.

Dickens' face lit up like a blazing fire. He surged into the glad crowd of friends and family, who encircled him, calling out cheers and good tidings. He shook hands and patted backs, all the while searching for some sign of Catherine or Katey or Mamie and any of the boys. *They must be here*, he thought, *they're home!*

Thackeray clapped his back. "Whatever differences we've had, Dickens, well, this book of yours is a national benefit, and to every man and woman who reads it a personal kindness!"

Thackeray's elder daughter chimed in, taking her father's elbow. "We've told Father he *must* write a book like one of yours!"

"But one simply has no chance!" added Wilkie Collins, coming to greet him.

Chapman was not far behind, proffering a gift. "And we've brought you a pen!"

Dickens took the pen gladly and shook Chapman's hand near off at the wrist. "Thank you. All of you! Thackeray! Macready! Hall! And Fred! Dear Fred! How glad I am to see you and your bride! I want to know everything, everything!" He put a warm arm around Fred's shoulder, instantly relieving him of the burden of thinking he was not the brother Charles wanted him to be, without one word more passing between them.

Over Fred's shoulder, Forster parted the crowd to get near. He had an empty champagne glass in each hand. "Don't blame me, Charles, if I love you for your talent! And your goodness!" Forster barrel-hugged him hard, not letting him go, possibly ever. "So, for God's sake, let us be friends again! I simply cannot get along without you."

"Nor I, you, John," said Dickens, returning the hug with full force. "It's I who beg your forgiveness."

"But that's what Christmas is for!" said Forster, taking a bottle of champagne from a tray and pouring their glasses full. "Forgiveness and friendship all around!"

Dickens toasted, all the while keeping one eye out for any of his brood. "Have you seen Catherine?" he whispered into Forster's ear.

Forster shook his head and put a sympathetic hand on his friend's shoulder. Topping was pushing through the crowd.

"Topping! Are they home?" Dickens shouted over the din.

"Not a word, sir."

"Then who did all this?" he asked, when Topping reached his side.

"Invitations'd been posted, sir. There were no stoppin' it. So I took it on my own account that it was the right thing to do."

"Oh, it was. It was."

"Mr. Forster helped. And his Mary. Thackeray's daughters did more than their part. Really, everyone."

"I don't know how to thank you—"

"No need, sir. Is there anything wanted at all?"

"No, no," he said, covering. "I can't think what would be missing."

He turned to the lighted tree, strung with cranberry vines and glowing with the teardrop flames of little wax candles. How his children would have loved it.

"The tree's a triumph, Topping," he said bravely, but his courage was dipping. He handed his champagne glass to his groom. "You know, I've a wonderful Christmas cognac I should like to share around. I'll just be a moment."

Dickens passed the dazzling tree and stood on the first stair, turning back to look out over the good people who'd come, and brought the party with them. He searched for Timothy and found him happily, hungrily filling a plate with meats and candies and filberts under the guidance of John Dickens, who was busy pointing out the things he mustn't miss, elucidating the merits and marvels of everything.

Dickens climbed the stairs to his study. There were fresh flowers on the table, everything dusted and just right. The gilt rabbit, the dueling bronze toads. Why, even the fusee clock was there on his desk, bruised and glued together, but back where it belonged. Surely he had Topping to thank for that, too. He wound it three times to the right with its heart-shaped key, pleased by the sound of its simple tick-tock. *Begin again*, he thought. *Second chances, everywhere.* He gazed out at the garden, resting under a blanket of peaceful white.

The cognac he found on a bookshelf. He gripped the bottle's neck, unable to pull himself away from the miniature portraits of his children. How perfect they were in their little gilt frames, with their bows and ringlets and stiff collars, not a hair out of place. But how he missed their imperfections, all. At last, his eyes settled on a portrait of Catherine. With the pad of a finger, he touched her eyes, her nose, her lips.

"My darling Cate," he whispered, leaning his head against it.

He felt someone watching him and turned to find Timothy a few feet away, standing in the open door. The young boy's chin was lowered, as if he somehow understood the intermingling of loss and hope, that only young children who have lost and hoped can know.

"I'm sorry, Mr. Dickens, if it's not enough Christmas."

Dickens took in a rough breath that ended with a sigh and a shake of his head. He collected himself and mussed the boy's hair gently, lifting his chin to look him right in the eye. "It's a fine Christmas, Timothy. A fine Christmas, indeed."

Timothy stepped beside him to gaze on the little portraits. Dickens reached for his hand. "But what I would not give for a kiss from any of my children. All the sovereigns in the world for just one sticky hug."

Topping appeared in the door, chirping with excitement. "Sir! Outside! Can you hear it?"

Dickens closed his eyes. He did hear it, the faintest sound of jingling bells and horses' hooves crunching downy snow. Timothy looked up at him, eyes round. Still holding his hand tight, Dickens rushed out of the study to the upstairs parlor overlooking the front of the house. He opened a window and leaned his head out as far as he could without falling, as a large park-drag coach rounded the corner of Devonshire Terrace and pulled up to the house. Dickens and Timothy shared a quick glance.

Christmas might be saved after all.

Just outside the front gate, young Charley, Walter, and Frank piled out of the carriage noisily, followed by the two barking Newfoundlands, and even a cat. Dickens flew out the front door to greet them, his heart pounding out of his chest.

"Look! My children! It's Flaster Floby! Chicken Stalker and Young Skull . . . And the dogs! Timberdoodle, Sniffery!"

The boys ran to meet him halfway up the walk, pulled at his pant legs, jumped into his arms, squeezed his neck, yelling the latest news of this and that and nothing that mattered and everything that did, while the dogs leapt around them and burrowed in the snow. Dickens lifted Frank into his arms—he was still just small enough—lightly pinched his pixie nose, and held him close.

"My boys, oh, my boys. How I've missed your shining faces," he said, showering them with kisses. "And your sticky fingers, Frank," he said, kissing each one in turn, down to the littlest. "And this, the tastiest one of all!"

Frank giggled and squirmed out of his father's arms to run inside with his brothers, all throwing snowballs as they went. Mamie stepped from the carriage with her usual quiet dignity and walked to her father. She pulled out a plain velvet bag pulled tight with a golden cord, heavy in her delicate gloved hand. She held it out to him.

"All the pennies you've ever given me. For the starving children of India."

Dickens took the bag, as he knew he must, then pressed it back into her hand. How lovely a girl she was, so much like her mother, and yet like no one he'd ever met. He put one hand on each side of her face and kissed her fair freckled forehead.

"My dearest Mild Glo'ster. How good you are, and true. I think you the kindest person I know."

Katey appeared behind her sister, nose high in the air, the best snub she could muster.

"Oh, Katey. Will your dance card be full this evening? I was so hoping for a waltz."

She folded her arms royally across her chest, turning her chin to the stars with an exaggerated huff.

"For a shilling, I will."

"A shilling it is," he said.

"Or a kiss."

She met her father's gaze. Her fern-green eyes matched the velvet of her carriage coat and bonnet.

"I shall give you two kisses," he said. "And be glad for the bargain."

Katey kissed one of his cheeks; Mamie the other. But the party couldn't be kept waiting a moment more, least of all for them.

As the girls skipped inside, arm in arm, Dickens walked toward the carriage, where a radiant Catherine stood by, having at last disembarked and come home. She held their newborn son in her arms. The baby was wrapped tight and warm in a wool blanket, but his little face shone in the moonlight. It was like seeing him for the first time, all of them, with fresh eyes and a clear heart.

"Oh, Catherine . . ." he said, taking the baby in his arms for only the second time since the child had come upon the earth. But he found it hard to go on.

"What is Christmas without our party?" she said softly, with a smile to match.

Choked with feeling, he looked at her. "I know that of late I've pitied myself a poor man—poor in love, in riches, in prospects. But I've learned, in these days of your absence . . . that whatever I suffered was a poverty of my own vision."

He raised his hand; she pressed hers to his. Their foreheads rested, one against the other.

"My dear Cate, forgive me for not seeing that I am rich in all ways . . . Wealthy beyond all imagining."

Catherine shook her head and nodded, both at once. "We have all that we need," she said, "right here."

"We do," he said, his voice faltering. "And we shall have such dinings, such dancings . . ." He was fighting tears, but losing.

". . . such kissings-out of old years," Catherine continued from memory, her own voice trembling, "and kissings-in of new as have never been seen in these parts before."

Dickens smiled, filled with the memory of their first Christmas, and every one since then. "I guess Christmas begins in the heart after all."

They leaned over their bundled newborn to kiss, warm and tender, the way only people who have loved each other a very long time can do.

When their lips parted, Dickens opened his eyes to find Catherine looking past him. The front door was open. Timothy stood in the foyer, by himself, watching the festivities from a distance. He seemed shy again, the boy he'd first met, who was afraid to speak, or had no one to speak to. Or had forgotten how.

Catherine's face bloomed beneath her fur-trimmed bonnet. "You must be Timothy," she called to him. The boy turned, surprised to hear his name on her lips. "Mr. Dickens wrote me all about you."

She beckoned him toward them with a wave of her glove. Dickens watched the boy step away from the safety of the threshold, unsure, as if his own fate hung in the balance. He stopped at Dickens' side and looked at the child in his arms.

"Wot's its name?"

"It so happens we're nearly out of names," she said. "Shall I take you up, show you the extra bed, and we'll choose one on the way?"

Catherine collected the skirts of her burgundy velvet in one hand and reached the other toward the boy. Timothy looked at her, incredulous at the offer of a kind hand and a proper bed all at once. He turned to Dickens, who blinked and nodded. He was a deserving boy, as all children are. But didn't yet know it himself.

"Mustn't keep Christmas waiting," Catherine said.

Dickens watched him slip his hand into hers, the most natural thing in the world, and grip it tight as she led him inside. Of course he missed a mother's touch.

How pleased Eleanor would be.

All the luggage unloaded, the carriage driver bade a good night and a merry Christmas to the household, which Dickens returned tenfold. As the bells on the horses jingled back the way they'd come, he stood on the walk outside the gate to cherish his first moment alone with his new son. He turned toward the house where, through the window, the Christmas party thrummed in all its splendor. Everyone, even Catherine and Timothy, gathered around the piano as Mamie played. All singing at once.

"Hark! the Herald angels sing Glory to the newborn King! Peace on earth, and mercy mild, God and sinners reconcil'd . . ."

It sounded brightly in his ears, a boisterous chorus of man and angels. He turned his face to the star-kissed winter sky, from which glittering snowflakes began to fall. He couldn't have been happier had he been transported to Paradise. Here it was, in front of him now.

Charles Dickens was filled with the spirit of Christmases past, present, and all that were yet to come.

He pulled his son close, kissed his tiny brow, and whispered in his ear.

"God bless us. Every one."

Author's Note

This is a work of fiction. It is spun out of threads from the lives of Charles Dickens, his family and friends, and even a nemesis or two. It is meant as a playful reimagining of how the second most beloved Christmas story in the world (after the original) came to be. I have twisted, embellished, and reordered the facts (and even his children) to serve the plot. Nearly all the characters are based on real people, and the best lines, to be sure, are things they actually said. Also true is that Dickens was a literary rock star in his own time, that *Martin Chuzzlewit* was a flop, that his publishers threatened to "deduct from his pay," that Dickens was overextended, and that his relatives—his father most of all (who did once go to debtors' prison)—depended on him for money. *A Christmas Carol* was born out of financial necessity. Most of the rest I made up from whole cloth.

Apologies in advance to Dickens aficionados and scholars who might bristle at the liberties I've taken. Please trust that I did so with abundant good cheer, admiration, and affection for the man who is my subject. The book is, most of all, a fan letter—

a love letter—to the "Inimitable Boz" himself that says, "I know you were a flawed man who had a heart as big as the world. That you saw Christmas as a time to reconnect with our humanity and revel in even our smallest blessings. And that you lived with so much darkness, inside and out, but leaned—urgently, frantically—always toward the light."

I hope this is a book about Dickens as much as it's a book about all of us. I owe a tremendous debt to his biographers. But I'm keenly aware that a good biography tells us the truth about a person; a good story, the truth about ourselves.

That, I think, is what Dickens did best. This book is my tribute to his prodigious gift, written with full awareness that he is, and always will be, inimitable.

Acknowledgments

I owe a debt of gratitude to my agent, Emma Parry, and my editor, Caroline Bleeke, for taking this leap with me. Without them, nothing. But there are others who believed for so long: Stacy Ericson, who sparked the idea years ago; my long-time manager, Matt Luber, who championed the screenplay through some heartbreaking near misses with the big screen; David Kirkpatrick, who urged me to adapt it; Tish O'Hagan, Lynn Hofflund, and Kim Philley, who read countless drafts. Josie Fretwell and Elizabeth Tullis, who never lost faith. And I'd be remiss not to thank my once-husband, Michael Hoffman, whom I credit for most of what I understand about storytelling. He believed, too.

I will be forever grateful for our three children, who lived this book so much of their young lives (and even came to consider Dickens one of the family). They helped me understand what it is to be flawed, and still love fiercely.

I lost my wonderful mother, Beverly Silva Kunert, while deep in the final edits of the book. I had to imagine, at so many turns, the utter delight in her voice if I'd been able to pick up the phone and tell her even the smallest good news. I would not be a writer if it weren't for her and my father, friend, and mentor, Mike Silva, who raised us to believe, above all things, in the power of words.

And to David Nevin, my Lydian stone, who makes every day feel like Christmas—all, and infinitely more.

Mr. Dickens and His Carol
by Samantha Silva

PLEASE NOTE: In order to provide reading groups with
the most informed and thought-provoking questions possible,
it is necessary to reveal important aspects of the plot of this
novel—as well as the ending. If you have not finished reading
Mr. Dickens and His Carol, we respectfully suggest that you
may want to wait before reviewing this guide.

1. Were you familiar with Charles Dickens' *A Christmas
   Carol* before reading *Mr. Dickens and His Carol*? Did
   Samantha Silva's novel change how you viewed the
   classic? Discuss the ways in which Silva referenced and
   departed from Dickens' original story.

2. The city of London plays a key role in this novel: "A map
   of it was etched on [Dickens'] brain, its tangle of streets
   and squares, alleys and mews a true atlas of his own
   interior. It was a magic lantern that illuminated everything he was and feared and wished would be true. It
   was his imagination—its spark, fuel, and flame." How
   does London inspire this story?

3. Clocks appear in many scenes, from Dickens' beloved
   fusee clock to the clock tower in the square, where he
   first meets Eleanor Lovejoy. What do you make of these
   representations of time? How does Dickens' view of
   time, and of his own history, change over the course
   of these pages?

4. When Dickens is suffering from writer's block, Eleanor
   tells him, "Then let the specter of your memory be the
   spark of your imagination." What is Dickens' relationship
   with memory, and with the past generally? How does
   his own life inspire *A Christmas Carol*?

5. Dickens is fascinated by costume, performance, and theater, and he dreams throughout the novel of going to India with Macready and performing Shakespeare. Why do you think acting holds such interest for him? How is it similar to and different from writing? What is the significance of his staged reading of *A Christmas Carol* at the end of the story?

6. In a couple of scenes, we see other famous Victorian writers, including William Makepeace Thackeray, discussing (and disparaging) Dickens' novels. Thackeray, a satirist, criticizes Dickens' "gushing displays of the heart," while for Dickens, "It was all heart, or nothing." How does Silva play with sentimentality and other "Dickensian" qualities in *Mr. Dickens and His Carol*? Discuss the writing style here and the effect it had on you.

7. Dickens' relationship with Eleanor is complicated: "He didn't understand the kinship he felt toward her, or gratitude maybe, or some ineffable affinity of nature and qualities." How would you characterize their bond? Is it at all romantic? Why or why not?

8. When Dickens learns that Eleanor is a ghost, he reflects, "How real she'd seemed, and if not, at least as true as anything he'd ever known. Maybe she'd sprung from his imagination, his own roiling conscience, but it didn't matter now." Were you surprised by the twist? How did you interpret Eleanor's existence?

9. In her author's note, Silva writes: "I'm keenly aware that a good biography tells us the truth about a person; a good story, the truth about ourselves." What do you think she means? What did you learn about yourself from this novel?